The Second Sister
Carrie Weaver

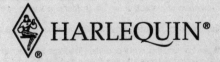

HARLEQUIN®

TORONTO • NEW YORK • LONDON
AMSTERDAM • PARIS • SYDNEY • HAMBURG
STOCKHOLM • ATHENS • TOKYO • MILAN • MADRID
PRAGUE • WARSAW • BUDAPEST • AUCKLAND

ISBN 0-373-71222-7

THE SECOND SISTER

DEDICATION/ACKNOWLEDGMENT

In loving memory of Annie McFadden (1940–2003):

To laugh often and much; to win the respect of
intelligent people and the affection of children…
To know even one life has breathed easier because
you have lived. This is to have succeeded.
—Ralph Waldo Emerson

The Second Sister is also dedicated to
Marilee Hill and Sandy McFadden, friends forever.

I would like to thank the CCCLP group:
Libby Banks, Connie Flynn, Cathy McDavid and
Pamela Tracy Osback—I'm blessed with your friendship
and insight. And a special thank-you to Cathy McDavid
for reading a little farther down the page than I do.

Books by Carrie Weaver

HARLEQUIN SUPPEROMANCE
1173—THE ROAD TO ECHO POINT

PROLOGUE

COLLEEN DAVIS paused inside the doorway to room 415. Her heart ached at the sight of her ailing father. Her instinct was to turn and walk away.

But if she didn't visit him, who would?

She forced herself to move to his bedside. "Hi, Daddy. How's my favorite guy today?"

He grunted in response. The remote lay slack in his hand, the TV blared.

She reached out and removed the remote, tucking his hand in hers. So fragile. So cold. Too bad she didn't have a magic elixir to give him hope. But maybe she could do the next best thing? Give him peace.

Colleen punched the off button and the TV went silent.

"Did you talk with the counselor today?"

Another grunt. Sparkling conversation had never been his strong suit.

"You know, the nice hospice lady—"

"Damn busybody."

Sighing, Colleen searched for an elusive shred of patience. God knew she'd used nearly all her reserve over the past couple of years. But she was his daughter. Not his only daughter, but the only one who cared whether he lived or died.

"It's her job. She's supposed to help you…us, I mean, gain some…closure."

"Bunch of touchy-feely crap. Don't need it."

"Daddy, look at me." Colleen gently held his stubborn jaw, so he couldn't evade the issue. "She's right. It's time you thought about contacting the family. I know you're not going to like this, but…I called Mom."

Hope sparked in his eyes. "Is she coming to see me?"

That's when she knew for sure her father didn't have much time left. Any mention of her mother in the past would have provoked a tirade or stone-cold silence.

Colleen couldn't quite meet his eyes. She didn't want to tell him that Maria Ruiz Davis Peralta didn't give a damn about any of them. "I keep getting her voice mail. Maybe she's, um, out of town or something."

"I understand." His chin quivered beneath her fingers and she almost lost her hard-won resolve not to cry. It hurt seeing such a strong man reduced to this pitiful shell. Maybe it was the fact that his condition was self-inflicted and totally avoidable that hurt most of all. Could she confront him about his illness? The counselor had suggested it was time for her to be honest with her father. That, no matter how much he resisted, Sean Davis needed to see exactly what he'd done to his children and ask for their forgiveness.

"I wish it were different, Daddy." In so many ways. "I'd bring Mom here if I could."

Sean pushed himself up on his pillow, breathing hard from the exertion. "All my fault...she left."

Colleen froze. It was the first time she'd ever heard her father acknowledge having any part in the breakup of his marriage. Her world tilted. How could her father be to blame when, all along, Colleen had been positive *she* had driven her mother away?

She shook her head slowly. There were so many questions left unanswered in the wake of her parents' broken marriage. Questions that rippled outward, widening in space and time.

"I couldn't be the man she wanted me to be." His voice was bitter. "So she up and left. Married that rich guy and never looked back."

This was the father Colleen grew up with. Always blaming someone else. Biting her tongue, she refrained from pointing out the truth—that none of them knew what kind of man he might have been if drinking hadn't ruled his life.

She also refrained from voicing any of the questions she burned to ask; her father's recall was skewed and unreliable.

"You're all I have left, Colleen." His voice was sad and wobbly, but it was a familiar song that bound her to him more effectively than chains.

Colleen smiled sadly. He loved her, in his own way, the best he was able. After all, he was the parent who had stayed.

"Here, lean back, relax." She repositioned his pillows. "It's not good for you to get upset."

"What about Violet? Did you call her?"

"Her number's not listed. Not under Davis, not under Smith, not even under her husband's name."

"You checked directory assistance?"

"Yes, Daddy. I did." Colleen managed to keep the impatience out of her voice. He was a sick old man. If he wanted to second-guess her actions, she should let it roll off. But that was terribly hard to do sometimes.

"How about her friends? Surely one of them has her number."

"She didn't have many close friends. And none of them have talked to her in years."

"Oh."

Colleen hated to see the disappointment cloud his eyes. He might aggravate the living daylights out of her at times, but he was her dad and she loved him. Nothing would change that.

"I even tried the Internet. No luck." Colleen pulled an envelope out of her purse. "But I think I have her address. It was on the envelope with her last check— for your glasses, I think. Echo Point, Arizona."

"Violet would come home if she knew how sick I was." The wistful note in his voice got to her.

Cupping her hand around his cheek, she said, "I'm sure she would."

Her throat tightened. She couldn't seem to summon her mother but she could darn well find her sister. And maybe find some answers in the process.

"I'll make sure Violet knows how sick you are, even if I have to go to Echo Point to do it."

The words surprised her as much as they surprised him. His eyes widened. He squeezed her hand with a strength he hadn't shown in months. "You're a good daughter."

What started as a rash promise grew into a makeshift plan. "This isn't the kind of news I want Violet to read in a letter. I'll leave tomorrow morning for Arizona. It's probably no more than a six-hour drive."

Averting his face, her father stared out the hospital window, surreptitiously wiping his eyes.

Once he'd regained his composure, he turned to Colleen. His old eyes, once green like hers, were rheumy. The whites were yellowed with jaundice. "She'll come back with you, won't she?"

"I'll ask her."

He nodded. "Be careful. Hurry back." It was phrased as a command, but she knew it was the closest this proud man would come to begging. He needed her.

"I won't be gone long, Daddy." She kissed him goodbye. "And I'll bring Violet home with me."

CHAPTER ONE

T EN MILES of desert brush and cacti separated Colleen from the service station she'd passed in Echo Point.

It might as well have been ten *thousand* miles.

She swiped her forearm across her face. Sweat trickled down her neck, her back and places she didn't even want to think about. Her knees ached from alternately kneeling and squatting next to her Benedict Arnold of a car.

Refusing to give up, she applied all her strength to the tire iron. Little black and white squiggles danced before her eyes. The veins in her forehead pulsed with her effort. But it was no use. The bolt, or whatever it was, refused to budge.

Colleen tipped her head to the side. Was that a car she heard? Hallelujah! Her prayers had been answered. A curve in the road kept her from seeing her would-be rescuer. And that meant his or her view of her…

She dashed to the shoulder of the road. And a good thing, too. Gravel crunched and dust flew as a white car came around the curve too fast. The vehicle lurched to a stop only inches from her Toyota.

The dust slowly settled, revealing an emblem on the side of the car. And red and blue lights on top.

Colleen stifled a groan. Maybe she'd luck out and the sheriff would be a kindly, gray-haired man who would have pity on a female in distress.

No such luck.

The driver exited the car. All six foot plus of him.

"Don't suppose you could've changed that tire a few yards down the road," he commented.

"I'm sorry. I didn't want to ruin the rim." She couldn't quite meet his eyes, shaded behind sunglasses. A guilty flush crept up her neck when she realized how irresponsible she'd been.

"Uh-huh." The man removed his shades and eyed her with interest. He had the warmest, kindest brown eyes she'd ever seen. She almost relaxed, until she realized the nerve in his jaw was twitching. He was either horribly angry at her or…

"Are you laughing at me?"

"Nah. Just kinda figured a couple more feet wouldn't have hurt that rim." He pointed to the sad reminder of her Corolla's treachery. The tire was shredded, the rim misshapen.

"Okay, I admit it. I wasn't thinking. I was distracted."

"That can be dangerous when you're behind the wheel of a vehicle."

Colleen's shoulders tightened, and she raised her chin. "I'm normally a very responsible person. But there's an emergency, an illness in the family. I need to tell my sister."

"Did you call 911?"

"Not that kind of an emergency. I mean, well, it's serious, but not immediately-this-second serious. I still need to reach her as soon as possible though."

The officer's gaze narrowed. "And your sister is…?"

"Violet Davis. Um, Smith. Her house should be just a few more miles down the road."

He looked her up and down. "You? Violet? Sisters?"

She crossed her arms over her chest. "And what's so hard to believe about that?" No doubt he'd seen Violet in town and was comparing Colleen's anemic-looking form with her sister's God-given beauty.

The man shook his head. "Nothing. You don't look much alike, but man…you've got Vi's attitude down to a *T*."

His grin told her the comparison wasn't necessarily a compliment. But it pleased her anyway.

She stepped closer and offered her hand. "Colleen. Colleen Davis."

Colleen could almost swear she'd heard him whistle under his breath before he nodded. "Vince Morena." His gaze never left hers as he accepted her handshake. "Does your sister know you're coming?"

"N-no. Like I said, it's an emergency."

"I wouldn't advise springing a surprise on Vi right now. If you tell me what the problem is, maybe I can help."

She was disturbed by an instinctive need to confide in this stranger. Sharing confidences went against everything she'd learned since she was a little girl. "It's personal. *Family* stuff."

"Hey, I'm just trying to help you figure out the best approach. Violet's kind of emotional right now."

"Thank you, Sheriff, but I think I can handle my own sister." It was a whopper of a lie, but he didn't have to know that.

"Um, it's not you I'm worried about."

"Is there something you should be telling me?"

"Noooo." He rubbed his jaw.

"Has something happened to Violet? Is she okay?"

"She's fine. It's just that I'm supposed to keep an eye on her while her husband's out of town."

"And that concerns me because?"

"Because I've never heard her talk about you. So either you're not who you say you are, or you're not at the top of her guest list and shouldn't show up unannounced on her doorstep."

Colleen was tired, sweaty and dangerously low on patience. "Do you want to see my driver's license?"

"First, why don't you tell me what this family crisis is all about?"

She kept herself from looking away. Her mission was too important to get sidetracked by her usual meek response to uniforms and authority. Straightening to her full five-nine, she hoped she achieved a don't-mess-with-me glare. "It's private. Now, Sheriff, you have two choices. Call a garage to send someone to help me, or I'll walk to my sister's house.

Then you'll have my death due to heat stroke on your conscience."

"You're just as stubborn as she is, aren't you?" He sighed and shrugged, glancing at the spare tire she'd propped against the fender. "Looks like that won't hold air. Come on. I'll take you to Violet's."

Ambling around the squad car, he didn't even turn to see if she was following. He simply opened the passenger door and waited.

His sudden cooperation made her uneasy. But not enough to stay by herself in the middle of nowhere.

VINCE EYED his passenger, trying to detect a resemblance to Violet. Her baby sister had dark blond hair with honey-gold streaks running through it—Violet's was black. Colleen had green eyes and freckles, long delicate fingers and a graceful, willowy frame. Violet was built like a bathing beauty from an old beach movie. The Davis sisters were as different as night and day. And he couldn't help but be intrigued by the contrast.

Vince shook his head. He couldn't afford to be distracted while Violet was his responsibility—if she weren't kept calm the consequences could be disastrous. And Lord only knew what kind of emergency sister Colleen wanted to spring on her.

"How long since you've talked to Violet?"

"Five, maybe six years."

"In my family five or six *days* earns me a tongue-lashing from my sisters. You wanna talk about it? It might help."

"No, I don't." She turned to look out the window, but not before he saw her flush.

"Hey, forget I offered. I didn't mean to upset you."

She didn't turn to look at him, just stared at the passing desert. Her voice was husky when she said, "Violet and my father had an, um, disagreement. She moved away."

"Hmmm. Must've been a heckuva fight for you guys to stay estranged for five years."

"She'd like to forget about us." The hint of resentment lurking beneath her wistful tone confirmed his first impression—there was more going on with this woman than she wanted to let on.

Vince cleared his throat. "So what is it you do for a living?"

"I transcribe medical records."

"Sounds interesting."

"It's not."

Her blunt answer intrigued him; she didn't like his prying. Tough, it was his job to pry.

"You plan on staying in town for a while?"

"A day. Two days at the most. I—I have to get back to L.A."

Vince opened his mouth to speak, then clamped it shut. The length of her stay didn't matter. Only Violet's reaction mattered.

Steering the squad car into a horseshoe-shaped gravel drive, Vince parked in front of the Smiths' adobe house. He turned off the ignition and started to open his door. "Thank you, Sheriff. You can just drop me off. I can take it from here."

"I need to check on Violet, anyway."

Colleen leaned forward and ran her hand along the floorboard beneath her seat.

"My purse. I must've left it in the car." Her voice held a note of panic.

"Hey, don't worry. We'll pick it up on our way out."

"You don't understand. It has all my cash and credit cards. And I didn't lock the door."

Vince wondered if she were simply trying to get rid of him. He searched her big green eyes for a trace of deception, but all he saw was genuine worry.

"We'll go back and get it."

"Would you mind going without me? I need to use the restroom, and I'm not sure I can wait that long."

Vince had learned a long time ago to trust his gut instincts. And his gut told him this woman meant trouble. He was determined not to leave her alone with Violet under the circumstances. "Look. We'll just pick it up on our way out. That road's usually pretty deserted and folks around here are trustworthy."

Colleen lifted her chin. "I—I have medication I need to take immediately." She was lying. It was apparent in every defiant line of her body.

"Lady, you're full of bull—"

"Isn't it your job to protect and serve, *Sheriff?* I don't think your superiors would appreciate you jeopardizing my health by refusing to help me."

Vince muttered a curse.

Her cheeks flushed, but her gaze remained steady. "Well?"

Vince started the car. "You don't leave me much choice. But I'll be back in five minutes tops."

The second Colleen moved away from the car, he jammed the gearshift into Drive and stepped on the gas.

AN INDULGENT SMILE twitched at Vi's lips as she watched her daughter finger-painting in the kitchen. The girl's blond head was cocked to the side, the tip of her little pink tongue stuck out in concentration.

Annabelle, their chocolate Lab, watched from her bed in the corner.

Vi rested her hands on her rounded tummy as she stepped closer to look over Rose's shoulder. She'd never known she could love a child as much as she loved her daughter. And in less than two months, she'd have another baby to love with her whole heart and soul.

"It's beautiful, honey. Just perfect."

"More."

"More what?"

"More hot colors."

Vi studied her daughter's creation. She had her late Grandma Daisy's inherent grasp of balance and color. And darn it if she wasn't right. The painting needed some spicing up.

"Would you like more red? And yellow, to make orange?"

"More red!" Rose clapped her hands with delight, apparently unaware that her hands splattered paint all over her face, neck and improvised smock—one of Ian's old dress shirts. Her golden curls bounced with her exuberant nod of approval.

Vi couldn't help but smile. Her daughter had that effect on her. On everyone, really. She'd inherited more than Daisy's artistic ability. She'd inherited her grandmother's zest for life and love for all things living.

Distributing more red paint on the aluminum pie plate, Vi was surprised to hear a knock at the door.

The dog raised her head.

"Uncle Vince," Rose guessed.

"Already? Somehow I kind of doubt that. But knowing your daddy, he probably asked him to check on us."

Vi reached around back to untie her own paint-splattered apron. She was rewarded by a vicious kick to the kidneys. Rubbing her back, she commented, "Your baby brother or sister is sure up to mischief this afternoon."

"Sister."

"Uh-huh. Well, we'll have to wait and see." She handed Rose an old dish towel. "Now wipe your hands and I'll answer the door."

Annabelle followed her to the front room, where Violet paused at the rustic, mission-style door. She rested her hand on the top of the dog's head.

When Ian was home, she didn't think twice about someone dropping by unexpectedly. But when Ian was out of town Vi wished the door had been fitted with a peephole. Thank goodness Echo Point was small and everyone looked out for one another. Still, they *were* out in the middle of nowhere.

Vi slowly opened the door to find a young woman she'd never expected to see on her doorstep. Those green eyes, the golden hair. Just like their father's.

"Colleen," she breathed.

"Violet?"

"Why…what are you doing here?" Vi braced her hand against the door frame to keep the room from swaying.

The familiar stranger touched her shoulder. "You don't look so good. May I come in? You better sit down and put your head between your knees."

"Uh, sure. Come in."

The Lab placed her body between the stranger and Vi.

"It's okay, girl. Go lie down."

Annabelle gazed up at her with huge brown eyes. Wagging her tail slightly, she ambled off and lay down in a corner.

Vi let her little sister lead her to the leather couch. Her breathing was labored, and she felt like she might pass out.

Gentle hands encouraged her to sit, to place her head between her knees. When had spoiled Colleen become so capable?

As her breathing slowed, her maternal antennae caught the scrape of stool legs on tile. God help her, she'd forgotten about Rose. Either the little monkey was climbing on the counters again or something equally as dangerous.

She started to rise, but then she heard the slap of bare feet on tile growing ever closer. Relieved, she sank down again.

"What's wrong with my mommy?"

"Your mommy?" Colleen's voice, more mature than she remembered, sounded strained.

Glancing up, Violet was shocked at her sister's pallor.

"Mommy's okay, honey. I just got kinda light-headed."

Colleen absorbed Violet's admission of mother-hood. She couldn't seem to take her eyes off the little girl, even though her instincts told her Violet needed her. Rooted to the spot, Colleen tried to assimilate the new information and the pain of betrayal. Close on its heels came the realization that her sister led a completely separate existence, almost as if she lived in another country.

"Who're you?" the pipsqueak demanded, small fists braced on her hips. Her chin was raised to a familiar stubborn angle. The child looked to be about four years old and her battle-ready posture left no doubt she was her mother's daughter.

Shooting an accusatory glance at Vi, Colleen was perversely glad to see her sister flush. Slowly, Vi nodded.

Colleen cautiously approached the girl. When she

got close, she knelt so she could take in the details of this precious, tiny being, at eye level. Colleen had always loved kids.

"I'm your Aunt Colleen, sweetie."

"Huh-uh. Don't like ants. They bite."

Colleen chuckled. "Not that kind, silly. I'm your mommy's sister. That makes you my niece."

The solemn brown eyes held her gaze. She could almost see the wheels turning in the child's head. Slowly, she nodded.

Grabbing Colleen's hand, she pulled her over to stand next to Violet.

"Mommy," she breathed. "You got a sister."

Violet raised her head, but her green pallor said it was a mistake.

"Yes, apparently I do."

Then she slapped a hand over her mouth and fled the room.

Colleen glanced at the girl, who shrugged her shoulders.

"Sometimes babies make ya sick."

"Um, yeah. That's what I hear."

They sized up one another in the silence. The clock ticked on the curving mantel above the beehive fireplace.

A knock at the door and the dog barking saved them from trying to make intergenerational small talk.

The little girl turned toward the sound. "Might be a stranger. You open it."

"Yes, ma'am."

Rose shook a finger at the dog then did an amazingly accurate imitation of her mother. "Quiet, Annabelle. Go lie down."

Colleen cautiously opened the door to find the sheriff standing there, her purse dangling from his fingers and a frown creasing his forehead. "It was under the passenger seat."

Colleen's conscience nagged at her. She *had* forgotten the purse, but the medication bit had been a lie. A necessary lie, she reminded herself.

"Thank you. I really *do* appreciate your kindness." She plucked her purse from his hands and started to close the door.

"No problem. Oh, and I called Ron's Auto. They'll have to special order your rims and they won't be in 'til Monday."

Colleen's heart sank at the news. Not only did special ordering delay her return home at a time when she couldn't afford delays, but it also implied a hefty expense. "That was very nice. Um, I'll figure something out. Goodbye."

He wedged his body between the door and the frame and glanced beyond her shoulder. "Hey, Rosie-Bug. I want a hug."

"Uncle Vince!" the girl squealed, clapping her hands with delight.

Colleen had no choice but to step out of the way as her niece hurtled past. *Uncle Vince?*

The sheriff swung Rose up in the air and twirled her around. He grinned when the little girl giggled with delight. It would have been a touching sight if she weren't so irritated with him. The smile transformed him from an interfering nuisance to…well… *a man*. The thought made her stop in her tracks. Eyeing him from head to toe, she noted the way his black hair had just a touch of a wave to it at the crown. Shorn close around the ears, the typical law enforcement haircut tapered to his muscular neck. As he swung Rose around in a circle, his short-sleeved uniform revealed tanned skin and some truly impressive biceps.

The spell was broken all too soon when he glanced around the room, his smile fading. "Where's your mommy?"

"Throwin' up."

"Again?"

Rose nodded.

Colleen could've kicked herself for standing there ogling the sheriff when her sister needed her. "I'm sure Violet will be right out. Or maybe I should go check on her…."

"I hope you didn't upset her." Vince brushed past her, Rose clinging to him like a baby chimp.

"I'm sorry it was such a shock for her to see me. I'd hoped for…a different reaction." The words practically stuck in her throat.

He raised an eyebrow. "Yeah, it's not often I make my sisters puke." The mischievous glint in his eyes softened the statement, but was almost immediately replaced by a worried frown.

Setting the child on her feet, he said, "Rosie-Bug, why don't you go check on your mommy."

She scooted off to do his bidding.

Vince turned to Colleen, his gaze solemn. "Just so you understand, Violet's obstetrician wants her to take it easy."

"It *is* kind of unusual that she's still got morning sickness at this stage of her pregnancy, isn't it?"

He crossed his arms over his chest. "Let's just say it's a difficult pregnancy. Stress of any kind isn't good for her."

"I can appreciate your concern, but the Violet I knew had no problem looking out for herself, pregnancy or no pregnancy."

"Then maybe she's not the Violet you knew." His voice was low. "So don't push her."

"I don't intend to 'push her.'" Colleen had a hard time meeting his steady gaze. She'd always been a terrible liar. But her sister was a stubborn woman, and if she made the wrong decision, Colleen would have no choice but to confront her. It wasn't a thought she relished. She'd never, *ever* stood up to Violet.

"Good. Ian's worried enough about Violet without you making it worse."

"Ian? Her husband, the writer?"

"Yes."

Colleen decided to change her tactics. "You two must be pretty close for him to ask you to watch out for his wife."

"We're like family. As a matter of fact, I'm Rosie's godfather."

"Ahh. So that's why she calls you Uncle Vince. I've never met Ian, but he sounds like a terrific guy. A good friend, devoted husband." Colleen hoped she could get the sheriff talking without appearing to pump him for information.

The taut lines of disapproval around Vince's mouth relaxed. "Exactly. He's on his book-signing tour. He didn't want to go at first, but Vi told him it would put more stress on her having his sorry butt around the house all day."

"Now *that* sounds like the sister I know."

"She misses him like crazy, I can tell. But he's wanted this for a long time—it was her gift to convince him to go."

Colleen was having difficulty absorbing Vince's take on her sister. From what she remembered, selflessness had never been one of Violet's attributes; she looked out for numero uno. It was one of the things Colleen had always admired about her big sister. Admired and detested. "I'd think she'd go with him. She used to want to travel. See America and all that."

"If she weren't pregnant maybe. But the last miscarriage really scared her. Took her a while to bounce back. That's why you can't upset her." Vince rubbed his jaw, eyeing her suspiciously

"I'll try not to." Then a horrible thought hit her. "Would travel jeopardize her pregnancy?"

"The doctor says flying is out. That's part of the

reason I'm here—Ian wants to make sure she doesn't decide to try to meet him somewhere. I'm supposed to see that she doesn't go off half-cocked—"

Just then, Violet rounded the corner, hand-in-hand with Rose. "Half-cocked? I beg your pardon? I do *not* go off half-cocked."

"Uh-huh," Vince grunted. He raised an eyebrow.

Colleen asked Violet, "Can we talk? If you're up to it, I have something important to discuss with you."

"You've come all the way out here to see me, I might as well listen." Violet gestured toward the front room.

Colleen sat on the couch, while Violet claimed a beautiful old rocker with Rosie perched on her lap. What little there was of it.

Vince sat at the other end of the couch. He wasn't overly close, it just seemed that way. She could feel his gaze on her face.

Violet leaned forward. "Okay, Colleen, what gives?"

"Could we discuss this alone?" She glanced at the sheriff."

"Vince is like a brother to me. He can stay. Go ahead."

Colleen fought the urge to squirm under her sister's direct stare. "I came here to help you…in a way."

It occurred to Colleen that she really would have loved for it to be true. For Violet to have called her sister and dearest friend to help during her difficult pregnancy. And devoted sister that she was, Colleen would have flown to her side. They would have talked late into the night, shared girlish giggles, played board games. Funny how quickly Colleen's old fantasy kicked in.

"Spit it out. You always did take the longest time to get to the point," Violet said.

Shaking herself out of her reverie, Colleen could feel a flush spread up her neck. "I—I know we haven't always been the closest family—"

Violet snorted, then covered with a cough.

Vince raised an eyebrow.

"Daddy's dying."

CHAPTER TWO

COLLEEN'S WORDS seemed to echo in the silent room. She regretted her bald statement almost as soon as it was spoken.

"So what else is new? He's been dying for years."

"This time it is the end. He's being moved to a hospice as soon as a slot opens."

Violet stopped rocking. The color drained from her face.

"H-hospice? That's where people go to die. I mean *really* die."

Rose turned to her mother and rested her pudgy little hand along Violet's pale cheek. "Mommy, who's gonna die?"

"Shhh. Don't worry, baby. Why don't you take Annabelle outside? Maybe give her a chew bone? Or play fetch…."

Rose nodded vigorously and dashed over to the dog. "C'mon, Annabelle. Let's go out."

When the sound of bare feet and jingling dog tags faded down the hallway, Violet raised her chin and demanded, "What gives? The old guy was okay last time I saw him."

Colleen studied her sister and wondered when she'd become so callous. But then she noticed the glimmer of moisture in Violet's dark eyes. And something else. Regret? Sadness?

Taking a deep breath, Colleen explained, "That was six years ago. He'd just started having liver problems then. Now he's in the end stage."

"Surely they can do something. Medication, a transplant."

Colleen squared her shoulders. "He's been on diuretics to keep his blood pressure, or portal pressure as they call it, down. A transplant's not an option. Not with his diabetes. Believe me, we've looked into everything."

"Portal pressure?"

"The veins to and from his liver. The pressure can go sky-high and cause internal bleeding." *Something you would be aware of if you bothered to visit once in a while.*

"Is he still drinking?"

Colleen shook her head. "He stopped two years ago."

"Did it help? His personality, I mean?"

"Some. Not much." She couldn't quite meet Violet's gaze. If anything, he'd gotten worse. During his really difficult times, she would try hard to remember flashes of the boisterous, larger-than-life man who occasionally took her out for an ice cream or to a baseball game when she was a little girl. These days, he was a bitter man, disappointed by the way life had treated him.

"Does Mom know?"

Violet's question surprised her. She'd assumed their mother kept at least *some* contact with her oldest daughter even if she ignored her youngest.

"I've left her messages." Glancing down at her hands, Colleen toyed with her purse strap. "She, um, didn't return my calls."

Violet raised an eyebrow. "So what do you want from me? Money to bury the old guy?"

"Keep your money. I'm here because he wants to see you." There, she looked Violet in the eye, her voice firm. In control. Yet her knees shook uncontrollably beneath her skirt.

"No way."

Colleen glanced at Vince.

He shrugged. "She's right. Violet has no business traveling in her condition."

Taking a deep breath, she plunged on. "The hospice counselor has been working with him at the hospital. She says he needs to set his personal life in order and do his best to make things right. It's apparently a necessary step for us all. Closure."

Violet stood and paced. "He *can't* make things right, not if he apologizes for a thousand years. I've done my part. Contributed to his expenses. That's all he's getting from me. And it's *way* more than he deserves."

Colleen was taken aback by her sister's vehemence. She'd only been eight when Violet had gone off to Arizona State University; her memories prior to that time were bits and pieces of a household in turmoil. She remembered lots of yelling and screaming until their brother, Patrick, was killed in a car accident at eighteen. She assumed it was grief that turned their house into a silent, stale vacuum. It only got worse after Vi left for college, followed by their mother's desertion.

"I don't pretend to understand all that's gone on between you and Dad—I was just a kid when you left and I made myself scarce when things got loud. But I think the counselor is right. It will help an old man prepare for his death. It's not my job, or yours, or anyone else's, to determine if he deserves forgiveness. That's up to God. But you and I can do our part. Meet with him. As kindly and as honestly as your conscience will allow. The rest is up to him."

"You don't understand, Colleen. You never will."

"I want to understand. I want to know what happened to our family."

Violet turned away. "It's an ugly story."

"But don't you see, it's your story, too? The way Dad treated you is part of who you are and what you've become. It may be ugly, but what if going back meant you could finally shut the door on the past?" She shook her head. "I—I don't think you've done that. You wouldn't hate him so much if you had." She reached out to touch Violet's shoulder. "Kids are very perceptive. And Rosie deserves a mom who isn't all tangled up with the past. Think about it?"

She watched the conflicting emotions flash across Violet's face: disbelief, anger, fear and finally, acceptance. Violet wiped her eyes. "You know nothing of what I've been through. But you're right about one thing. Rosie deserves better than to have all this crap handed down to her. I thought I'd dealt with it until you showed up at my door."

Vince jumped to his feet and strode over to Violet's side. "What're you saying?"

Violet sighed. "I'm saying I have to face the old bastard before he dies. Not for him, but for *me*."

"You can't go," he insisted.

"It's not your choice to make."

"The hell it isn't. The doctor said no travel and Ian—"

Violet's voice was chilly as she cut him off. "Nobody forbids me anything. *Nobody*. Besides, the doctor never said anything about car travel."

Vince blanched. He seemed to reconsider his approach. "Hey, Violet, you know me. Sometimes I say things all wrong. But I remember how it was each time you lost a baby." He paced restlessly, running a hand through his hair. "I don't want to see you and Ian hurt again."

Violet's face softened, fondness shone in her eyes. "I know you mean well, Vince. You always have. The last thing I want to do is jeopardize this baby."

"Then don't go."

"Why not call your doctor, Violet?" Colleen countered. She'd sorely wanted to keep her promise to a dying man, but she wouldn't ask her sister to travel if it meant putting the baby in danger. "Vince says my rims won't be in 'til Monday. But we could rent a van if car travel is okay with your doctor."

"Yes, I think I will call Dr. James. Then if he okays a road trip, I'll call Ian, maybe think about it overnight. That ought to satisfy both of you. Then, whatever my decision, it wasn't made in haste."

"I guess that'll have to be enough." Vince's eyes narrowed as he turned to Colleen. "And I'm sure your sister will agree to those terms, too."

Colleen flushed at his tone. "Of course. I don't want my sister or her child in danger."

Violet's head was held high. "It's settled then, for now. You'll both stay for dinner?" She didn't give him time to answer. Instead, she turned to Colleen. "And you'll stay the night."

Colleen opened her mouth to protest, but the stubborn tilt of her sister's chin told her it would be pointless. Besides, she couldn't let Vince have the opportunity to persuade Violet not to go.

COLLEEN SURVEYED the courtyard and sighed. Peace and a warm, jasmine-scented breeze washed over her. Violet's adobe home was square with an open courtyard in the center. Weathered bricks made up the walkways between beds of desert plants. A mesquite tree reigned in the center.

"It's beautiful," she commented.

Vince stood a few feet away. "Uh-huh."

"Would Violet tell me if she needed help with dinner? I offered, but she said no. I don't want to be a bother."

Vince raised an eyebrow. "A little late for that."

"I only wanted to give Violet the chance to reconcile with our dad while she still can."

Holding her gaze, he said, "I believe you mean that. But I also believe you could cause a whole lot of trouble."

Colleen scuffed the toe of her sandal in the gravel. "I would never intentionally do that. But it's time she faced whatever she's been running from."

"Running?"

"Leaving our home at eighteen and never looking back, except for a few brief visits."

"You can't force something like this on her. She needs to deal with it in her own time."

"There *is* no time. It's now or never."

Vince stepped forward and grasped her forearm. "Can you live with yourself if she miscarries because of your interference? Because that's what's at stake here. A baby, a human being. A life."

Colleen shook off his grip. She turned away so he couldn't see the doubt in her eyes.

"You don't have an answer, do you?" He was so close she could feel his breath stir her hair as he spoke.

She forced herself to lift her head. The uniform, combined with his intensity and nearness, intimidated her. But she refused to let it show. Her voice only wavered a bit when she responded to his question. "It won't come to that. I'll abide by what the doctor recommends. Will you?"

The seconds ticked by.

"You don't have an answer, do you?" she mimicked.

"I'll do what I feel is necessary. Doctor or no doctor. I promised."

Colleen opened her mouth to ask more about the promise, but she was interrupted by a miniature whirlwind.

"Uncle Vince, Mommy said you could entertain me while she cooks." The little girl screeched to a halt. She squinted up at him, then Colleen. "Are you guys mad?"

Vince stepped back. His scowl relaxed into a smile. "No, *chica*. We're only having a discussion."

"That's what Mommy and Daddy say when they're fighting."

Colleen smothered a chuckle.

"Your aunt and I have come to an understanding."

"We have?"

"Yes. We've decided to declare a truce for tonight. Because bickering would only upset Violet and Rose." He turned to Colleen and raised an eyebrow. "Agreed?"

"Truce. Yes. I guess so."

Rose grabbed her by the hand, pulling her toward the end of the courtyard. "I bet you know how to play hopscotch, huh?"

"Um, it's been a while."

"Come on, Uncle Vince, you can play, too."

Colleen glanced over her shoulder, surprised to see him following.

His eyes glinted with mischief. "I'm very good at hopscotch. How about a friendly wager? Loser does the dishes tonight?"

Colleen couldn't help but laugh at his challenge. There was no way this guy could keep his size twelves within the crooked lines Rose had obviously drawn.

"You're on, Sheriff."

COLLEEN TOYED with a piece of garlic bread while she watched Violet. Her sister was strangely quiet. Sure, she'd nod her head at something Rose said, flash a smile here and there. But it seemed as if her mind were a thousand miles away. L.A. perhaps?

By some sort of tacit agreement, the subject of their father had been avoided. Nor did they discuss their mother and her second husband. Vince's prior warnings might have had something to do with it, but Colleen had to admit she didn't want to spoil the meal. For a few moments, it had almost seemed like the family dinners she'd always wanted. Lots of love, lots of laughter. Totally devoid of tension.

She glanced at Vince. He'd gone home to change into a faded, navy blue Remember NYPD T-shirt and jeans. Leaning toward Rose, who had insisted on sitting next to him, he asked, "Hey, Rosie-Bug, want me to make a quarter come out of your ear?"

The little girl clapped with pleasure. "Yes, Uncle Vince, yes!"

His expression was deadpan as he held his hands out, palms up. "Ladies, you will see that I have no quarter."

Colleen eyed his hands as he turned them over. She tensed in spite of herself. There had been a strict rule at the Davis household—no clowning at the table. Dinner was a serious, silent affair if their dad hadn't been drinking. If he *had* been drinking, there was a torrent of hollering and nasty name-calling.

Glancing at Violet, she saw only mild interest, no fear, no anxiety.

"Madame, please confirm that my hands are empty." Vince stretched across the table.

"They look empty," she murmured.

"And now I will produce the magic coin from my lovely assistant's ear."

With a flourish, he produced a new, shiny quarter from behind Rosie's ear. He grasped the girl's hand and pressed it into her palm.

She giggled with pleasure.

"And where does the quarter go, Rosie-Bug?"

"In my piggy bank. For college."

"You bet. That's my girl." He ruffled her hair.

"Can I do my trick now?" Rose asked. "Mommy hasn't seen it yet."

"Go ahead, *chica.*"

The little girl picked up her spoon and pressed the concave part to her nose. "See, magic. It stays all by itself."

Colleen couldn't help but chuckle at her niece's

antics. They were fast friends now that they'd conquered hopscotch together. "Wonderful, Rose."

Violet smiled indulgently at her daughter. "Enough, Rose. You need to eat your dinner."

"Now you, Aunt Colleen. Do a trick."

Drawing a blank, Colleen stammered, "I don't know a trick."

"Sure ya do. You can use my spoon trick," Rose offered magnanimously.

Her niece's gesture went straight to Colleen's heart. A warm, fuzzy feeling washed over her. So this was what it felt like to belong.

Picking up her unused spoon, Colleen pressed it to the tip of her nose, just as she'd seen Rose do. It stuck there. She crossed her eyes to survey her handiwork, and for good measure, stuck out her tongue.

Rose clapped. Vince whistled.

The spoon lost suction and dropped to the pine table with an irritating clang.

And Violet was very still. Her mouth tightened into a disapproving frown.

Colleen had violated the unspoken rule. She didn't really belong at all. "I—I'm sorry. I shouldn't have done that." Then she mumbled something inane, like, "Bad manners…adult example…"

Vince smiled at her reassuringly. "Hey, this is a *family* dinner. You're allowed to cut up once in a while. You shoulda seen some of the stunts my sisters pulled when I was growing up. And one of them is a pastor's wife now. With *excellent* manners."

He helped himself to more lasagna. "Personally, I think you're very talented. A woman who can balance a spoon on her nose is very hard to find."

His smile was so warm, so sincere, Colleen could almost believe she was welcome here.

"Mommy, look. Uncle Vince and Aunt Colleen're making goo-goo eyes."

"So I see." Violet's voice was flat. She didn't seem very pleased. "If the horseplay's over, maybe we can eat."

"Are you mad, Mommy?"

Colleen shifted uncomfortably in her mission-style leather seat and fervently wished the floor would open up beneath her chair.

Vince's gaze was warm with approval. Turning to Rose, he said, "Your aunt Colleen did nothing wrong. Your mom is just a little grumpy tonight."

Now Colleen *really* hoped the ground would swallow her up as she watched all the color, including the greenish, sick-to-her-stomach pallor, drain from her sister's face. Her eyes, however, snapped and crackled, indicating an explosion of epic proportion was imminent. "I beg your pardon? Did you say *I'm* grumpy? As if I don't have a good reason to be thrown for a loop by all this?"

Uh-oh. That quiet, restrained tone wasn't good. Neither was the rhetorical question. Not at all. The poor man was a goner. But he didn't seem to know when to quit.

"Thrown for a loop, yes. Unkind, no. Colleen is a

guest in your home and you're not making her feel welcome. I, for one, enjoyed your sister's performance."

Vi's face flushed.

Colleen cringed, waiting for the explosion. But it never came.

Violet dropped her gaze.

"I apologize, Colleen. I was rude."

Colleen's jaw dropped.

"Please excuse me." Violet's voice was husky, her eyes bright with emotion. She tossed down her napkin and fled the table.

"What's wrong with Mommy?"

Vince leaned toward Rose, his tone serious. "She might have that leaky eye thing again. You know, the one we talked about?"

"Yep. She cries, but she's not really sad."

Vince ruffled her hair again. "You got it, kiddo. But maybe you can go check on her in a couple minutes just to make sure."

Rose nodded solemnly.

Colleen was mortified to have been the cause of such a scene. "I wish you hadn't done that. I'm used to Violet's…um…outspokenness."

"Rudeness you mean? I love Vi like a sister, but I couldn't just sit there and watch her ruin your evening when you did nothing to deserve it. It looked like someone needed to step in, so I did."

"I told you I could handle her."

Vince frowned. "Then why didn't you?"

"It would have made a scene."

"And cleared the air." His voice dropped a notch as he leaned closer. "Look, I'm sorry if I was out of line. Sometimes I jump into things that are none of my business. But I couldn't just stand by and watch Violet lash out at you."

"I can handle it."

Vince eyed her closely. He nodded slowly. "I'll stay out of it next time. Deal?"

Colleen smiled in relief. "Deal."

Vince held her gaze, speculation gleaming in his eyes. "You ought to laugh more often. You've got a beautiful smile."

She didn't quite know what to make of this man. He was entirely different from the men she knew. Her father saw only the grim side of any situation and expected everyone else to agree with him. The guys she occasionally dated tended to be strong, silent types who didn't seem to believe in showing emotion or bestowing compliments. Or even rescuing damsels in distress.

"Um. Thanks."

Vince stood and started stacking dirty dishes. "Who's ready for dessert? I happen to know there's a carton of triple chocolate ice cream in the freezer. Vi can sniff it out a mile away. If that doesn't bring her back to the table, I don't know what will."

"I'll clear, if you dish up the ice cream," she offered.

"No way. I lost at hopscotch and I always pay my debts. Next time, I'll challenge you to some one-on-one and I guarantee you'll have dish detail." His grin was wicked.

"One-on-one?"

"Yeah, as in basketball. What else?"

Basketball. Of course. She'd been out of circulation for way too long. For a minute there, she'd thought he might be propositioning her.

CHAPTER THREE

THE KITCHEN WAS empty when Colleen tiptoed around the corner at a few minutes before eight in the morning. There was no coffee perking, no sign of life.

She found the coffee tin on the kitchen counter next to the coffeemaker. Removing the lid, she inhaled the dense aroma and scooped out enough for a full pot.

Colleen leaned against the counter as the brew began to perk. Contentment stole over her as she surveyed Violet's kitchen. Like the rest of the house, the warm, brown Saltillo tile gave the kitchen the feel of an old Spanish mission. Her gaze traveled around the room, missing nothing. The walls were rough textured and whitewashed—the cabinets made of dark, distressed wood, with ornate wrought iron fittings. Wooden beams bisected the white ceiling and a selection of copper pots hung along one wall. It was homey, solid, comforting.

A trace of girlish laughter tickled her ears and made her smile. *Rose.*

The little girl was a treasure, her joy infectious.

Even Violet had ditched her somber mood last night and rejoined them for a rousing game of Chutes and Ladders. And fortunately for Vince, he was a lot more adept at board games than he was at hopscotch.

Hearing another giggle, Colleen headed down the hallway to intercept Rose before she could wake Violet. She was too late. The little girl hauled her mother by the hand.

Colleen surveyed Violet from head to toe. She looked like hell. Dark circles, puffy red eyelids. The vacant stare of the undead. And a pallor to match. If she didn't miss her guess, Violet still hadn't become much of a morning person.

"Morning, sunshine," Colleen chirped. It was cruel, but she couldn't resist.

Violet squinted at her as if she were some sort of alien being. An ambiguous grunt was her only reply.

"Mornin'," said Rose as she brushed by.

Colleen followed them to the kitchen.

"It's going to be a beautiful day."

Another grunt. Followed by the refrigerator door swishing open.

Intrigued, she watched her sister fill a coffee mug at least two-thirds full of milk. When Violet turned toward her, Colleen raised an eyebrow at the mug's sentiment, Ruggers Do It Down And Dirty. She sincerely hoped it was Ian's rugby cup.

Violet was grumpy-poetry-in-motion as she expertly switched her mug with the coffeepot, allowing not a drop of coffee to hit the sizzling burner. She topped off her cup, then completed the same maneuver in reverse.

Colleen couldn't help but smile as she watched Violet inhale the aroma and sigh with contentment. Then she shuffled out of the kitchen without another word. A blissful slurping sound followed her down the hallway.

By the time Violet returned, Colleen had Rose seated at the table eyeing a big stack of pancakes. Her sister's gaze was brighter, more alert. The greenish tint to her skin remained, though.

Colleen gestured toward the table. "Have a seat. I'll get you some pancakes."

"One's plenty. Thank you."

Colleen itched to ask her if she'd made her decision, but didn't. She knew when it was best to keep her mouth shut. Dealing with her father had taught her that.

A loud pounding on the front door startled her out of her reverie.

"I'll get it." Rose vaulted off her chair and headed toward the front room.

"Rose Adrienne Smith, you get back here right now," Violet snapped. "You know you're not allowed to answer the door."

But she was talking to thin air. The girl moved like a gazelle when she wanted to.

Violet started to rise, but Colleen stopped her. "I'll go. I'm already up."

Colleen rounded the corner to find the door wide open.

"It's Uncle Vince, it's Uncle Vince." Rose hopped on one foot, excitement sparkling in her eyes.

Vince stood just inside the doorway, frowning. His tone was stern when he asked, "Rose, does your mom allow you to answer the door?"

Looking down at her feet, the girl mumbled something indistinguishable.

"Rose. This is not a game. Look at me." He stepped close and tipped her chin. His tone was grave. "Your mommy and daddy want you to stay safe. So do I. So promise me you won't do that again."

She looked up into his face, tears clinging to her long lashes. "Please don't be mad, Uncle Vince."

Rose's plea made Vince feel like a big jerk. She was just an innocent and shouldn't have to worry about monsters, human or otherwise.

He knelt on one knee so they were eye-to-eye. "I'm not mad," he murmured. *I'm scared.* "I just want you to remember what I told your preschool class about Stranger Danger. Policemen and sheriffs are here to help kids. So I want you and the rest of the kids to stay safe."

She nodded and swiped away her tears. Taking him by the hand, she said, "Come on. Aunt Colleen made pancakes."

Exhaling with relief, he stood.

"Come on." Rose tugged on his hand.

Colleen cleared her throat. She was still standing in the doorway to the kitchen. She held his gaze, her expression thoughtful.

"Come in and have some pancakes."

"Mmmm. Pancakes. My favorite." He followed her into the kitchen and greeted Violet with a brotherly kiss on the cheek. "Morning."

"Don't think I've forgotten your overbearing behavior last night. A dish of ice cream doesn't buy my forgiveness."

"Aw, come on, you had it coming. Somebody's gotta keep you in line while Ian's gone. And I got elected. Besides, I let you win at Chutes and Ladders."

Violet crossed her arms across her chest. "You did not *let* me win and I do *not* need to be watched like a child." Her face softened, her eyes lit with amusement. "But I appreciate it anyway. So does Ian."

The good-natured ribbing helped to ease the tension gripping his neck and shoulders. Maybe he'd overreacted a little when Rose answered the door, but dammit, she needed to stay safe. His view of the world was still colored by some of the stuff he'd seen when he worked the streets of South Phoenix.

"Here you go," Colleen said.

Accepting a plate of pancakes and cup of coffee from her, he pulled out the chair next to Rose. "Ian call last night?"

Violet nodded. "Uh-huh."

"How's the book tour going?"

"He…didn't say much about it." Her cheeks grew pink. "Good, I think."

Vince sighed in mock exasperation. "You two

burning up the phone lines again with all that romantic phone stuff?" If truth be told, he was just a bit envious of Ian and Violet's passion.

"That's none of your business, buddy."

"I know, but I like teasing you anyway. Cut to the chase. Are you going to California or aren't you?"

Violet pushed a piece of pancake around her plate with a fork. "The doctor said I could travel by car."

"That's wonderful news." Colleen poured herself a cup of coffee and joined them. "I'm so glad."

Vince eyed her for a moment, wondering if Colleen was glad because the baby appeared to be safe or because it looked like she might've gotten her way.

"I'm relieved, too," Violet said. "After I told Ian the doctor said car travel would be fine, Ian left the decision up to me."

Vince knew better. He'd bet his friend had done everything in his power to persuade Violet to stay home and rest.

Colleen pulled out the chair across from him and sat down. It looked as if she were hanging on to the coffee mug for dear life. She leaned toward Violet, expectation flashing in her eyes. "And?"

"I'm going."

Vince's heart sank at the news. He'd hoped that Violet would be sensible and postpone the trip. Raking a hand through his hair, he asked, "So Ian's okay with this?"

"As long as it's just a couple days and I don't overtire myself."

Colleen went around the table and gave her sister a big hug. "You won't regret it, I know it."

"This doesn't mean I've forgiven Dad, or that I'm convinced we can be one big, happy family. It simply means that I'll try."

"That's all I ask." Colleen's voice was husky, her eyes suspiciously bright.

He wondered if stirring up all this trouble might not be worth it when all was said and done.

Caught up in his thoughts, the sound of his cell phone barely registered. It was the sound of his name that brought him out of his reverie.

"Vince." Violet pointed to the cell hanging on his belt.

"Um, thanks. Hello."

"Hey, Vince." It was Ian. "Violet talk to you about California?"

"Uh-huh. She's right here. I'm at your place."

Violet's expression softened when she realized he was talking to her husband.

"You don't sound too enthusiastic about the trip," Ian said.

"I think it's a mistake. But it's not my call to make."

"You do have *some* say in the matter."

"Um, I appreciate you trying to make me feel included and all, but—"

"Of course you're included. How else do you think Violet's gonna get to Los Angeles? Wait a minute—she didn't ask you, did she?"

"Ask me what?"

"To take her there. Make sure she's safe."

Vince glared at Violet accusingly. She refused to meet his gaze.

"No, she failed to mention that part."

"Ahhh, letting me do the dirty work."

"I wouldn't call it that. I'd say she was just hedging her bets."

Ian chuckled. "Yeah. She likes to get her way. So will you go?"

"L.A. isn't one of my favorite cities." That was a gross understatement. Vince would have preferred the Mojave Desert in August.

"You lived in L.A. for years, didn't you?"

"That's why it's not my favorite city. Besides, I was only a kid then."

"I know it's asking a lot, but will you go? I'm counting on you, man. You're the only one I trust. You or one of your sisters. But Vi says Marisol's busy and Teresa has finals."

"I know Marisol would love to go. Must be a BMX competition for the boys."

"See, you're my only hope."

Vince glanced around the table. Violet and Colleen both gave him the kind of puppy dog look that generally brought him to his knees.

He started to sweat. The pressure was worse than a midcourt shot in the last three seconds of a tie game. How could he possibly say no?

"There's gotta be someone else? Hey, Colleen will be with her."

"Come on, Vince, you know the stuff that can happen to two women traveling alone. Besides, the history between them is intense. Let me just say Violet will need you *more* with Colleen around. And when she sees her dad. I don't even wanna think about it…. You know what, forget I said anything. She needs me right now and nothing, I mean *nothing* is more important. Not even the damn book tour."

"Hey—hang on a minute. We can figure something out."

Violet shot him a dirty look, as if she could sense the direction in which his conversation with her husband was headed.

"Nope. I'm done hanging on. My wife needs me and I'm on the next flight outta here."

Vince pushed away from the table and stood. He escaped to the hallway, where he hoped he wouldn't be overheard. His voice was barely above a whisper when he said, "You know that'll upset Vi. She's wanted this tour for you. Wanted you to have your day in the sun and all that. It might be more stressful for her if she knows she's responsible for you ditching the tour."

"Damn, I hate this. I'm halfway across the country, my wife's having a difficult pregnancy and now this. I miss her, and I miss Rosie."

Vince winced at the frustration in his friend's voice and remembered all the times Ian had pulled his butt from the fire.

"I'll do it." The words dropped out of his mouth

before he could reconsider. Before he could even think what returning to L.A. would mean.

"You will?" Ian's obvious relief made Vince's conscience ping. He shouldn't have put his best buddy through this suspense, no matter how valid his reasons. "Sure. I've got some vacation time I was gonna lose anyway. And they've been after me to get some R&R. Let's see, tomorrow's Friday. If we leave early in the morning that'll give us a long weekend, maybe we'll even stay 'til Monday."

"I owe you. Big-time. I'll never forget this." Ian's voice was husky.

"Forget it. You'd do the same for me."

"You know it."

VINCE EYED the hood of the minivan through the wide expanse of windshield as they pulled into Marisol's driveway on Friday. Morning sunshine reflected off the silver paint. It changed his whole perspective, this extremely domestic vehicle. To be behind the wheel was almost surreal. Almost as if he might catch a glimpse of his future if he turned his head quickly enough. A future within his reach if he could find the right woman or *stay* with the right woman once he found her. He tried to picture what his children might look like, but failed. The empty passenger seat next to him spoiled the illusion of family solidarity.

"Hey, I feel like the chauffeur. One of you ladies needs to sit up front after Rose gets out."

Annabelle poked her brown head between the front seats. She propped her huge paws on the console and grinned, then slurped the side of his face with her tongue.

"Ugh." Vince wiped his face with his forearm. "No way, Annabelle, you get out here, too."

Vi shook her head. "Not me. Front air bags, remember?"

"That leaves you, Colleen."

"Um. Sure."

It wasn't the enthusiastic reply he would have liked, but he was confident she'd grow to appreciate his conversation.

"I'll get the sliding door." He went around to the passenger side and opened the van door. "You ready, Rosie-Bug?"

Rose was bookended in the rear seat by her mother and aunt, her legs crowded by Annabelle's rear end. The girl crossed her arms over her chest in a very accurate portrayal of her mother. "I don't wanna stay with Missus Marisol."

Violet's eyes were bright with unshed tears. "I'm not sure this is such a good idea."

"No, a good idea would have been postponing this trip until after the baby's born. But if you insist on going, this is the best place for Rosie to stay. She adores the boys, gets along great with my niece and will feel secure with Annabelle there." Vince lowered his voice. "Besides, kids her age aren't allowed to visit the hospital."

"I guess you're right."

"Sure I'm right. She'll be happy here with my sister and her kids."

He winked at Rose. "Won't you, Rosie-Bug? I hear Missus Marisol needs your help to bake some chocolate chip cookies."

His goddaughter frowned in concentration as she apparently considered her options. He'd given her his best pitch—plenty of playmates and chocolate chip cookies, it didn't get much better than that for a four-year-old. Heck, it didn't get much better than that for most adults.

"Okay, Uncle Vince." She turned and shook a finger in her mother's direction. "Call me. Tonight. Promise?"

Violet nodded emphatically, her eyes bright, apparently not trusting herself to speak without bursting into tears. She hugged her daughter fiercely.

Colleen smothered a laugh. "Rose, you are totally precious. You be good, okay? And remember what I said?"

Rose nodded solemnly. "You're gonna send me a present."

"I sure am."

BLYTHE, CALIFORNIA, was remarkable only for being so unremarkable. It could have been any small town north of the border between California and Texas. Judging by the store signs, Spanish was just as prevalent as English, maybe more so. It made Colleen wish for a moment that she'd known her grandmother long enough to learn fluent Spanish. But she'd been just a toddler when her Abuela Rosa had died.

Twisting around, Colleen glanced at her sister sleeping scrunched against the door. She'd refused to remove her seat belt, even if it meant she could stretch out more comfortably. Colleen had been a bit confused by Violet's views on safety until Vince explained the accident statistics involving pregnant women. Apparently seat belts were generally considered helpful, while airbags weren't.

Colleen marveled at the changes in Violet over six years' time. Her face had softened, her features refined. She bore a striking resemblance to the old black-and-white photos of Rosa.

Both women had lush figures, dark brown hair and eyes that flashed with laughter or anger, depending on the mood.

Colleen, on the other hand, had received the scrawny Davis genes. All knobby knees and elbows during her teens, she'd never blossomed into anything approaching Violet's voluptuous figure.

"Hey, Earth to Colleen." Vince's voice held a hint of amusement. "We're here."

Colleen rolled her eyes at her own flight of fancy. "Sorry. My dad says I always have my head in the clouds."

"Nothing wrong with that. It just means you're intelligent and have an imagination. But I'd like to get Violet settled in ASAP—this trip has been hard on her." He nodded toward the back seat, where Violet shifted in her sleep.

Colleen didn't have time to analyze Vince's assessment of her daydreaming, but it pleased her just the same. "You're right. Why don't I go get us checked in, and you can stay here with the air conditioning running?"

Vince grinned. "I love a resourceful woman. Here, put it on my credit card." Removing his wallet, he held out his Visa.

"Not necessary. You've sacrificed enough to help us. I'll handle the hotel."

"That's a little too resourceful," he grumbled.

"Take it or leave it, Moreno."

"Man, eighteen hours with Violet and you've picked up even more of her attitude. I didn't think that was possible."

"I've had it all along. I just hide it better than she does." Colleen grinned.

He raised an eyebrow and whistled under his breath. "You are one dangerous woman, Colleen Davis."

Colleen shook her head, wishing he were right. Wishing she felt a bit dangerous once in a while, rather than always practical and reliable.

Closing the van door with a quiet click, she headed for the lobby area. She could feel Vince's gaze following her progress.

He greeted her with a worried frown when she returned with the room key cards.

She glanced to the back seat to see that Violet was awake. Awake, but not very coherent. And not very well-rested. Dark circles rimmed her eyes, her skin was pasty white.

As soon as Vince pulled up near the outside elevator, Colleen hopped out of the van and opened the sliding door. Her sister needed a place to put up her swollen feet and rest comfortably.

Reaching out to Violet, Colleen was surprised to see Vince's large, tanned hand beat her to it.

"I'll help her inside," he said.

"That's not necessary," she insisted.

"It *is* necessary. Ian trusted me to care for her."

"But I'm her sister—"

Violet shoved both of their hands out of the way. "Oh, would you two stop. I'm not a Thanksgiving wishbone for goodness' sake."

Colleen grasped one of Violet's arms, while Vince took the other. Between them, they steadied her as she stepped down from the van. And a good thing, too, because Violet closed her eyes and swayed.

Colleen wrapped an arm around her sister's waist and eased her toward the elevator. "Come on. We'll leave the bags until we get you settled in our room. You look like you're still absolutely exhausted."

Vince held up his hands in defeat. "I'll get the bags. You ladies go inside where it's cool."

"Thanks," Colleen murmured.

She helped Violet to the door and waited as Vince unlocked the door and carried in their overnight bags.

He had a calm strength. Though he seemed easy-going on the surface, Colleen got the feeling he was ever alert, as if he processed information on several levels at once.

Colleen shook her head, aware she'd been watching his every movement as he unloaded their luggage and carried it to their rooms.

"Don't get too involved, baby sister. Vince is a complex guy."

Colleen glanced sideways at Violet and was surprised to see the shrewd glint in her eyes. She'd thought Violet was too tired to pay attention to much of anything.

"I don't know what you're talking about."

"Oh, yes, you do. Just be careful."

Colleen puzzled over Violet's observation as she settled her in their room. She led her to one of the two queen-size beds. "Kick your shoes off and get comfortable."

Violet slowly complied.

Busying her hands, Colleen plumped a pillow and wedged it behind Violet's back.

"Why'd you do that?"

"Do what?"

"Put the pillow behind me."

"I don't know. I just did."

"How'd you know that's exactly where I needed it?"

Colleen stilled. "Because that's where Daddy likes it."

Violet's eyes widened. Then a single tear slipped

down her cheek. She reached around behind her and grabbed the pillow, flinging it to the ground. "I'm *not* like Dad, and I don't need the stupid pillow."

Colleen stood rooted to the floor. She couldn't have been more shocked if her sister had hit her; the rejection was the same. Wrapping her arms around her middle, she willed the pain away.

"Hey, I brought some snacks."

She turned slowly to see Vince standing in the doorway to the connecting room. He was holding the large, teal and white ice chest as effortlessly as if it were filled with packing peanuts instead of an assortment of healthy goodies and drinks.

He acted like he didn't notice that neither of the women spoke or made eye contact, though he had probably heard Violet's outburst. Placing the cooler within Violet's reach, he touched her arm. "You need some rest. We'll get out of your hair. Kick back, take a nap. We'll bring you something to eat if you get tired of fruit and cheese."

Violet frowned. Her eyes were dull as she nodded slowly. "Go."

CHAPTER FOUR

COLLEEN SCOOTED into the booth opposite Vince, avoiding his gaze. Her emotions were too raw and confusing for polite chitchat. While she was glad her promise to her father would be fulfilled, she couldn't shake an uneasy feeling about the impending reunion. Violet's unpredictability concerned her.

Colleen shook her head. She'd been incredibly naive to think she could bring them back together and everyone would hug and make nice.

"Hey," Vince said. "You're sure Mexican food is okay with you? We could scout up some burgers."

"Mexican's fine." Glancing around, she noticed the place was quaint in a tacky sort of way—lots of baskets, terra-cotta pots and an occasional oddly shaped piñata. "I'm just a little distracted."

"By Violet losing her temper at the hotel? Sorry, I couldn't help but overhear."

She nodded. "I was kind of thrown for a loop."

"You were only trying to help."

"Violet's always been hotheaded. But today was different. I'm worried."

"How was today different?"

"I can't really explain it. She seems afraid." Colleen hesitated for a moment. "She was almost hysterical."

"I'm not a big fan of dredging up the past, but I gotta admit today proved Violet has kept some stuff bottled up. I'm beginning to think that counselor might have been on to something. Maybe Violet *does* need to see this through or else she'll explode, big-time."

"The counselor didn't know the extent of, well, how badly my dad treated her. I didn't either. I see now more than ever how important it is for him to apologize, ask for forgiveness. And I wonder if his apology might heal Violet like nothing else could. But what if things don't go well and she ends up getting hurt?"

"I won't let that happen. Believe me, your dad steps over the line and I'll have her back home in no time."

"And what if my dad gets hurt? I hate what he did to Violet, but he's still my father. He's *dying*—I won't turn my back on him."

Vince raised his hands. "Violet is my top priority. You're going to have to handle your dad."

"In other words, I'd better get ready to referee."

"Hey, you pretty much took on that job the minute you decided to come to Echo Point."

"Somehow I overlooked the possibility." Colleen's heart sank at the thought. "Or maybe it was just wishful thinking."

"Whatever the reason, it looks like you put yourself between a rock and a hard place. Question is, how are you going to handle it if things explode in your face?"

"I don't know," she murmured. "I just don't know."

"Look on the bright side. It could be worse. At least you've got some time to come up with a plan before we hit L.A. around noon tomorrow."

"That makes me feel *so* much better." Colleen didn't even try to keep the sarcasm from her voice.

Vince smiled crookedly. "Glad I was able to help. Now, let's flag down a waitress and order. I'm starving."

By unspoken agreement, they set aside the subject of Violet and her dad while they ate. Mostly they talked about Rosie, which made for easy conversation; Vince seemed to adore her niece as much as she did.

When he leaned back and gave a satisfied sigh, she asked, "You know about my family. What about yours?"

He hesitated for a moment. "Fair's fair. You've met Marisol. She's the oldest. Then there's Linda, she's a year and a half older than me. She lives in New Mexico. And Teresa, the baby."

"All of you live in Echo Point? Besides the sister in New Mexico?"

"Yep. There have been Morenos in Echo Point for four generations. Sometimes a few leave to find work, like my dad did, but they always come back."

"Sounds nice. Like you're close."

Vince chuckled. "Yeah, we're close all right.

Sometimes too damn close. My sisters make it their mission to keep tabs on my social life."

"Oh?"

"They're afraid I'm not gonna settle down. My relationships tend to be kind of…short." His cheeks flushed beneath his olive skin.

Colleen had been out of the dating scene for a while, but she surmised that "short" was a euphemism for one-night stand.

"So that's why Violet warned me."

He rubbed his chin. "I have a little bit of a reputation, I guess. Totally undeserved, of course."

"Of course." Colleen bit back a smile. She had a hard time reconciling him as a love-'em-and-leave-'em kind of guy when he was apparently so devoted to family. "And what do your parents think? Or don't the rumors get back to them?"

Vince's eyes went bleak for a moment. "Mom's dead and Dad's recuperating from a heart attack in New Mexico, so they're kind of out of the loop. Besides, according to my sisters, I'm Dad's favorite and can do no wrong. See, rumors aren't a problem."

Colleen's heart contracted at his awkward attempt at humor. His forced smile told her he found the subject far from funny.

Placing her hand on his, she squeezed. "Hey, you know what? I believe people we love can see us from heaven. I bet *both* your parents are proud of you."

He looked away. "I wish that were true."

"Wh—"

"Do you bowl?" Vince asked as he stood and picked up the check. He tossed a generous tip on the table.

Colleen experienced mental whiplash with the sudden change of subject. "Bowl?"

"Yeah, you know with the pins and the balls?"

"Once."

He raised an eyebrow. "Only once? We definitely need to remedy that. I saw a bowling alley down the street—wanna give it a try? I'm way too wound up to sleep yet."

"I'm not very good."

"Don't have to be. Just need to have fun."

Fun. What a novel idea. It had been so long since she'd done something purely for the enjoyment of it. Longer still since she'd done something spur-of-the-moment. Her mood was lighter already.

Smiling, she said, "Well, if that's the case, I could use some fun. Count me in. I just need to make a quick call to the hospital. Make sure everything's okay."

"I'll pay up front. Why don't you meet me outside when you're done?"

Colleen nodded, reaching for her cell phone.

When she joined Vince a few minutes later, she tried to recapture her earlier enthusiasm, but didn't quite succeed. Her smile felt wooden. "I'm back."

"How's your dad doing?"

"I didn't get to talk to him. The nurse said he was

sleeping and his condition was stable. I hope he doesn't think I deserted him."

"You'll be back in no time. He's being cared for. There's not a whole lot more you can do."

"I suppose."

"I'd say you're long overdue for some R&R," Vince said, touching her on the arm. "And bowling's just the ticket. Come on."

NOISE ASSAULTED Colleen's ears when she and Vince entered through the glass doors. Raucous laughter, the crack of a ball connecting with pins, the clatter of pins against the glossy hardwood floor. Hoots and catcalls. It was orchestrated chaos.

Colleen's pulse jumped with the energy of the place. It was so very alive, when she'd felt nearly dead for a long time.

Excitement shot through her like an adrenaline rush. She clapped her hands together, unable to contain her enthusiasm. "Where do we start?"

Vince's blank expression told her he hadn't heard a word she'd said over the commotion.

Standing on tiptoe, Colleen touched the sleeve of his shirt.

He bent closer.

The noise and bustle faded to background music as his fresh, masculine scent washed over her. Colleen tried not to focus on how touchable his clean-shaven neck looked. Clearing her throat, she yelled, "Where do we start?"

Colleen's breath was warm on Vince's skin. He pretended not to hear her simply for the pleasure of getting closer.

"Where do we start?" she repeated.

"This way." Vince pulled her by the hand toward the shoe rental counter. After they received their shoes, he navigated the crowd, her hand tucked in his. He told himself it was to keep from losing her in the crowd, but the truth was, he liked being near her.

When he'd met Colleen on the road to Echo Point, he'd thought she was an uptight bundle of trouble. The past twenty-four hours had shown him that she was gentle, caring and a heckuva lot of fun when she allowed herself to cut loose. Not many women could hopscotch like she did, though her Chutes and Ladders skills were rusty. Too bad she led a life where fun was apparently a luxury.

He dipped his head closer to hers. "See what I mean? Bowling is like one big party. There's no way you can worry here—it's physically impossible."

"Well, duh. Wearing these, how *could* I take myself seriously? I'll look like Bozo the clown." She eyed the regulation shoes dangling from her fingertips.

"Exactly. And once you get into the game, I guarantee you'll be hooked. No pun intended."

"Pun?"

"Yeah. When you release the ball and it has a curve to it, it's called a hook."

"Oh. Hooked." Colleen's eyes lit with amusement. "Good one."

He was glad to see her relax. When she talked about her father, she seemed almost like a different person. Worried, unsure, hyperresponsible. Or maybe he was simply guessing based on how sick she said her dad was. Vince couldn't even imagine caring for someone terminally ill.

Watching Colleen change into her bowling shoes, her movements light, her smile quick, he decided to make sure she had fun for the next few hours.

Vince sat down next to her and explained scoring while he changed shoes. Colleen seemed to hang on his every word, as if trying to memorize every nuance of the game. Her big, green eyes never left his face.

Given different circumstances, he might have been thinking about seducing her. He was on vacation, away from home, and would probably only see her for another day or two. They could have mind-blowing sex and never see each other again. The perfect fling. Only two things stopped him. Her inherent goodness, obvious even to a testosterone-driven guy like him, and the fact that she was Violet's sister.

Vince shook his head. Colleen was definitely off limits for a fling. So it was only with friendly interest that he watched her tie her shoes with a flourish and stand, almost shaking with excitement. "Okay, Boss, what next?"

He had a hard time meeting her eyes. He could only hope she was completely unaware of his wayward thoughts.

Bowling. Concentrate on bowling.

That was safe ground. There was nothing remotely sexual about bowling. He reminded himself of all the wholesome afternoons he'd spent at the bowling alley as a kid. Successfully redirecting his focus, he asked, "You know how to release the ball?"

Nodding solemnly, she said, "But sometimes it goes behind me instead of toward the pins." She grinned wryly. "That's not good, is it?"

Vince stifled a chuckle. "We want the ball to go *forward*. Preferably in your own lane."

"Hmm. That could be a problem. Sometimes it bounces into another lane."

Vince resisted the urge to smack his forehead. Instead he grasped Colleen by the arm. "Here. I'll walk you through it. Line up behind the fault line."

"Okay. This much I remember. It's just the other stuff I'm kind of fuzzy about. Don't I need a ball?"

"What was I thinking? Wait here, I'll get you one. Why don't we start you off with a ten-pounder?" Vince selected a ball off the rack and handed it to her. "How's that feel on your fingers?"

"Like I stuck them in a cement block with holes."

"Good. That's how it's supposed to feel. As long as it doesn't hurt."

"No."

"Good. Now face the pins." He guided her and stepped back. "Toes there. Make sure you don't go over the line or you'll get a fault. Pull back your arm."

Colleen did as she was told.

"No, keep it straight. Take a couple steps, draw

back the ball and release it before you reach the other line. Be sure to follow through."

Nodding slowly, she nibbled on her lower lip as she studied the pins. Two jerky steps and she drew back.

Thud.

Vince sidestepped the ball as it landed at his feet. The successive bounces weren't as loud as the first, but still drew plenty of attention. He received sympathetic glances from the lane on the left, a group of seniors having a night on the town by the looks of it. The bowlers on the right, however, weren't nearly as kind. One beer-bellied guy had the nerve to snicker, his partner out-and-out guffawed.

Colleen flushed, the sparkle fading from her eyes. "Maybe this wasn't such a good idea."

Vince could have gladly grabbed the two guys by the neck and cracked their heads together. Instead, he moved closer to Colleen, blocking her view of them with his body. "This was an *excellent* idea."

She glanced down at her feet. "Maybe I shouldn't—"

He raised her chin. The defeat in her eyes hit him viscerally, almost like a direct blow to the gut. "Hey, don't let them bother you. We're here to have fun. Why don't you watch me throw one?"

Smiling crookedly, she nodded.

He selected a ball off the carousel. The pins crashed as he knocked down all but one. "Did you see the way I followed through? Don't release the ball too early and you'll be fine. Focus on the pins. Tune everything else out."

"That was terrific. Do you think you can teach me to do that?" Her voice was hopeful.

"I *know* I can." Handing her the ten-pound ball, he hoped he was right. It would kill him to see her disappointed a second time. He hit the reset button and said, "Now try again."

Colleen lined up as before. She concentrated on the pins until Vince thought she might bore a hole through one by sheer force of will. She stepped. She waited to release until the correct moment and the ball went…

Straight into the gutter.

The lane next to them erupted with laughter.

Vince didn't even wait for her to react. He knew if he didn't do something fast, she'd hate the game and never try again. Grabbing another light ball off the rack, he led her by the hand.

"We'll do it together."

"I don't—"

"Here." He handed her the ball.

She opened her mouth to speak.

He grasped her shoulders and turned her to face the pins. Stepping a few paces behind her, he instructed, "Put your fingers in the holes. Now, draw back."

She obeyed, her arm wobbling.

Vince closed the distance between them and reached around to grasp her wrist. "Keep your arm straight."

He wrapped his left arm around her waist to steady her. Of course, that necessitated pulling her close to his body. He ignored the fierce protectiveness washing over him in waves, triggered by her nearness and the jeering from the next lane. "When I say 'now,' let it go."

She nodded.

"Now," he instructed, his voice husky. He sent a silent prayer heavenward. He knew in his heart that God was a bowler and would understand.

Vince watched her release. It wasn't good, but it wasn't bad, either. The ball stayed in their lane and rolled slowly down the glossy wood floor. Colleen didn't move a muscle. He suspected she was holding her breath.

Then she exploded with excitement when the ball wobbled into a single pin and knocked it over. Jumping up and down, she clapped her hands. "I did it. I did it."

Thank you, God.

Colleen turned to him. Her smile lit up the alleyway like a halogen light on steroids.

He sucked in a breath at her sheer beauty. She'd only knocked down one pin, but it could have been a strike to her. Throwing her arms around him, she gave him a hug. "Thank you."

No, thank you. For reminding him that sometimes the small victories counted as much as the big ones.

"Way to go. That was perfect." And he meant it. The woman couldn't bowl worth a damn, but her spirit and heart made up for it. He wrapped his arms around her.

Whistles and catcalls interrupted his thoughts.

Glancing to the right, he caught Beer Belly in the midst of a lewd pelvic thrust. "That'll get you in her pants," the guy hollered.

Anger battled with disgust. His intentions had been pure for once and he hated anyone spoiling it. Or insulting Colleen.

"Hey," Colleen said. "Don't let him get to you."

He didn't know whether it was her soft voice or the dignified tilt to her chin, but he let the insult go. There had been a time when he would have gladly beaten the guy to a pulp, but not tonight. "He's a jerk."

"He is. But let's ignore him." Her breath was warm on his face.

Awareness seeped through him. He'd been so focused on Colleen's accomplishment that he'd forgotten he had an attractive and possibly willing woman in his arms. His body stirred in response.

He disentangled himself from her and stepped backward, hoping to hell she didn't know he was turned on. Hoping Beer Belly's crude performance wasn't simply an insightful reflection of Vince's true character. Hoping to hell he was a better man than that.

Vince closed his eyes. No woman was worth jeopardizing his self-respect. Nor was any woman worth the punishment he would receive if Violet found out he'd even thought of putting the moves on her sister—being drawn and quartered came to mind. The visualization technique was more effective than a cold shower.

When he opened his eyes, Vi's very lovely and enthusiastic baby sister was studying him. She was still close enough that he could see the pulse beat at the base of her neck.

"You okay?" she asked.

"Uh. Yeah. The fluorescent lights got to me for a minute. I think you've got the hang of it. Now, go again and see if you can knock down the rest of the pins."

Vince made sure he stayed a safe distance away this time. Not only was she dangerous with a bowling ball, she was dangerous for his equilibrium, too.

"WE'RE HERE." Colleen gestured toward her hotel room door, as if Vince couldn't see for himself. Embarrassment warmed her cheeks.

"Hey. Colleen. I had fun tonight." The concern in his eyes made her want to hide. Or throw herself at him, one of the two.

"Thank you. For dinner, for teaching me to bowl. You were right, I had fun."

"No problem. You're a quick study." Vince chucked her under the chin.

Colleen stifled a groan, more frustrated by the brotherly gesture than his out-and-out lie about her bowling abilities. He'd said he preferred short relationships. She was a let's-take-it-slow-and-see-what-develops kind of woman. She was also a woman who had spent way too much time around death and·dying.

Longing washed over her. What she wouldn't give to be held in a man's arms again, skin to skin, heartbeat to heartbeat, reveling in the give and take of making love.

Tipping her head to the side, she studied Vince. The curve of his mouth, the line of his jaw. The way his dark eyes made promises he probably wasn't aware of.

She wanted to make love with him.

Tomorrow she could be responsible again, but tonight she needed to be loved.

She moved closer to him, lifting her face. Willing him to understand what she needed.

Awareness flashed in his eyes, then he stepped back.

"Well, good night," he said, his voice husky. He raised his hand as if to shake good-night, then let it drop. "We've got a busy day tomorrow. You need your sleep."

He started to turn.

"Vince? Can I ask you a question?"

He hesitated, then turned back toward her. "Sure. Shoot."

"How do you see me?"

"Um, with two eyes." His grin was forced, as was the bad joke. He acted as if he were almost afraid of her.

"Look at me. I mean *really* look at me. What do you see? If you didn't know I was Violet's sister, would you try to hit on me? Or would you not even notice? Just walk on by?"

"That's not a fair question. I *do* know you're Vi's sister."

Colleen wanted to pound her fists on his chest. He was being deliberately evasive.

"Close your eyes," she commanded.

"Huh?"

"I said close your eyes."

He complied.

She moved closer to him, 'til there was only the barest space between them. Close enough that he should feel her nearness. Had to feel the heat generated by two bodies.

"No cheating. I can see you looking."

Sighing, he squinched his eyes shut.

She raised her fingers to his cheeks, touched them lightly, then drew his face to hers.

His eyes flew open. She could feel his jaw tense beneath her fingertips.

"No peeking," she murmured. The sheer beauty of the man awed her.

Once he'd closed his eyes again, she pressed her lips to each eyelid, whisper soft.

His quick intake of breath told her he hadn't anticipated this. Neither had she. He might never admit it, but something strange and fragile happened in the dim hallway. Her soul connected with his, intertwined, never to be separated.

Her fingers trembled against his face as she stroked his jaw. She ached to touch him all over.

"Col—"

"Shhh."

She stilled him with a kiss.

He rested his hands on her hips as if he weren't quite sure what to do with them.

She slid her palms down his shoulders, his arms, his wrists. Then she grasped his hands and guided his arms around her.

He surrendered with a sigh, pulling her to him, caressing her back through the thin cotton of her blouse. He made love to her, fully clothed, with only a kiss to approximate the act. But she wanted more.

The stillness of the hallway exploded into a wealth of sensation. She gave him everything she had, everything she would ever have, crystallized in that one awesome, never-ending kiss.

Murmuring her name, he pressed her against the door. She barely noticed the handle digging into her back. She couldn't think, couldn't breathe, could only go with the moment. Because it was so spectacular it might never happen again.

Vince lifted her off the ground. She wrapped her legs around him. Needed to get closer.

Her head was swimming, her eyes tearing, and Lord how she wanted this man.

Vince broke off the kiss, pulling away from her. His breathing was ragged, sweat beaded his forehead.

His gaze was possessive as he grasped her hips and shifted her oh-so-slightly. Just enough so that they fit together perfectly, braced against the door.

"Vince," she whispered.

"Shhh."

He dipped his head and kissed the tender spot at the base of her throat. His mouth was hot and wet, his tongue teasing. He nipped at her skin.

She wound her arms around his neck, murmured wordless encouragements.

He pressed her hard against the door.

It was then, through the fog of destiny and need, that she remembered what she'd wanted to tell him.

"The door handle—"

His mouth covered hers and she lost whatever rational thought she might have had. She was falling. Falling in love? In lust? She wondered hazily if it were a dream.

But it was no dream when she hit the hard floor. Before she could draw a breath, Vince landed on top of her.

Then she saw stars. Bright specks of light floating in an aura around Violet's angry face as she glared down at them from above.

CHAPTER FIVE

VINCE ROLLED OFF her. Or at least Colleen assumed he did, because it felt like a great weight had been lifted from her chest.

"Are you okay?" His face wavered above her.

Unable to speak, she nodded.

Vince's face was replaced by Violet's. She made a peace sign only millimeters from the bridge of Colleen's nose. "How many fingers am I holding up?"

Colleen crossed her eyes to focus, but couldn't seem to stifle an errant giggle.

"You think we should call the paramedics?" Violet whispered.

"We better. She acts like she's got a concussion."

"I'm fine," she wheezed. "Once I catch my breath. Really."

"Let's help her into bed," Vi suggested.

Vince gently propelled Violet away. "Not you. *You* go sit down and put your feet up. I'll take care of her."

But instead of sitting, Vi paced.

Vince slid one arm under Colleen's shoulders, the

other behind her knees. Lifting her off the ground, he gently deposited her on the bed.

Colleen was tempted to wrap her arms around his neck and never let go.

"Where the hell were you?" Violet was still pacing.

"We went—"

"Don't you think you're overreacting a bit?" Vince interrupted. Colleen was grateful he was there to calm her sister. She didn't have the energy at the moment.

"Overreacting? Me? I don't think so. You told me you were going to get a bite to eat. *Four* hours ago."

"We went bowling after dinner. I told Colleen you'd be so sound asleep, you'd never notice."

"Well, I did notice," Vi barked.

"I'm sorry, Violet. I didn't mean to worry you," Colleen said.

"Well, you did. The hospital's been calling for the past half hour looking for you. I left three messages on your cell phone." Her voice dropped. "Dad's been vomiting blood and his pressure's dropped."

Colleen was upright and completely alert in seconds. "That's impossible. I called, what, two hours ago?" She glanced at Vince for confirmation.

He nodded.

"And my cell never rang. Unless it was too noisy for me to hear."

Violet's hand shook as she scraped her hair back off her forehead. "When I couldn't get ahold of you, I was…scared. They wanted permission for testing and endoscopic surgery. I didn't know what to do. Finally the administrator said they had a power of attorney from you and would proceed…otherwise he might go into shock."

Colleen tried to think beyond her confusion. One minute she'd been in Vince's arms, celebrating the end of a lovely evening, celebrating her return to life. The next, her dad was in immediate danger of dying.

Swallowing hard, she said, "I should have been here. I'm sorry you couldn't reach me."

"What can I do to help?" Vince asked, guiding Violet to a chair.

Colleen stood. Her head swam, but she ignored it. The sight of the tears trickling down Violet's face made it seem all the more real. She went to her sister and wrapped an arm around her stiff shoulders.

Violet wiped the moisture away with the back of her hand. "They want you to call ASAP, Colleen."

"Vince, will you make sure Violet's okay while I call the hospital?"

"Sure thing."

"It might be a good idea to help her pack while I'm on the phone—"

"Why don't we see what the hospital says first?" Vince appeared calm.

Colleen turned to him. "We may not have time. If they can't get the bleeding stopped, he could go into shock and die. It happened to another patient. One minute he was stable, the next he was gone." She snapped her fingers, as much to get his complete attention as to demonstrate how lightning-quick something like this struck.

His voice was low, concerned, when he said, "I didn't realize. I'll help Vi with her stuff."

Picking up the phone, Colleen dialed the number she knew by heart. Her favorite nurse explained the status. Though her voice was kind, it didn't lessen the impact of her words.

Numbness swept over Colleen as she placed the handset on the receiver. The warmth of Vince's hand on her shoulder was the only thing keeping her grounded.

"Well?" Vi asked, clutching a tissue as if it were a lifeline.

"He's in surgery. They're going to tie off the blood vessel with a rubber band-type thing. He's lost a lot of blood, his pressure's dangerously low. They'll know more in a couple hours."

Colleen's knees buckled and she sank to the bed. "They have my cell number to give me updates—I'll check to make sure it's working." Glancing at her watch, she calculated quickly. "We should get to L.A. in about three and a half hours. By 2:00 a.m. at the latest."

Vince frowned, pacing. "The doctor specifically instructed Vi to rest overnight."

"I have to see him before he dies. It's something I've got to do," Violet said.

Vince grasped Violet's hand and led her to a chair. "Sit down. You're shaking like a leaf."

Colleen looked more closely at her sister and didn't like what she saw. She was paler than Colleen had ever seen her. Dark circles ringed her eyes. And Vince was right, her whole body shook as if she'd been out in the cold all day.

She went to her and knelt beside her. Grasping her hand, she said, "I want you to have peace, closure, or whatever it is. But not if it causes you to lose the baby because you disobeyed doctor's orders." Colleen rose, thinking aloud. "I can rent a car. You can follow with Vince tomorrow when you've rested more."

Vince shook his head. "Remember the waitress said something about a road rally coming through town this weekend. Apparently every hotel room and rental car for a hundred miles was booked. We were fortunate there was a last-minute cancellation for these rooms or we wouldn't have had a place to stay tonight."

"Damn." Squeezing her eyes shut, she tried to think. But rational thought had fled the minute she heard her father was hemorrhaging.

Violet stood. There was a new determination in her voice when she said, "I'm not going to lose this baby. At least not by riding in the van. I've had a good nap and I can probably sleep better at the house than in this darn hotel room. Get the stuff loaded up and help me out to the van."

Vince stared at Vi. "You're sure this is what you want to do?"

"Yes."

Slowly, he nodded his head. "I'll do everything in my power to keep you safe. That means I drive 'til we hit the outskirts of L.A. Then, Colleen, I'll turn it over to you since you know the territory."

THE HAIR on the back of Vince's neck prickled when they passed the Welcome to Los Angeles sign. As traffic grew more congested, even at this hour, sweat beaded his upper lip. His pulse whooshed in his ears, and he felt like he couldn't pull enough air into his lungs.

"Are you okay?" Colleen asked, her hands steady on the steering wheel.

"It's a good thing you're driving now. 'Cause I think something I ate didn't agree with me."

"You're a little pale." Glancing in the rearview mirror, she commented, "But our other patient appears to be doing better. Her color's coming back."

Vince twisted around and was relieved to see Violet sleeping again. She was sitting upright, seat belt in place, her head resting against the travel pillow.

The silence lengthened. He'd been thinking about what had happened between him and Colleen, or what had nearly happened between them. "About what happened, you know, back at the hotel…"

"I don't need distractions while I'm driving. Can we talk about this later?" Colleen's gaze was focused on the road, her voice soft.

He had to agree with her logic. He just felt he

should say something noble and apologetic. Instead, he went for helpful.

"Want me to try the hospital again?" he asked.

"Would you? Please?" She handed him her cell phone.

He was glad to relay good news a few moments later. "The procedure was a success. The bleeding's stopped. He's weak, but doing well."

Colleen's shoulders relaxed, she exhaled slowly. "I'm so relieved."

"I know you are. So am I. And the news'll be good for Vi, too."

He just wished he could get rid of the uneasy knot in his gut. The crisis was averted, Vi was doing better, he'd almost safely delivered them to their destination. So what the hell was his problem? Whatever it was, he doubted it was food poisoning. He and Colleen had both eaten chimichangas for dinner, and she seemed fine.

That left a bad case of intuition, and he couldn't for the life of him figure out what his digestive system was trying to tell him. Sure, all the stuff going on with Vi and Colleen made him want to hightail it home. But they'd resolved their problems for the moment. And he and Colleen had managed, through sheer bad luck and timing, not to fall into bed together. As long as he didn't repeat the mistake everything would be okay.

So what in the hell had him so on edge? Glancing out the window, Vince's chest tightened.

Familiar landmarks whizzed by—L.A. had changed considerably in the nearly twenty years since his family had lived here, but there was a sameness about it. The smell of diesel fuel and smog, the dark streets illuminated by streetlights. It struck a chord in him. Home. But it wasn't his home anymore. Echo Point was the place he belonged. This city held only painful memories.

But Vince refused to let the memories dominate him. He ignored his aching stomach and the way his shirt clung damply to his back. Shifting in his seat, he felt for the lever on the lower edge. "If you're okay to drive the rest of the way, I'm gonna catch a few winks."

"I'm fine. Maybe you'll feel better after you get some sleep."

He grunted, closing his eyes as he lowered the back of his seat.

Old images flashed through his brain. A gas station. Blood. The knowledge that life would never be the same again.

VINCE AWOKE, disoriented and alone.

He knuckled the sleep from his eyes and looked around. Colleen was no longer in the driver's seat. Twisting around, he noted that Vi was gone, too.

Darkness surrounded the van like a cocoon. He shook his head, trying to figure out how long he'd been asleep and exactly where they were.

A tap at the window drew his attention. Colleen peered in at him from the other side.

Her pensive expression made him want to kiss away her worries. Just like last night. Except things had gotten way out of hand in a matter of seconds and a repeat performance would complicate an already tense situation.

Opening the door, he noticed they were parked in the driveway of an old, faded, yellow ranch-style house. A streetlight illuminated the yard, where the small patch of grass was brown and shaggy. A lone palm tree, its fronds shriveled, threw odd shadows. The whole place had an aura of being unloved. As if the owners just didn't give a damn.

"Are we in Monterey Park already?"

"Yes. This is um, my house. My dad's house, I mean."

Vince tried to clear his sleep-fogged brain. "So how come Vi says she grew up in East L.A.?"

"We lived there 'til I was three. Then Dad got a better job and we moved here. Violet spent most of her life at the first house."

"Makes sense. From what I remember of East L.A., it was pretty rough. I lived there when I was a kid, too. Small world, huh?"

"Yes, small world. Violet had said something about you living there a long time ago. By the way, she's in no condition to go to the hospital yet—I've got her settled in my room. I'll call and check on Dad, then get Patrick's room ready for you."

Vince stepped out of the van and winced. Stretching, he rotated his neck. "Who's Patrick?"

"Violet never mentioned him?"

"No. She was very closemouthed about her family. I figured out pretty quick that it was a touchy subject so I didn't push." Now he wished maybe he had. Then he wouldn't have been blindsided by the whole situation.

"Patrick was our brother. He died in a car accident, must be sixteen, seventeen years ago. But somehow we never got around to clearing out his stuff."

"That's rough, losing someone so young." All this talk about death was making him uneasy.

Colleen nodded. "He and Violet were especially close, but losing him hit all of us hard. Maybe Mom most of all. Things were never the same after that."

Things were never the same. How many times had he thought similar thoughts. It was painfully easy for him to pinpoint exactly when his life had changed forever.

Colleen tentatively touched his arm. "I really do want to talk about…well, what happened between you and me at the hotel. But first I need to make sure everything's ready for you inside and then get to the hospital."

"You need some sleep."

"Like I said, I'll call the hospital. It looks like Dad's out of the woods. If he's resting, then I may catch a few hours sleep and go tomorrow morning."

"Sounds like a good idea."

"Oh, and Vince?"

"Yes."

"Thanks for caring."

"Um. Yeah. But about what happened at the hotel…well, I'm sorry."

"Don't be." She lowered her eyes. "I needed you last night. I just thought I'd let you know that."

"When the news came in about your dad? I was glad to help."

Colleen cleared her throat. "No, I mean I needed you to…hold me."

Vince felt as if the earth dropped out from under him. Her honesty touched him. Her vulnerability touched him. And holding her had definitely been *his* pleasure. The jumble of emotions scared the hell out of him. "Um, like I said, glad to help."

Oh, that was a smooth line. *Glad to help.*

But it didn't seem to bother her. She stared up at him, her eyes luminous, her lips slightly parted.

Warning bells went off in his head. "Look, I don't do relationships. It's better you know up-front. I should probably rent a hotel room for the night."

Shaking her head, she said, "That's too bad. That you don't do relationships." She shrugged, tucking a strand of hair behind her ear. "A hotel room is out of the question. I dragged you hundreds of miles from home, the least I can do is give you a comfortable place to say."

"I really don't think it's a good idea."

Crossing her arms, she tilted her head to the side and studied him through narrowed eyes.

Vince felt like a suspect in a lineup. Only instead

of holding up a cardboard number, his identifier had Coward written on it.

"And who will be here to make sure Violet stays calm? Isn't that your job?"

He nodded slowly.

"Don't worry, I'll bunk with Violet in my room. You'll be perfectly safe in Patrick's room—there's even a lock on the door." She turned and headed for the house.

Swearing at fate under his breath, Vince noticed the way the breeze plastered Colleen's sundress to her body. Her movements were graceful, her chin tilted to a proud angle. He hoped to hell there was a lock to keep him *in* as well as to keep her *out*. Because something about her made him wish he *could* do relationships.

CHAPTER SIX

VIOLET SPLASHED cold water on her face, hoping the shock would jolt her out of the weird time warp she seemed to have fallen into.

Patting her face dry, she studied herself in the mirror. The confident adult was gone. In her place was a young Violet striving to cover a black eye with makeup or rearrange her hair so the missing clump wouldn't be noticeable. Shrinking Violet, as she'd thought of herself then. The girl whose only protector died and left her to fight her battles alone.

Tears of loss welled in her eyes. *Patrick.* She missed her brother as much now as she had then. There would always be a small piece of her heart missing, a piece that belonged to the boy who had sacrificed so much for her.

He'd seen something worth saving in that petrified girl—seen beyond the pathetic mixture of defiance and fear. Violet ran her fingertips along her cheek. Her eyes looked huge, afraid. Her skin was chalky.

Anger washed over her in hot waves. She'd only

been home a few minutes, and she was already reverting. It was as if she'd instantly lost all the ground she'd won in the intervening years.

Shaking her head, she wondered how in the hell she was going to last a couple days in this house without falling to pieces. The answer was simple. The way she always had—through sheer grit and determination.

She squared her shoulders and left the refuge of the bathroom, hoping to leave her old self behind. Because if she didn't, the old Violet colliding with the new meant things were going to get pretty crazy.

FLUFFING UP the pillows, Colleen wondered if Violet would be warm enough? A blanket maybe?

No, that would be overkill. Why was it so important that Violet find the place acceptable? This had been her home, too, after all.

Picking up her stuffed Scooby Doo, Colleen hugged him tight. She'd only been eight when Vi had left, but she remembered vividly the feelings of loss and betrayal. Because Vi had let her know in no uncertain terms how glad she was to be escaping from the family, escaping from *Colleen.*

And the ache in her chest was just as intense as the day Violet had hurled the ugly words at her.

Colleen shook her head, willing away the déjà vu. She carefully placed Scooby on the white wicker dresser. Smoothing the sheet on the twin bed, she pulled up the faded pink bedspread. It clashed horribly with the rust-colored shag carpet. Funny, she'd never noticed before.

"I feel like I've landed in an alternate reality or something. This place was a dump when I left and it hasn't changed a bit." Violet's voice clashed as badly as the bedspread.

Colleen tried not to let her sister's criticism get to her. "Dad's comfortable with things the way they are."

I'm comfortable with things the way they are.

Or at least she had been.

"You always were a daddy's girl," Violet commented as she placed her overnight bag on the dresser. Scooby toppled to the floor.

Violet stepped over him to survey the framed corkboard that contained Colleen's high school memorabilia. National Honor Society, the Science Club, her clerical internship.

"How would you know? You were never here."

Vi turned, raising an eyebrow. "I was here enough. The little princess could do no wrong. While I, on the other hand, could never do anything right."

"That's not true."

"I didn't figure you'd admit it."

"Why are you being so awful?" Colleen was starting to lose patience. She'd tried to give her sister leeway because she was pregnant, ill and out of her element. But there was only so much she was willing to take.

"Because that's what I do best. It's what I've always done best. According to Dad, I'm a bitch on wheels."

Colleen heard the hurt underlying her sister's brash words. The whole situation saddened her. So much pain with no one around to heal it. And the one man who had the power to hand their lives back to them wasn't exactly reliable. She only hoped her dad would see past his own needs and give Violet the apology she deserved and Colleen the unstinting love she'd always craved. In return, they could give him the forgiveness that would allow him to die in peace.

"You're wrong, Violet. Dad loves you." Colleen hoped her words were true. Hoped that their father hadn't simply been indulging in a moment of clarity, too fleeting for any real change. "He misses you. If only you'd seen him in the hospital asking for you."

"Dear old Dad is facing the gates of hell. That's why the sudden interest in me." Violet's laugh was brittle. "But you know what? He can burn in hell for all I care." She tossed her hair the same way she had as a teen.

"Who can burn in hell?"

Colleen turned toward the unexpected male voice. Vince leaned against the door frame.

"Colleen and I were just taking a trip down memory lane."

"Doesn't sound like a very pleasant trip."

Smoothing an imaginary wrinkle from the bedspread, Colleen responded, "Violet and I have different…perspectives on our family. Our dad in particular."

"And Daddy's Girl doesn't want to hear anything bad about her father."

"I didn't say that. I'm really trying to understand. But it's hard. And you're not making it any easier, Violet. You may not believe this, but I'm *not* the enemy."

Violet sighed. "I'm sorry, Colleen-Jellybean. When you're ready to hear the truth, let me know." She turned to Vince. "Do you think I could call Rosie first thing in the morning? I don't want to wake up Marisol and the boys tonight."

"Sure thing. They're usually up early."

Violet nodded and headed for the door, massaging her tummy. "Nature calls. Junior must be tap-dancing on my kidneys again."

Colleen released a shaky breath once her sister rounded the corner.

Colleen-Jellybean. Patrick and Violet used to call her that when she was a little kid. The nickname brought back vague memories of the few times they'd allowed her to join their tight-knit circle of two. All she remembered was the warmth of finally belonging.

Shaking her head, she muttered, "I thought I was ready. But this is so hard."

"Who says you guys have to resolve all the past stuff in a matter of days? Or even be best buddies? Sure, Violet needs to see your dad, but maybe rejoining the family fold is too much to expect of her right now. Give it some time."

Colleen had been so lost in thought she'd almost forgotten Vince was there. "Easy for you to say. You have a big storybook family, all close and cozy. But you know what, Vince? Being an only child sucks. I want my family back."

Vince held up his hands. "Okay, okay. I get it. You don't want my advice."

Colleen could see she'd offended him. But the emotional roller-coaster ride she'd been on the past couple of days was finally catching up to her. The effort to explain seemed monumental, but she gave it a try. "I didn't mean to take it out on you. I'm just…well…on edge. I've been worried about Dad, worried about Violet and then we got here and she started all this stuff."

"Hey, it's okay. We're all a little on edge. You want to talk about it? I've got a lot of experience handling sisters."

Colleen shrugged. "You've seen how she is here. Nothing like she is with you and Rosie. It's as if she blames me."

"Blames you? For what happened with your dad?"

She nodded. "Yes. And Mom, too."

Vince cupped her cheek. "I've answered more domestic calls than I can count, and I can tell you the kids are never to blame. And I don't think Violet blames you deep-down."

The warmth of his hand on her face was both comforting and confusing. His actions said he cared about her, while his words the night before had told her he never could.

She started to pace. "You heard her. She resents

the heck out of me. Maybe she figures if I hadn't been here, Dad would have treated her differently. I don't know."

Colleen had wondered the same thing many times, trying to make sense of a tragic situation.

"And your mom? What's the deal with her?"

Colleen turned away from him. "I can't go there right now. I'm on overload already."

"Okay. But remember, Vi's bark is worse than her bite—try not to take it personally. Things will look better in the morning. After you sleep in your own bed." He nodded toward the twin bed.

Colleen didn't want to be alone. There were too many confusing undercurrents. Too much at stake. She needed to be held, needed to be loved. Remembering his tenderness a moment ago, she stepped closer to Vince. "What if I said I needed you tonight? Even knowing that you don't do relationships?" she asked.

His eyes were dark with emotion. Clearing his throat, he said, "I'd have to tell you it's not a good idea."

"But would you say no?"

Vince hesitated, clenched his jaw.

Colleen held her breath. She willed him to take the few steps separating them and wrap his arms around her, make all the bad stuff go away, if only for a while.

His voice was stilted. "I would say no."

VINCE SAT at the kitchen table the next morning, mentally chewing himself out for being a bumbling idiot.

He'd probably never forget Colleen's wounded expression or the quick way she had recovered her dignity. He'd hurt her when he'd been trying to do the opposite. But somehow he'd been unable to put together the words explaining that his refusal had everything to do with him and nothing to do with her.

He tried to tell himself he'd done such a piss poor job because he wasn't used to turning down women. But truthfully, her plea had reached way too deep for him to ignore. His knee-jerk reaction would have been to carry her off to bed, make love with her all night long and promise she would never be alone again. Only he knew it was a promise he couldn't keep. So he'd refused. Baldly, with no tact, no finesse.

"Dad's doing much better this morning," Colleen commented as she entered the kitchen.

She looked good. Her dark green pantsuit made her eyes look deep green. Her hair was pulled back from her face in a sleek ponytail. He studied her face, noting the faint circles under her eyes.

Colleen poured a cup of coffee and took a sip. "He had a good night."

Obviously she wanted to put last night behind her, pretend nothing had happened.

"I'm glad."

"I'm headed to the hospital to see Dad. The hospice lady's going to meet me there— I have no idea what this setback will do to his chances of getting into a hospice group home. Then I have to run by the office and pick up more tapes. I'm behind on my transcribing."

"You said you don't really like transcribing?"

"Not really. But it pays the bills and allows me to work from home and keep an eye on Dad."

Her flat description floored him. He loved his job. Everything about it. Well, maybe everything but writing reports.

"So it's the working from home part that keeps you doing it?"

"Yes. I tried college, but Dad took a bad turn and I had to drop my classes. I'm thinking about going back later, after, you know…"

"Yeah. It would probably be good for you."

She nodded. "It's hard, though. To make plans for when Dad isn't here anymore."

Vince shifted uncomfortably. He couldn't make love to her, couldn't promise to chase away the loneliness, but maybe there was something he *could* do for her. "I guess I'll be hanging around the house 'til you get back with the van. Anything I can do to help around here? I'm pretty handy. Those dead shrubs out front need digging up. And I wield a mean paintbrush—"

"No. Thank you, but that's not necessary." The color drained from her face. "It's kind of you to offer, though."

"I bet it'd take a load off your old man's mind to have some of this stuff taken care of."

Colleen stiffened. "I said no, thank you."

"But—"

"My father likes things to stay the same. No changes, no surprises."

Vince didn't know how to respond. From Colleen's description, it sounded unlikely her dad would ever return home. Apparently she didn't see it that way.

"This would be a good surprise, though, wouldn't it?" he asked.

"There are no good surprises as far as Dad is concerned. He'd go ballistic."

The more he heard about Mr. Davis, the more certain he was that the man couldn't be human. And though Violet seemed to think Colleen had gotten the good end of the deal, he wondered if she might have been damaged just as deeply as Violet. He could easily imagine Colleen as a young girl, trying in vain to please everyone. Just as she was still trying to do.

SEAN DAVIS appeared much the same as when Colleen had left. He looked like a man who was dying, slowly, from the inside out.

She reached down and grasped his hand. "Hi, Daddy. I hear you've had it pretty rough while I was gone." She didn't really expect him to respond, but thought he might find her voice soothing even in his sleep.

His eyes flickered open. He tried to say her name.

"It's okay. Just rest. The nurses say you're doing much better. You had me scared there for a while."

Fear flashed in his eyes. She wondered what his thoughts had been before they sedated him and took him in to surgery. Surely he'd known he might die. Did he regret that his daughters weren't there? Did he want to apologize for the way he'd wrecked their family? Their lives?

"I've got some good news. I brought Violet home."

His lips quivered. His eyes darted from side to side. Slowly, he lifted his head and glanced around the room. When he realized they were alone, he let his head drop back to the pillow.

"Violet's at home, sleeping. She's pregnant, Daddy. And her doctor has advised her to get lots of rest. The last thing I want is for her to lose the baby."

He nodded, apparently satisfied.

There were so many questions bouncing around in Colleen's head, but her father was too weak to answer them. What if she never got the chance to ask again?

She had to give him the benefit of the doubt. "Daddy, when Violet was home, did things get out of hand? I mean, did you ever…hit her?"

He closed his eyes tight and turned his face to the wall.

"Dad, you've got to face the truth, whatever it is, when she comes to see you. You…may never have another opportunity."

COLLEEN PULLED into the driveway a short while later and stopped the van. But she couldn't get out. Couldn't face her guests.

She'd tossed and turned most of the night. The couch had seemed like a haven from her sister, but turned out to be highly uncomfortable.

Vince stepped out the door and glanced at the van. When he'd apparently assured himself that nothing was wrong, he went back in the house.

Sighing, Colleen squared her shoulders. She was tired and crabby and the last thing she wanted to do was play hostess. But she'd started the whole thing and she would see it through to the end.

After retrieving the box of tapes from the passenger seat, she headed for the front door. "Hello? Violet? Vince?" she called, closing the door behind her.

Vince wandered around the corner from the kitchen, as if he hadn't just been outside checking up on her. "How'd it go? At the hospital?"

"Fine. Is Violet awake?"

"Yes, Violet's awake," the woman said as she came into view. "I just move slower than Vince."

He grunted. "Only because you wanted to grab the last muffin while I was gone."

"You know me too well, Moreno." She licked crumbs off her fingertips. "And it was good, too."

Colleen couldn't help but smile. The cheerful banter was a welcome relief. Vince and Violet treated each other like siblings. She had vague memories of Patrick teasing Violet in much the same way.

"Well?" Violet prodded.

"I saw Dad this morning. He's weak, but he's doing well. He wants to see you. I told him you were resting. If you're up to it, we can go during the afternoon visiting hours."

"Th-this afternoon? There's no rush now, I mean he's out of danger."

Colleen saw fear flash in her sister's eyes. She wanted to hug Violet and tell her to take all the time in the world. But then she remembered her father's disappointment.

"He's anxious to see you. Visiting hours are from one to five. I thought maybe three o'clock?"

"Don't rush me. This isn't a simple family reunion. There's…stuff. I—I'm not sure I'm ready."

Colleen studied Violet. She'd changed since they'd arrived in L.A., swinging from one end of the emotional pendulum to the other. Colleen had never seen her this unsure before.

Approaching her sister, Colleen swallowed hard. "Violet, I'm trying to see things your way. I asked Dad about what you told me—that he hit you."

"And what did he say?"

"He was too weak to talk, and I couldn't tell from his expression. But I told him he should be ready to talk to you about it. That he might not have another opportunity."

Violet's eyes shimmered with tears.

Colleen sighed. She didn't know what to believe anymore. "He might still be weak this afternoon, but at least a quick visit will break the ice. I've, um, got a few things I need to discuss with him, too. But my stuff can wait."

Violet nodded slowly. "I guess the sooner I get it over with, the better."

Colleen wrapped her sister in a quick hug. "Thank you. I know how hard this is for you. But it will mean so much to him. And to you. Let's get some lunch." She urged Violet toward the kitchen.

"Vince, you'll come with us, won't you?" Violet glanced over her shoulder. Her eyes were wide, something akin to panic flared.

Vince cleared his throat. "Um, no. This should be a private, family moment."

"You're almost family," Violet said.

"Yes. And you've done so much for us. You're certainly welcome to come," Colleen added.

"No, no. I insist on staying here."

He looked a little green around the gills. Maybe he had gotten a touch of food poisoning while they were on the road.

She shrugged. "If that's what you want."

"It is. But please keep a close eye on Violet. I want you to promise you won't let her get upset or overdo it."

"I promise."

Ha! She could promise nothing of the sort. But it would work out, or so she told herself. All she had to do was get Violet to the hospital and talking with her dad. "Now, what's it going to be for lunch? I can order pizza or Chinese."

"Pizza," said Vince.

"Chinese," said Violet.

"You know I don't like Chinese," he protested.

"Tough." She turned to Colleen. "You decide."

Colleen sighed. Yes, they certainly acted like siblings.

"The lady is pregnant so she gets two votes. Chinese it is."

Vince grumbled good-naturedly, but when the food arrived he managed to polish off a good share of the fried rice and moo shoo pork, along with several egg rolls.

He appeared right at home in their kitchen, as if he'd been the boy next door, dropping by on a daily basis.

Colleen frowned. She couldn't for the life of her remember Violet bringing boyfriends to the house, though she knew there had to have been some. Violet had been the popular one.

With Colleen, it had been a different story. Dad's health had started going downhill, Mom didn't seem to give a darn about anything. And Colleen had found refuge in learning.

She vividly remembered sitting at this same battered, oak dining table to do her homework. For a while, she could tune them out. The sound of Dad opening the refrigerator door and popping the top on his first beer. Her mom nagging him not to drink so much. It was a nightly exercise in futility. Because one beer led to another and another.

Then the homework was cleared away and she set the table for dinner, where they all pretended Dad wasn't schnockered. Only Dad didn't need to pretend—he really *believed* it. Even though he slurred his words and dropped his utensils, he believed he was sober. Because if he believed hard enough, that made it so.

Shaking her head, Colleen willed herself to live in the present. Despite the fact that everything in the kitchen was the same—the avocado-green refrigerator, the brown-and-gold tile, the dark cabinets.

It was hard not to get sucked into a mental time warp, but she focused on Vince. "You know what, Vince, I think we'll take you up on your generous offer of help with the yard. Feel free to spruce it up. But don't feel obligated if you want to do some sightseeing or something."

"Nope. I've seen enough of L.A. I'd like to do some physical work, get my hands dirty."

"I appreciate your help. What'd your fortune say?" she asked.

He picked up the small rectangular strip of paper. "It's silly."

"Tell us." Violet leaned forward.

"It's nothing."

"Come on. What did it say?"

He sighed and picked up the tiny paper. "'The past is the future, the future is the past.' What the heck is that supposed to mean?"

Violet chewed slowly, then swallowed. "That *is* kind of strange. Maybe reincarnation and all that?"

"Who knows. You try one." He handed Colleen a cookie.

She snapped it open and withdrew the slip. "It

says, 'Fortune shines on you.' How much more generic can they get?"

"But yours is almost normal. No fair." He handed a cookie to Violet. "Your turn."

"'Your destiny lies within the circle.' How weird." She tossed the scrap of paper on the table. "Good thing I don't believe in that stuff or I could drive myself crazy looking for circles."

"Anyone want that last cookie?" Vince was already reaching for it.

Both women shook their heads.

"I'm not even gonna look at this one." He snapped open the cookie and removed the fortune, tossing it aside. Popping both halves of the cookie in his mouth, he crunched slowly, his expression thoughtful.

Violet stood and stretched. "Don't suppose you'd let me take a nap first? Before the hospital?"

"No way, big sister. And by big, I mean *big*." Colleen chuckled and gestured toward Violet's tummy, attempting the same bantering tone Vince had used.

Violet sniffed with mock disdain. She tossed her to-go container into the trash can and rinsed her glass. "I was going to clean up the kitchen, but after that remark, you deserve KP detail. I'll change clothes and put on a little makeup."

"Colleen, you mind if I look in that shed out back for some gardening tools?" Vince asked.

"If you promise to keep the improvements small. And only as long as you don't have anything better to do."

Vince held up three fingers, Scout style. "I promise I won't do anything too outrageous."

"I appreciate the help. I've been meaning to get to it for ages." She'd been keeping things going at home for so long, she couldn't remember having help. She supposed her pride would survive a little assistance from Vince.

He grinned. "Hey, you're doing me the favor. I need something to keep me occupied. All this waiting gets to me."

Colleen shrugged as he let himself out the back door. She could understand the need to keep busy. It was how she managed to stay sane sometimes.

Replacing the lid on the container of won ton, she noticed the slip of paper Vince had tossed aside. Her curiosity got the better of her and she picked it up.

The future is the past, the past is the future.

He'd received the same fortune twice.

VINCE RAKED the dried grass into a pile and wiped the sweat out of his eyes. The physical exertion felt good after so much time in the van.

Glancing up at the late-afternoon sun, he noticed the smog. It was like a great, gray-brown haze blanketing the sky. He missed the crisp air of Echo Point. The evenings were getting cool now as autumn approached. He could walk out his door in the evening and feel like he could reach out and touch the stars.

Not like here, where everything seemed layered with grit.

He hated L.A. That's what it came down to.

Standing the rake up against the faded yellow house, he picked up a hacksaw and went to work on the dead palm tree fronds low enough for him to reach.

The wail of an ambulance made his hackles rise. The sound, combined with the scents and textures of L.A., made him want to puke.

The future is the past. The past is the future.

Damn fortune cookie. It was as if fate were taunting him. First, this trip. Then all this talk of the past. He might as well have parked his butt in a psychiatrist's office.

It wasn't that he had anything against remembering the past. He just didn't think it deserved all the focus counselors seemed to insist on. Sure, he'd seen a shrink while he was with Phoenix P.D. He knew all about closure and feelings and all the rest of that happy crap. But he hadn't been able to figure out, at the time, what that had to do with a female bystander being killed in cross fire. It hadn't even been *his* revolver, dammit. So why the guilt trip and the nightmares?

After weeks and weeks of sessions, he still hadn't understood why his hands trembled every time he took a call. Or why he woke up in the night terrified, but not knowing what caused his terror.

His shrink said it was probably rooted in his past and the trauma of the shooting had brought it all back. That's when he'd said *adios* to Phoenix, the shrink and the idea of living anywhere but Echo Point. Echo Point was home—a safe haven. The past was better left alone.

Vince shook his head, refusing to spend more time rehashing it.

He lost himself in the repetitive motion of sawing. A few minutes later, he had several fronds at his feet. Shielding his eyes from the sun, he admired his handiwork. The tree looked tidier already, so did the lawn. As if someone cared.

He turned at the sound of a vehicle pulling into the driveway. Glancing at his watch, he frowned.

"Short visit," he called to Colleen as she got out of the van and started toward him. He picked up a push broom to sweep grass clippings off the driveway.

"Talk to her." She jerked her thumb over her shoulder, where Violet was slowly making her way around the front bumper.

Vince's shoulders bunched with tension. He stopped sweeping to really take stock of the situation. Colleen's eyes flashed with impatience.

"What happened?"

"You mean what didn't happen?" Colleen's tone was laced with irony. "Violet didn't go in. Wouldn't even set foot inside the hospital doors."

CHAPTER SEVEN

COLLEEN COULDN'T keep the disappointment from her voice. "I thought today was going to be the day. And then, nothing."

"Is Violet okay?"

Nodding, Colleen blinked back hot tears. "She seems fine. Just a little shaky. Dad, on the other hand, was so sad when I told him she couldn't come today."

"I'm sorry, Colleen. I just couldn't do it." Violet's voice was low, husky, as she approached. She paused on the steps to the porch. "I haven't panicked like that in years."

"Are you feeling okay? Any contractions? Any pain?" Vince asked.

Violet shook her head. "The baby's fine. I'm fine. Mad at myself, but fine."

He frowned, turning to Colleen. "What happened?"

"Violet did all right 'til we got to the sliding glass doors. Then she froze. I understand that she didn't mean to panic, I understand she couldn't control it, but still I'm…"

"Angry," he supplied.

Colleen's shoulders sagged. "Yes. I'm angry. I'm mad at my dad for causing all this. I'm mad at God for allowing it. And I'm mad at Violet for leaving when things got tough."

Violet crossed her arms over her chest. "You're not just talking about today, are you?"

Colleen's eyes burned. She brushed away angry tears. This wasn't the way it was supposed to be. She'd brought Violet home to patch things up with their dad, not drag out a bunch of their old problems. It was too much to deal with at one time. But she couldn't seem to hold it in anymore. "I'm talking about today and every other day I needed you. You left me and never looked back. Even after you knew Mom left, too. Even though you knew that Dad wasn't the greatest father in the world."

"I had to leave," Violet said. "It was the best thing for me to do."

"But what about me?" The plea came from deep within, the place in her heart where a sad little girl hid. A little girl who'd been abandoned by everyone she loved. Everyone, that is, except her father. And soon she would lose him, too.

Violet lifted her chin. "I wasn't strong enough to save both of us." She turned and went inside.

Colleen had never felt so alone in her life.

I WASN'T STRONG enough to save both of us. Violet's words echoed in Vince's ears long after she went inside. He watched helplessly as the tears trickled down Colleen's face.

He left a smudge on her cheek where he wiped with his thumb. Cupping her neck, he kissed her fleetingly on the forehead. "It'll be okay."

"It seems like everything's falling apart." Her voice was raw with emotion. "But I'm not giving up."

Vince stepped back. Colleen's pain grabbed him viscerally and wouldn't let go. Running a hand through his hair, he tried to reconcile all the undercurrents and innuendo. She'd been through hell, abandoned by almost everyone she loved, and still came back giving it her all. Still tried to reunite a family that might be better off apart.

He said, "Um, I'll give Violet a couple minutes by herself, then check to make sure she's okay."

"Yes, that'd be a good idea." Colleen stood on the steps, staring him at with eyes that seemed to plead, "What about me?"

She made him feel restless, as if there was something he should be doing to help. Instead, he started gathering the gardening tools.

"Vince?"

"Huh?"

"What did I just do?" Colleen's voice wavered.

He stopped, a pair of hedge clippers grasped in his hand. It was on the tip of his tongue to tell her that she'd opened Pandora's box, but knew it wouldn't do any good now. The truth could be softened in this case. "You told Violet how you felt."

"Wh-what if she leaves?"

"She won't."

"How can you be so sure?"

"Because I've never seen Violet back down from a fight. And it looks like this might be one of the biggest fights of her life. It won't be easy—for either of you."

She shook her head. "No, not easy. But it's got to be done. I was wrong. I thought all the old stuff was between Violet and Dad. Me and Dad. Kind of like spokes on a wheel, with him at the center. Our spokes never intersected. But that's not right. It's all connected, more like overlapping circles." She frowned, thoughtful.

"You lost me there with the circles."

"That's okay." Colleen nodded. "It means something to me. I better go work things out with Violet."

He angled his head to the side, refusing to acknowledge the churning in his stomach. Colleen seemed to feel better and had a sense of purpose— that alone should have reassured him. But all he could think of was the chaos she could cause by rocking the family boat, damaged and leaky as it was. It went against his instincts to stay hands-off, but she was a big girl, capable of making her own decisions and so was Violet. "Just try to keep it low-key if you can. She's had a lot of upset today."

"I'll be gentle." Colleen's gaze was warm, her voice held a teasing note.

Vince swallowed hard. His heart started beating double-time. She was getting to him and there wasn't a damn thing he could do about it.

"I've, um, just got a couple more things to do out here. Go on ahead inside. I'll be in soon."

SHAKING HIS HEAD, Vince removed his work gloves, smacking them together to remove the dust. The late-afternoon sun beat down on his back.

He listened for raised voices, but the coo of a dove was the only thing to disturb the quiet afternoon. Well, as quiet as it ever got in the city. The muffled sound of traffic was ever-present.

He'd tried using physical labor to sweat Colleen, Violet and the whole Davis family out of his system, but no such luck. He wanted to wring Mr. Davis's neck for hurting so many people—it almost seemed fitting that the man should be dying a slow, uncomfortable death as penance for his sins.

As for Violet, he just wanted to get her back home safe and sound. He couldn't force her to face a father who had treated her so cruelly and wasn't so sure whether it was a good idea anymore. All he knew was that he would protect her as much as he could.

Then there was Colleen. With eyes that mirrored everything in her soul and touched him deeply. She had grace, beauty and a compassionate heart. And she was the Davis family member he suspected might be the hardest to escape, drawing him further into her life with every minute they spent together.

He dismissed the thought before it could take hold—getting involved romantically wouldn't be a good idea.

Shaking his head, he went to the backyard. The small plot of dirt and gravel needed some help, too. After returning the tools to the shed, he wiped his feet on the mat and entered the house through the back door. He stood in the kitchen, tilting his head to the side. He heard female voices. They didn't sound friendly, but they didn't sound hysterical, either.

He grabbed a glass of water and went into the front room. Colleen was standing toe-to-toe with Violet, her chin raised to the same obstinate angle. If he'd had any doubt that these two were sisters, those doubts were now erased.

The women were apparently arguing over nail polish.

Vince scratched his head. His sisters had arguments like that and they could last for days, until the women finally got down to the *real* reason for the fight.

"I told you," Colleen said. "It was an accident."

"I just bet it was. You knew it was my favorite color."

"So shoot me. I spilled your favorite nail polish."

"On my favorite sweater. The day of Patrick's funeral, no less. Maybe somebody should have taught you to stay out of other people's stuff. Oh, I forgot. You were too perfect to need discipline."

"Maybe somebody should have taught you the world doesn't revolve around you. Oh, I forgot, you didn't stick around long enough for that."

Vince glanced from one to the other.

Violet's shoulders sagged, the light of battle in

her eyes flickered and died. "If I'd stayed any longer…I don't think I would have survived." There was a childlike vulnerability in her expression. She touched Colleen's shoulder. "I didn't mean to desert you. I truly thought you'd be okay—that he'd never hurt you."

Colleen's chin came down a notch. Her voice was low when she said, "It was an accident. The nail polish. I'd watch you put it on and you were so b-beautiful." Her smile wobbled. "I wanted to be just like you."

"I remember. You were only a little bitty thing, not much older than Rosie." She brushed Colleen's hair off her face. "At the time, I thought you were kind of a pest. Now I know you were just being a kid. Aw, sweetie, you were too young to know any different. And I yelled at you, too, didn't I?"

Colleen nodded.

"You really wanted to be like me?" Violet murmured.

"Yes. I'd try on your shoes, put on your makeup and pretend I was you." Tears trickled down Colleen's cheeks.

Violet drew her into a hug, rocking her from side to side as if she were Rosie. "Shhh. It's okay, baby."

Vince cleared his throat. His eyes burned—probably dust.

Colleen drew back to gaze into her sister's face. "Know what, Vi? We'll get past this. Next visit to the hospital will go better. I'm sure of it."

"I *was* trying." Violet's voice was soft. "Maybe I can do better tomorrow after a good night's sleep."

Vince's stomach sank. He didn't want to stay in L.A. any longer than was absolutely necessary—the place gave him the creeps. "They have visiting hours in the morning. We could leave for Echo Point by midafternoon."

Both women turned and frowned at him.

"Okay, okay. It was just a suggestion. A bad suggestion. Take as long as you need."

"I wonder why he's in such a big hurry?" Violet mused.

"He's been acting kind of tense, too." Colleen eyed him.

"You don't need to talk about me like I'm not here. Sure I'm tense. Listening to you two argue would give any guy a nervous twitch. And as for being in a hurry, I do have a job to get back to."

Violet tipped her head to the side. "Aren't you off work 'til Thursday?"

Vince nodded. He felt trapped. His instincts told him to get the hell out of Los Angeles before something bad happened. Before someone he loved got hurt.

"So what's the big deal?" Violet asked.

He debated telling them the truth. Shaking his head, he realized both women, Colleen in particular, would pounce on the information and make him relive every second. For his own good, of course. Closure.

"It's not a big deal. Um, just thought I could get some things done at home. And I'm sure Colleen wouldn't mind having her house to herself."

"I'm fine." She patted Vi's arm. "You're welcome to stay as long as you need."

"Great." *Just fricking great.* "Now if you ladies don't mind, I'm gonna take the van and check out the nearest hardware store."

Colleen gave him directions to a store a few miles away.

"I intended to get gas—the gauge is almost on empty. You might need to stop for some. There's a station across the street from the hardware store."

"Sure. No problem."

Vince let out a long breath when he got in the van. He'd go to the hardware store and lose himself in the familiarity of tools and gardening equipment. But first, gas.

The station was a nondescript, neighborhood garage with a minimarket attached. Swiping his debit card, he started the pump.

A maroon Impala pulled up at the next pump. Two Caucasian males got out and headed toward the minimarket.

Vince started to sweat. He tried to concentrate on the electronic display, but the numbers seemed to move in slow motion. He wanted to hurry it along.

Glancing around, he noticed the men exit the market and head toward him.

His breath caught in his chest. His pulse pounded.

He saw flashes of another gas station, another time. Blood, lots of blood.

It was all he could do to turn off the pump, replace the handle and get in the van. His legs felt like rubber.

The guys pumped a few dollars' worth of gas into the Impala's tank and drove out of the parking lot a few minutes later.

And still Vince sat, unmoving, in the van.

Somewhere a siren wailed.

The smell of diesel fuel and day-old tacos was thick in his nostrils. He saw flashes of two different crimes, two different cities and knew without a doubt he was in a dangerous place.

"HAVE YOU NOTICED anything weird about Vince?" Violet asked as she sliced carrots for the salad.

Colleen shook her head. Heat warmed her cheeks. She'd noticed *a lot* about Vince, none of it weird. "How long have you known him?"

"I met him the first week I was in Echo Point. He's indirectly responsible for me meeting Ian."

"Oh?"

"He investigated the accident. Annabelle darted out in front of my car. I was going too fast and barely even saw her. Anyway, Ian came charging out of the brush at me and I kind of freaked out. He scared me, so I left the scene. Vince gave me the ticket."

"You were afraid of Ian? You're not afraid of any-body…except maybe Dad."

Violet gazed out the kitchen window, a carrot in

one hand, the vegetable peeler held loosely in the other. "Everyone's afraid of something, little sister. There was a while after we first got married that I thought I might lose Ian." Violet's eyes were suspiciously bright as she gazed out the window. A tear trickled down her cheek. "I miss him so much. This is the longest we've been away from each other since Rosie was born."

Wiping her cheek with her sleeve, Violet said, "I miss Rosie, too. I called her this morning, but she was having so much fun with Vince's niece and nephews, she could barely spare a minute to talk to me."

Colleen got a lump in her throat simply from listening to the love in her sister's voice.

"Here." She went to Violet and gently pried the carrot and peeler from her hands. "Why don't you go call them? I bet they miss you like crazy, too."

Vi smiled through her tears. "I think I will."

Colleen assembled the salad by rote after Violet left the kitchen.

What would it be like to love a guy as much as Violet loved her husband? Or even better, be loved by a guy as much as Ian apparently loved her?

A wave of longing caught Colleen by surprise. Her life was okay, wasn't it? Sure, it could be more exciting. Her job was kind of tedious, but it allowed her the flexibility to care for her dad. And caring for dad was tedious at times—

Colleen cut short the thought. She shouldn't resent him. If, years ago, he'd known the outcome of his drinking would be chronic illness, he would have quit. At least that's what she told herself, what she was desperate to believe.

A prick to her index finger reminded her to pay attention before she really did some damage with the knife.

But the thoughts kept coming. She was fooling herself. Her dad probably wouldn't have quit drinking even if he'd suspected it would eventually kill him. Had he known and just not cared? Not cared about her? Violet? Their mom?

Colleen seethed. The unfamiliar anger percolated inside her. And grew. And grew. Until she wanted to break something. She slammed down the knife.

Taking a few deep breaths, she reminded herself that anger was a normal emotion. It simply meant she was human.

So why did it make her feel so crummy?

Colleen folded her arms on the counter and rested her head there. Tears came, hot tears of rage and despair. She cried for herself, she cried for Violet. And she even cried for her father and the sad way he'd wasted his life.

As the tears gave way to hiccups, Colleen became aware of someone caressing her back.

"You okay?"

Colleen raised her head and looked up into Vince's face. "H-how long have you been here?"

"Just a couple minutes." His hand stilled between her shoulder blades. It was warm and real and reassuring. "What's going on? Did you and Vi fight again? Is she okay?"

"She's f-fine. She's talking on the phone with Ian. I guess I just kind of hit the wall. With everything that's been going on."

"That's understandable." He grabbed a tissue from the box and handed it to her.

"Thanks," she murmured, embarrassed that he saw her with red, puffy eyes and a runny nose.

"No problem. I've got three sisters, remember? I'm used to it."

"You were gone a long time."

Vince's smile looked forced. "Lots of bargains at the hardware store."

She could almost feel him drawing away from her. He probably thought she was a total wimp. "I'm not usually like this. I mean, I hardly ever cry."

"Hey, you don't owe me any explanations."

"I thought I'd pretty much worked through this stuff with the hospice counselor. I guess I was wrong." Colleen shrugged.

Vince hesitated. "Maybe you should ease up on this whole family reunion thing."

"I can't. I don't have time to ease up. Vi and my dad need to make up before it's too late. And there's some stuff I need to work out with him, too."

"You did your part. You brought Violet home."

"What if they waste the opportunity, though?"

"Then it's their deal. Or don't you think they might be able to fix their own messes without your involvement?" His gaze was probing as he studied her. "Or is that maybe what you're secretly afraid of?"

"What a horrible thing to say."

Horrible, but true?

Vince shrugged. "Hey, it was just a shot in the dark."

Colleen swallowed hard. His shot in the dark had been a direct hit. "So you're asking me if I enjoy being in the middle?"

"I guess so."

"I don't know.... I hope not." Did other people see her that way? Pushing her nose in places she didn't belong? Getting some sort of satisfaction out of it?

"Whether you enjoy it or not, you've got to take yourself out of the middle."

"But—"

"Otherwise somebody's going to get hurt. I don't want it to be Violet." He stepped closer and brushed a strand of hair off her cheek. "And I don't want it to be you."

COLLEEN WATCHED Vince through the living room window; his back flexed as he squatted to pull weeds. She'd thought about what he'd said. Maybe he was right. Maybe her concern for Violet and her dad was only the tip of the iceberg.

Sure, she'd desperately wanted the two to reconcile. Both for their benefit and for her own. She wanted to be a part of a family again—having Vince and Violet here in the house only intensified that need. The three of them had formed a little family group and it felt right, even the squabbling. She didn't want to go back to being an only child. And she didn't intend to.

Colleen mulled the problem from all angles. If Vince felt more included, he'd be less inclined to want to get out of L.A. as fast as possible. So she would make darn sure he felt included.

Stepping outside, she called, "Vince, will you come with us to the hospital?" She picked her way across the yard. Shading her eyes from the angle of the morning sun, she looked up in Vince's face. "I think Violet might be more reassured if both of us are there. If you drive, I'll sit in the back seat with her and keep her distracted."

"She seemed calm enough a few minutes ago."

"That's now. Being at the hospital is a whole different story. You do want her staying calm, don't you?"

"Of course I do. But I don't like hospitals."

"They're not my favorite places, either. But she'll do much better if we can provide a united front. Let her know she has our support."

Sweat trickled down his face, and he used his shirt to wipe it off. "I'll drop you off, wait in the van. That's all."

"If it's that you don't want to go inside all dirty, we can wait—"

"That's not the point. I'm not going in. Not now, not ever. It's not that I wouldn't love to help you out. I'd *carry* Violet up there if I thought it would help."

She shook her head, mystified. "Then what's stopping you?"

Vince picked up a push broom and started to sweep the already pristine driveway.

Colleen flushed. She had been ignored a lot in her life—it went along with trying to be a good little girl, being seen and not heard and all that outdated crap. But this man was not going to ignore her.

She walked up to him and grabbed his arm. "I said, what's stopping you?"

Vince paused, resting his hands on the top of the broom. "I haven't been inside a hospital in years. You're on your own."

You're on your own.

She'd been on her own all her life. She'd hoped now would be different.

Opening her mouth, she then clamped it shut.

Vince wasn't the kind of guy who avoided responsibility. He'd stepped up to the plate every time they'd asked for help.

There had to be a very good reason he couldn't or wouldn't help now.

Understanding dawned. "You really can't go inside, can you?" she murmured. "Like some people can't get on an airplane?"

He nodded slowly.

"How do you manage? With your job?"

"Paramedics handle most of the injuries. But if I'm involved, I take 'em as far as the outer doors. The hospital staff takes over there."

Colleen tried to assimilate this new facet of Vince, so unexpected, so sad. This courageous, intelligent, stubborn man was afraid of hospitals.

"Can't you even do it for Violet? She needs you."

"You'll be there for her. Just make sure she takes it easy."

"She needs all the moral support she can get. But if you can't, you can't." Colleen suppressed a twinge of remorse for playing on his sense of duty.

He turned away, but not before she saw the frustration in his eyes.

The same frustration that was there an hour later when they parked the van in the visitors' parking lot and Violet refused to get out. But his voice was strong and reassuring when he said, "Go on, Vi. Everything will be okay."

"Everything will be fine," Colleen soothed.

"It makes me so damn mad. Look at my hands, they're shaking." Vi demonstrated. "My father no longer has any control over me, but he can still mess with my mind."

"He can't hurt you. He's too sick, even if he wanted to," Colleen said. "Everything will be fine, you'll see." She said it to convince herself as much as her sister.

"If it's too much, all you have to do is turn around and come back. We'll leave, no questions asked," Vince said.

Colleen hesitated, thrown off guard by his caring. Here he'd had some serious issues with hospitals but he'd brought them anyway, as far as he could take them. It was something her father wouldn't have done in a million years.

Guilt made her queasy. She'd played on his emotions, his sense of duty, and essentially forced his hand. All in the name of orchestrating something that maybe wasn't her concern. Putting herself in the middle, as Vince called it.

Colleen swallowed hard, giving herself a mental pep talk on the greater good and all that. She gripped Violet's elbow. They'd come this far, they might as well see it through. She vowed to apologize to Vince when this was all over.

"I know it's not easy for you." She helped her sister out of the van. "You're doing great. This'll be a piece of cake."

Violet seemed to draw strength from her with each step. When they approached the sliding glass doors, she took a deep breath and charged through. It was as if she thought momentum would make up for her lack of enthusiasm.

The elevator ride to the fourth floor seemed like an eternity. Violet didn't say a word. Neither did Colleen.

When the elevator opened, Vi didn't move.

"Come on. This is Dad's floor."

"I'm not doing it. I don't know what to say. How he'll react. It's just not worth it."

"He won't say anything bad, I promise."

"You can't promise that, Colleen. Fact is, none of us know what the old bastard is going to do from one minute to the next. You even admitted his personality hadn't improved much since he quit drinking."

Colleen knew they only had a few seconds before the doors shut. "We can talk about it over there. By the waiting area."

"It's no use, Colleen. It's turning me into a nervous wreck. He could say something that destroys any hope I have of forgiving him."

The doors swept shut.

Colleen took a deep, calming breath.

"He won't do that. I know it. He's been looking forward to seeing you."

"I just can't do it."

"How about for me?"

Violet smiled sadly. "Not even for you, little sister."

The finality in her voice told Colleen it would be pointless to argue.

Her heart sank with the inevitability of it all. Frustration melded with loneliness to form a tight ball in her chest.

"I'll walk you out to the van, then I'll go explain to Dad."

This was one of those times when being in the middle really sucked.

CHAPTER EIGHT

COLLEEN TIPTOED into room number 415. Part of her hoped Dad was asleep. That way she wouldn't have to hurt him. Yet.

As if through some sort of sixth sense, he shifted, rolling over to face her.

His cheeks were gaunt, but there was a spark of expectation in his eyes.

When he saw she was alone, the expectation died, replaced by a question.

"Violet's not here, Daddy. She, um, needs more rest before she comes in."

His chapped lips quivered. His hand shook as he reached for the cup of water.

Colleen went around the bed and handed the cup to him.

He mumbled a thank-you, though his tone had more "screw you" in it than gratitude. But Colleen knew how to read between the lines, or so she told herself, relying on distant memories of a kinder, more patient man. Some days, she wondered if she'd invented the memories just to make herself feel better.

"How're you doing today?" Her tone was chipper. "Violet?"

"I told you, Daddy, she couldn't come."

She tried to be patient, but it hurt that she was here busting her rear to take care of him and all he thought about was Violet. Colleen swallowed her anger. She refused to think about the pang of jealousy. It didn't matter. He was a sick man.

"Tomorrow?"

"I hope so.

COLLEEN'S STEPS slowed as she neared the van. The visit with her dad had drained her. She didn't want to see Violet, didn't want to be supportive and encouraging. She wanted to go home, crawl into bed and cry her eyes out.

But she wouldn't. She was the perfect one, as Vi put it, always dependable, always levelheaded. There didn't seem to be room in her life for Vince's theory that she was entitled to human foibles.

A dull ache started somewhere behind her right eye. She rubbed her forehead.

She still managed some semblance of a bright smile when she reached the van. The vehicle vibrated quietly to the hum of the engine, the air conditioning was probably going full-blast. She rapped on the passenger window, and Violet jumped.

When Colleen opened the door, Violet said, "I came up here because it was easier to talk to Vince. We can switch seats."

Colleen waited for her sister to lumber from the van.

When they were eye to eye, Violet studied her face. "How'd it go?"

Colleen's head started to throb as she searched for the appropriate half truth. But the beginnings of a migraine made it impossible to think. "He was…disappointed."

"I'm sorry," Violet murmured.

Sighing, Colleen said, "I know you are." She closed the sliding door with more force than was necessary and claimed the front passenger seat.

Vince took one look at her and said, "That bad?"

"That bad." She lowered her voice so her sister wouldn't overhear. "Once he knew Violet wasn't coming, he rang the nurse for pain medication. I stayed with him until he fell asleep. I hope you guys weren't too uncomfortable."

"Hey, we did just fine. Cranked up the AC and the stereo, and it went by in no time." He turned toward the back seat. "Right, Vi?"

"Um, right. Can we leave now?"

Vince frowned. "Are you okay?"

"I'm fine. Just a little tired. Let's go…home."

"Home it is."

When they arrived a few minutes later, Colleen couldn't believe her eyes. "You painted the trim this morning. I didn't notice on the way out."

"Yeah. I was able to get the same color, so it's really not a change. It shouldn't bother your dad and it gave me something to do."

"That was so sweet. And the yard, you've done wonders with it," she breathed. "It's never looked this good."

"No problem." Vince smiled. "I enjoy working with my hands. It keeps me occupied."

Colleen could have reached across the seat and kissed him for his generosity. But she didn't.

Instead, she helped Violet into the house—her sister looked about ready to drop. "Why don't you go take a nap."

"I'd prefer to sit on the couch. I don't feel like being alone right now."

Her admission of weakness surprised Colleen. It also worried her. "Here, I'll make you comfortable."

She started to place the pillows behind Violet's back, then thought better of it, remembering when her sister had thrown the hotel pillow against the wall. Colleen handed them to her instead.

When she checked the answering machine, she heard an unfamiliar male voice with a message for Vi.

"Ian," Violet breathed. Her smile was luminous.

"You better call him back ASAP. He said he has a surprise."

Colleen handed the phone to her, curious about the man who seemed to light up her sister's world.

She knew Violet probably wanted privacy, but she couldn't seem to make her feet obey. It was fascinating to watch Violet talk. Her gestures were animated, her voice tender. All traces of her exhaustion had vanished. And along with it, the tense, brittle woman afraid to face her past. Amazing.

Violet covered the mouthpiece and whispered, "He'll be here in a couple hours."

Thank God. Maybe he could talk Violet through her fears.

Colleen went in search of Vince and found him in the kitchen, making a sandwich. "Ian called. He'll be in town in a couple hours."

Vince raised an eyebrow. "I hope he's not doing something stupid, like quitting the tour. Although, I have to admit, I'd be more than happy to hand over the reins to him."

"It sounded more like a short visit. I think Violet would have been angry if he were quitting the tour."

"Furious more like." He shook his head. "But she needs him right now. Seeing him will do her a world of good."

"That's kind of what I thought."

Their suspicions were confirmed when Violet floated into the kitchen.

"Somebody's on cloud nine," Vince commented, smiling affectionately.

"Ian's coming." Vi's voice was vibrant, her eyes sparkled. It was hard to believe she was the same woman. "He's taking me to dinner."

Colleen couldn't wait to meet Ian. He had to be one heckuva guy to cause such a drastic change in her sister.

"How'd he work that? He's not ditching the tour, is he?" Vince asked.

"Oh, no, nothing like that. He finagled his schedule so he can have his signing in L.A. tomorrow. He'll be here for two whole days."

"Um, I guess you guys could have Dad's room. If you don't mind sleeping in an adjustable hospital bed. It's not very romantic, though."

Vi wrinkled her nose. "Perish the thought. Ian said something about making reservations at a hotel nearby. The man thinks of everything."

"Apparently," Colleen murmured.

"I've got to go get ready. He'll be here in two hours. First, a nice long bubble bath…" Violet's voice trailed off as she wandered out of the kitchen. "What will I wear?"

Vince raised an eyebrow. "You'd never know they've been married for five years, would you?"

"No." Colleen suppressed the wistful longing that seemed to creep in whenever she saw how happy her sister was in her marriage. "I wouldn't."

But then again, she would never have believed she'd meet a guy like Vince, one who could be strong without being domineering: open, encouraging and funny, a man who loved with his whole heart. She could detect it in the way he treated Vi and Rose, the affection in his voice when he talked about his sisters, his father. When he loved a woman, he would give his all. How in the world had he decided relationships weren't his strong point?

"Hey, wanna go to the plant nursery?" Vince asked. "We can pick up a couple shrubs to replace the dead ones?"

Colleen eyed him speculatively. "Sure. Give me a couple minutes to change."

COLLEEN UNLOCKED the front door a few hours later. She turned to Vince and said, "I can't believe you convinced me to get all those plants." She gestured toward the assortment of potted plants on the front porch.

"They're low-water, low-maintenance. How could your dad object?"

"Oh, he'd object all right. But I guess I have to face the possibility he won't be able to see this house again. His medical needs make in-home care nearly impossible." The thought made her sad, just as it had made her sad the day she'd decided to contact the hospice people.

Vince's hand was warm on her shoulder. "Hey, a few minor changes'll perk things up around here. And if your dad takes a turn for the better, he'll probably be so darn glad to get out of the hospital he won't even notice."

Colleen nodded, content to let him look on the bright side, even if it was just an illusion.

The house was incredibly quiet when they stepped inside.

"Violet?" she called.

"Surely she's not sleeping?"

"She'll be glad we stopped to get milk and bread." Colleen hefted the grocery sack she carried into the kitchen.

Vince picked up an envelope on the table. "Has my name on it. Huh."

Opening the seal, he pulled out a piece of lined notebook paper. Something fluttered to the floor. Vince picked it up, whistling low when he read the print. "Tickets for tonight's Diamondbacks vs. Angels game."

Colleen stood on tiptoe to see over his shoulder. "What's the note say?"

"It's from Ian. He and Violet are staying in a hotel tonight. They'll drop by to see us tomorrow or hook up with you at the hospital. Hmm. Ian must've convinced Violet to give it another try. If anyone can get her through this, it's Ian."

"I'm so glad she's going to try again. And you're right, Ian's presence might just do the trick." Colleen couldn't contain her curiosity another moment. "Does it say anything about the tickets?"

"Yeah. Down at the bottom there's a P.S. The tickets are for me—a thank-you gift for bringing Violet here." Turning to her, he grinned broadly. "Ian knows I love baseball. Love the D-Backs."

"It'll be a great game."

"D'you like baseball?" he asked.

"Are you kidding? I'm a *huge* Angels fan. My dad used to take me to Edison Field."

Vince raised an eyebrow. "The game starts at six. I'd ask you to come with me, but there's one problem."

Colleen's heart took a nosedive. "Problem?"

"We'll be rooting for opposing teams. It could get

tricky. What if you're a sore loser?" His face was serious, but he had a wicked gleam in his eye.

"It won't matter, because the Angels won't lose. What I'm more concerned about is whether *you're* a sore loser."

"Oh, you think so, huh? Wanna make a little wager?"

"Sure."

"Loser takes winner out for a drink afterward. Or ice cream. Pick your poison."

"Hmmm. A margarita to toast the Angels' win. That sounds good."

"You got it. Only you'll be toasting the Diamondbacks' win."

"I don't think so, Moreno. You've got a bet. Deal?"

"Deal."

As Vince waited in line at the concession stand, he tried to remember the last time he'd been to a major league baseball game. Not since he'd lived in Phoenix, at least. He watched the games on TV these days, but it just wasn't the same. There wasn't the noise and excitement of the crowd, the aroma of junk food, the occasional obnoxious drunk spilling beer.

Vince hadn't felt this good in ages.

He made his way back to their seats. Colleen wore a red T-shirt and jeans, presumably to show her spirit along with the zillion other Angels fans who made up the sea of red. She waved a team pennant. Her eyes sparkled with excitement.

"Here you go." He handed her a pop and a hot dog. "There's ketchup and mustard. No onions. Just the way you requested."

Colleen inhaled deeply. "There's just nothing like a ballpark hot dog."

"You know it. How old were you when you saw your first game?"

"I was a little bitty kid, couldn't have been much more than three. How about you? With the Diamondbacks?"

"When I lived in Phoenix."

"I didn't realize you lived there."

Vince shrugged. "Yeah. I was only there a couple years—I was a rookie in South Phoenix. Trial by fire, as they say."

"Oh?"

"It's one of the rougher areas of town."

Colleen tipped her head to the side and studied him. "I have a hard time seeing you as a city cop. Sheriff suits you better."

"It does. I love my job. I get to do so many more positive things than I did in Phoenix."

"Is that why you made the change?"

Vince hesitated, bit into his hot dog and chewed. It gave him time to formulate an answer. "I didn't know then that sheriff was the job for me. I loved being a cop. But seeing so much bad stuff, day in, day out, it got to me."

He didn't tell her that it had been one episode in particular that had sent him into a tailspin. Didn't tell her about the nightmares, the sessions with the shrink. Sessions he'd cut short because the guy wanted him to revisit childhood trauma practically back to the womb—and didn't believe him when he said there *wasn't* any trauma.

"So when the job opened up in Echo Point, I applied. I was elected before I knew it." He shrugged.

"You're pretty young to be a sheriff. Does anyone give you a hard time?"

"Not for long. Like I said, I patrolled some pretty scary places in Phoenix. I don't back down easily. Word gets out quick."

"I bet it does. I envy you. You have a job you love."

"Isn't there something you've always wanted to do? What was your major before you quit college?"

She hesitated, glanced away. "Marine biology. I wanted to research ocean life or train animals someplace like Sea World."

"You're kinda far inland for that."

"Dad started getting sicker my senior year in high school. I had a choice, stay here or go to the University of San Diego. I chose to stay and attend the community college—figured I could get my required courses out of the way." Regret flashed in her eyes, then was gone. "But I had to quit."

"That's a tough choice to have to make. My dad lived with me after I returned to Echo Point. It was a pretty good arrangement for a few years, but he went to live with my sister in New Mexico last year."

"How come?"

"He had bypass surgery. My sister Linda really wanted him to stay with her while he recovered. Since she had the time and resources to take care of him, it was a no-brainer. He seems to like it there and that's what counts. I saw Ian struggle with caring for his mom and I'm grateful I didn't have to face the same decisions he did."

"Violet said something about Ian's mom having Alzheimer's?"

He nodded. "It got pretty ugly. Then he found a place for her to live that specialized in Alzheimer's patients. I took my dad to visit her a couple times. It was a nice place—she seemed happy."

Colleen frowned, chewing slowly. "When your dad moved, did it kind of leave a void? Like you didn't quite know what to do with yourself?"

"I still miss the old guy. I go home intending to tell him the great joke I heard at work and he's not there. The place is kinda empty without him." Vince cleared his throat. He needed to plan a trip to New Mexico *pronto*. It'd been way too long since his last visit.

Colleen murmured, "I wonder how I'll handle it when my dad…isn't there anymore. A part of me thinks, wow, I'll be able to do whatever I want. Travel, date, go back to school. The other part is lonely without him around. What will I do when nobody needs me?" Her voice was soft, vulnerable.

Vince wrapped his arm around her shoulder. "You'll do fine. It'll be rough at first, I imagine. But it gets better. I've seen that with Ian and Vi. They were heartbroken when Ian's mom no longer knew them. Then she passed away and that was a fresh wound. Now, I think they enjoy remembering the good times. Telling Rosie about her."

"I have a hard time visualizing Vi caring much about her mother-in-law."

"She met Daisy before the Alzheimer's got bad. She loved Daisy and Daisy loved her. They were more like mother and daughter than most blood relatives."

"Like I said, I have a hard time seeing it. Violet and my mom weren't close. Of course, I don't think my mom was close to anybody."

Vince was tempted to ask about the mysterious Mrs. Davis, but the subject of mothers hit a nerve left exposed simply by being in L.A. "Hey, looks like they're gonna start in a couple minutes. Who's your favorite player?"

Colleen started to reply, when an elderly gentleman moved beside her. She half rose in her seat to make more room for him to get by. He was carrying an old ball glove and an Angels pennant.

Vince stood to let the old man past. The proud way the guy held his head reminded Vince a little bit of his dad. He smiled and said hello.

The teams took the field and the crowd went wild. But Vince enjoyed watching Colleen the most. She seemed to want to absorb the experience and remember it forever.

Too bad she seemed to have missed out on so much to take care of her father. But he had to respect her loyalty. She was one terrific woman. He'd watched her handle Violet and the crisis with her dad and he admired her spunk. She might seem calm and shy to some, but to him, he saw passion. Passion for the people she loved and passion for life.

He tried hard to tell himself his interest was purely platonic, but he knew better. She was beautiful, caring, giving. It wouldn't be hard to fall for a woman like Colleen.

Vince was jostled out of his reverie by the old man next to him. The guy's elbow apparently got away from him as he cheered himself hoarse for the Angels.

Vince leaned nearer to Colleen and shouted, "You guys have me surrounded. I'm the lone Diamondbacks fan in a crowd of Angels fans."

Colleen glanced around and nodded. She leaned closer to him, her mouth inches from his ear. Her warm, sweet breath raised goose bumps on his neck. "You're a brave man, Moreno. A little misguided in your choice of teams, but brave nevertheless."

Pulling her close, he kissed the top of her head. "You'll just have to woo me to the other side."

She looked up at him, her eyes sparkling. "Maybe I'll just do that," she murmured.

"What do you have in mind?" Vince could have bitten his tongue but it was too late. Flirting was an automatic reflex.

Tipping her head to the side, she seemed to consider her answer. "I'll surprise you."

"You already have." Oh Lord, what was he getting himself into? He had a pretty good idea that whatever it was, it would be over his head. But even that knowledge couldn't persuade him to move away from her. He felt too good having her tucked beneath his arm, snuggled against his side.

He gave up and just savored having her close until the Angels shortstop hit a home run. Then she jumped up, waving her pennant like crazy and yelling for all she was worth.

A feeble yell on his left drew his attention. At first he was afraid the old guy was having a heart attack or seizure or something. But a closer look told Vince he was merely cheering on his team. The man waved his pennant for about two seconds, then let his arm drop. He didn't look well.

"Did you see that?" Colleen plopped back in her seat, grinning from ear to ear. "Home run, Moreno. You're gonna owe me that margarita."

"It ain't over 'til it's over, as the great one used to say."

Several more innings went by and the Angels were up by two runs. "It's starting to look like I might owe you that drink."

"I'm glad you can admit when you're wrong."

"Only in baseball."

She eyed him speculatively. "You do have a stubborn streak, don't you?"

"Yep. I'm *very* good at getting what I want." He grinned wickedly, focusing on her lips.

"Oh?" Colleen raised an eyebrow. "What would that be? Other than a doomed desire to see the Diamondbacks win, that is?"

"I'd like more opportunities like now." He shrugged. "To get to know you. To date you." The words slipped out so easily as if he were asking her to the high school prom. He hadn't *dated* a girl in years. Bedded yes, dated no. But he realized that was exactly what he wanted. Regular, old-fashioned dates where they got to know each other slowly and built a future instead of falling in lust.

Whoa. His heart just about jumped out of his chest.

Colleen slipped her arm through his and leaned against him. "I'd like that, too." She raised her face to his, her lips parted, her eyes deep and dark.

He forgot what he'd ever had against dating in the first place. A relationship with this woman was a no-brainer. Only an asshole would consider a one-night stand with a woman as terrific as this.

Grasping her chin, he lowered his head, anticipating the same passionate response as the last time he'd kissed her.

Vince felt a tap on his left shoulder. "Young fella, would you do me a big favor?" the guy seated next to him asked.

He reluctantly withdrew his arm from around Colleen and sat up straighter. "Um. Sure."

"My grandson has a birthday coming up. He

wants an authentic Angels autographed game ball. If I were thirty years younger, I'd catch it myself. But, as you can see." He held out his hand and it trembled. "This darn Parkinson's makes it difficult. Would you consider taking this glove and if a fly ball comes our way, catching it?"

"Sure thing." He accepted the mitt from the man. The glove was old and brittle. It chafed when he slid it on his left hand.

He turned to Colleen, intending to pick up where they'd left off. The second baseman for the D-Backs made a double play and Vince nearly forgot he had the glove on.

A few minutes later, he almost cheered for the wrong team when the Angels scored a run and Colleen threw her arms around him. The noise of the crowd faded. Time seemed to stand still as he held her. Baseball, distance, visitation logistics and everyday problems shifted to the background. He was aware of only Colleen.

She glanced up at him and he could tell she felt it, too. Her beautiful green eyes glowed, a reflection of her smile.

The old man nudged him. "This guy is good, the next Sammy Sosa. Get ready. I've a feeling this is the one."

Vince smothered a retort about bad timing, annoyed at himself for being annoyed at the guy. So he sat down and waited.

The first pitch was a little low and to the outside.

But the player swung anyway. The second pitch was a strike, too. He connected on the third and it was a fly ball to center field.

It looked like a white dove as it arced up, up in the sky. The fans, as if a single unit, shielded their eyes from the lights to watch its descent. The ball was headed in their general direction.

A hush fell.

Vince sucked in a breath while the thing hurtled toward them. He positioned himself, raised his glove and—

Felt a searing, white-hot pain in his left hand.

Stunned, he turned to the old guy and held out the baseball. "For your grandson, sir."

Tears welled in the man's eyes. "You've made a seven-year-old boy very happy, son. And his grandpa, too."

Vince pressed the ball into the man's trembling hand. Slowly, he removed the glove and returned it to its owner.

Flexing his hand, the scent of sweaty leather caught him by surprise. It was a familiar odor, one he hadn't smelled for nearly twenty years. And with it came an avalanche of bad memories.

Vince swallowed hard, trying unsuccessfully to hold back the images clamoring for attention. Images of blood, an emergency room and, later, a casket.

He barely heard Colleen's congratulations or felt the pats on his back from other fans.

All he could do was let the memories wash over

him in wave after disturbing wave. He knew, without a doubt, the last time he'd pulled off his sweaty glove, never to wear it again.

It was the day his mother died.

CHAPTER NINE

COLLEEN SLID her hand in Vince's, waiting for the commotion to die.

She would remember this evening always—the way Vince caught the fly ball, the sheer emotion of watching him press the ball into the old man's hand. The way he made her feel like the world was about to open up to her.

"That was so sweet of you to do that for him."

"No big deal."

"Yes, it *was* a big deal. Not all guys would have done that."

He shrugged.

"Are you okay? You seem kind of distracted."

"No, I'm fine."

Colleen didn't press him further, but knew something was wrong. She pointed to the scoreboard where their images were projected. "Look, we're on TV."

Vince barely glanced at the screen. Then when his gaze rested on her, it was as if he didn't see her.

"Is your hand okay?"

He turned his hand over slowly, studying it. A frown formed.

"Vince?"

Shaking his head, he seemed to come out of his trance. "Um. Yeah. It's fine."

The rest of the fans started to take their seats.

Vince sank to his.

Colleen eased next to him. She wondered if he was in shock. His hand was cold, but sweat beaded his brow. The color drained from his face.

"You're not acting like it's fine. Let me see."

Releasing his right hand, she inspected his left. His palm was red. She gently moved his fingers one by one. No yelps of pain, no sign of fracture.

"Everything looks okay."

"I'm…all right. Just stunned, I guess."

He was silent for what seemed like hours, gazing toward the field, but not reacting to any of the plays.

Colleen tried to regain her former joy in watching the game, but it wasn't the same. "Hey, Moreno, Johnson just struck my guy out. Where's all that team spirit?"

Shaking his head, Vince seemed to make an effort to follow the game. He even cheered when one of his guys hit a home run. But his heart just wasn't in it, she could tell.

The Angels won. But it was a hollow victory for Colleen because there was no good-natured bantering with Vince. No sense that they were sharing something more than a love of baseball.

People streamed toward the exits. He grasped her hand and led her through the crowd, his authoritative presence encouraging folks to move out of his way. Anyone looking at him would immediately know he was used to being in command. The part they probably didn't see was his innate kindness.

When they reached the parking lot, Vince stopped and glanced around, apparently searching for the rental van.

"There it is. Come on, I owe you a drink." His tone was matter-of-fact.

Under other circumstances, she would have joined him for a drink anytime, anywhere. "I can take a rain check. I get the feeling you'd rather be somewhere else."

"Why d'ya say that?"

"You've barely said a word. I don't think you really saw the game. You're distracted as hell." She tried not to let disappointment creep into her voice. She didn't want the evening to end. It was exciting to see a live game again and it was exciting being with Vince. And a part of her, the part that had been so serious and dependable for so long, hoped they could take up where they'd left off at the hotel in Blythe.

But she didn't want to be with a man who felt obligated to be there.

Vince stopped again for no apparent reason. The crowd flowed around them like a school of salmon heading upstream.

The Harlequin Reader Service® — Here's how it works:

Accepting your 2 free books and gift places you under no obligation to buy anything. You may keep the books and gift and return the shipping statement marked "cancel." If you do not cancel, about a month later we'll send you 6 additional books and bill you just $4.69 each in the U.S., or $5.24 each in Canada, plus 25¢ shipping & handling per book and applicable taxes if any.* That's the complete price and — compared to cover prices of $5.50 each in the U.S. and $6.50 each in Canada — it's quite a bargain! You may cancel at any time, but if you choose to continue, every month we'll send you 6 more books, which you may either purchase at the discount price or return to us and cancel your subscription.
*Terms and prices subject to change without notice. Sales tax applicable in N.Y. Canadian residents will be charged applicable provincial taxes and GST. Credit or debit balances in a customer's account(s) may be offset by any other outstanding balance owed by or to the customer.

GET FREE BOOKS and a FREE GIFT WHEN YOU PLAY THE...

SLOT MACHINE GAME!

Just scratch off the silver box with a coin. Then check below to see the gifts you get!

YES! I have scratched off the silver box. Please send me the 2 free Harlequin Superromance® books and gift for which I qualify. I understand I am under no obligation to purchase any books, as explained on the back of this card.

336 HDL D2AS   **135 HDL D33Y**

FIRST NAME	LAST NAME

ADDRESS

APT.#	CITY

STATE / PROV.	ZIP/POSTAL CODE

7	7	7	**Worth TWO FREE BOOKS plus a BONUS Mystery Gift!**
🍒	🍒	🍒	**Worth TWO FREE BOOKS!**
♣	♣	♣	**Worth ONE FREE BOOK!**
🔔	🔔	🍒	**TRY AGAIN!**

www.eHarlequin.com

(H-SR-08/04)

Offer limited to one per household and not valid to current Harlequin Superromance® subscribers. All orders subject to approval.

© 2000 HARLEQUIN ENTERPRISES LTD. ® and TM are trademarks owned and used by the trademark owner and/or its licensee.

DETACH AND MAIL CARD TODAY!

"Nonalcoholic?" Colleen nodded toward his beer bottle. "Are you in a program?"

"Program? Oh, AA. No. But I'm frequently the designated driver. I've investigated too many fatalities where drinking was involved."

"I shouldn't have assumed you'd drive—"

"It's not a problem. You won, remember. I owed you a margarita. But you did assume I had to be a recovering alcoholic if I refused a drink. Is it that black and white to you?"

Colleen shredded a cocktail napkin. "Sometimes. I make assumptions based on what I've observed. My dad has no middle ground where alcohol is concerned. It's all or nothing. So I guess I'm quick to jump to conclusions where men are concerned."

"But not women?"

Colleen shook her head. "Now that I think about it, no. Only men I'm…interested in. It's a protective mechanism, I guess."

Her honesty caught him by surprise. It pleased him, too. He reached across the table and cradled her hand. "So you're interested in me?"

"Yes."

"Good. I've enjoyed being with you tonight. I'm sorry if I spaced out on you there for a while. Something about catching that ball just kind of, I don't know, got to me." Vince hesitated. "How about if we start the evening all over, okay?"

The uncertainty in Vince's voice tugged at Colleen. She barely skipped a beat. "No need to start over, just continue. Tell me about your family, what's it like having three sisters?"

He leaned back in his chair and chuckled. "Chaos most of the time. Lots of laughter. Lots of arguments. You and Vi reminded me of my sisters—the whole bit about the nail polish."

"It *was* kind of weird, wasn't it?"

"No, it was very normal. Right down to the hugging and the tears. Women sure are hard to figure."

"It's normal to fight like that? I've never really had much of a relationship with her before, she's so much older. And there was almost twelve years between me and Patrick. Sometimes it's hard to remember him…." A thought popped up out of nowhere. "Except he used to call me *'chica,'* like you call Rose. My *abuela* died before I started talking, so I know very little Spanish."

"Vi's mentioned her—that's where Rosie's name came from."

Colleen nodded. "That's what I figured. She's a special little girl. I hope she and I can become close, now that Violet and I are kind of communicating again."

"You were communicating all right. Loudly." Vince grinned.

Her cheeks warmed. "I've never yelled at anyone like that before."

Vince threw his head back and laughed. "Hey, that's what siblings are for. You oughtta hear my sisters get on my case."

"Does it do any good?"

His gaze became thoughtful. "Not until now. They'd like you." Reaching across the table, he grasped her hand. "So do I."

Colleen saw a spark of something in his eyes. Attraction? Affection? Whatever it was, she tucked it close to her heart. "Um, I like you, too."

How totally inane could she get?

But Vince didn't seem to notice. He brushed his thumb over her knuckles, sending arcing currents through her bloodstream.

Every nerve ending in her body was on high alert.

"I'm glad you and Vi are working things out. Family's important."

"Family *is* important." Colleen tried to figure a way to explain the jumble of emotions and insight she'd experienced in the past couple of days. "It's so strange, I feel like I have a sister for the first time in my life. And I love it. Even the bickering. I'm lucky, you know. I was so busy concentrating on her and Dad, I didn't realize how much all our issues were connected. I knew I wanted a family more than anything, but I just didn't know how to go about it. Facing the stuff with Violet was as necessary as facing the stuff with Dad. It *all* has to come out."

"How are things going with you and your dad?"

Colleen sighed. "I've talked to him some, but not much. I figure there's only so much turmoil a sick old man can handle at once. Now is Violet's time. I'll have mine after she leaves. By then, maybe I'll know what to say."

"You'll know. You're smart and courageous and kind."

Glancing away, she swallowed hard. "Thank you." Her voice was husky.

The waitress arrived with their meals, breaking the spell.

From there, their conversation headed toward safer ground. They discussed baseball teams and playoffs, debating the merits of the Angels and the Diamondbacks. It seemed like a harmless conversation on the surface, but Colleen was acutely aware of his every inflection, every gesture.

They talked long after they'd finished eating. Vince never took his eyes off her.

When his fingers brushed her wrist, she couldn't look away, couldn't form a coherent thought. It was the most intimate, erotic gesture she had ever experienced. Not the actual touch, but the promise in his eyes.

They'd stepped over some sort of line, and Colleen wasn't entirely sure when or how it had happened. Vince thought she was smart, courageous and kind—high praise coming from a man who didn't do relationships.

VINCE WAS TONGUE-TIED for probably the first time in his life.

He watched Colleen's fingers tremble as she tried to fit the key in the lock. Gently, he took it from her and unlocked the front door.

Stepping into the house, he felt strangely out of

his depth. He could have seduced any other woman pretty much by rote. But this woman reduced him to a bundle of nerves.

What if he said something wrong? Did something wrong? Offended her by even suggesting intimacy?

Then he cursed himself for being every kind of fool. Colleen was exactly what he'd been trying to avoid. A woman who touched off emotions in him he'd never experienced. This uncertainty was unknown territory for a guy who generally was smart enough to avoid entanglements. It scared the hell out of him and had his libido racing all at one time.

"Vince?" She touched his arm. Her eyes shimmered in the weak light seeping through the curtains. "Stay with me tonight?"

He groaned, pulling her close, kissing her deeply, aware only of the scent of her, the feel of her and the absolute rightness of her response.

She ended the kiss what seemed like hours later. Her palms were warm as she laid them against his face. "Make love with me?"

The last vestiges of Vince the Chivalrous prompted him to ask, "Are you sure?"

"Very sure," she murmured. "Come on." Tugging on his hand, she pulled him toward Patrick's room.

Vince stumbled in the dark and swore. Colleen giggled, collapsing on the bed, taking him with her. Then her lips found his, and he accepted the invitation. The sound of his breathing and her murmurs seemed to echo off the walls. Her skin was like silk beneath his fingertips, so soft and supple. Her scent surrounded him. Burying his face in her hair, he inhaled deeply. She smelled so sweet.

He wanted to explore her body, inch by inch, with the slow dedication she deserved. He slid his hand under her shirt, and she shivered when he traced the outline of her bra. The shirt had to go. He removed her Angels T-shirt with tenderness and care, first one sleeve, then the second and finally pulled it over her head.

Continuing his exploration, Vince marveled at her delicacy. A wave of protectiveness washed over him. She was so very precious.

Her wrist was tiny, but her pulse beat strong and sure beneath his lips where he kissed her soft skin. He trailed caresses up her arms and shoulder and teased her with his tongue.

Her breath caught when he found the sensitive spot at the hollow of her throat and nibbled.

Sliding her arms behind his neck, she tried to draw him to her for a kiss.

"Not yet," he murmured. "Let me love you."

Colleen made a noise low in her throat, half moan, half laugh. "You're torturing me."

"Want me to stop?"

Sighing, she dropped back against the pillows. "Not on your life."

He reached above the bed and opened the blinds a fraction, allowing enough light in so he could see her better.

Faint stripes now stretched diagonally across her

torso. He traced one of the shadows with his fingers until he met the solidity of her bra. Removing the garment, Vince continued where he'd left off, only this time he traced the line from breastbone to belly button with the tip of his tongue.

Colleen moaned. She sat up only long enough to remove her pants at his request.

He admired the elegant lines and curves of her body. She had an almost regal perfection—like a young Grace Kelly, willowy and fragile.

"You are so beautiful," he whispered, his voice hoarse. He needed her. Needed to be inside her and absorb her pureness of heart.

He covered her body with his and connected with every blessed inch from mouth to thigh.

But he stopped short.

A sniffling sound sent alarm bells off in his head. "Colleen?"

The sound stopped, but she didn't answer.

He leaned over her and clicked on the bedside lamp. Blinking in the sudden glare, he focused on Colleen. What he saw destroyed his desire and his self-respect.

"You're crying." Reaching out, he wiped the moisture from her cheek. "What did I do?"

She smiled up at him through her tears. "You did everything right. It's just so perfect. *You're* so perfect."

The adoration in her eyes should have pleased him. But it didn't. It scared the hell out of him. There was so much responsibility that went along with that kind of emotion. Not to mention the knowledge that he could never live up to her adoration.

He stifled a groan. He felt even worse than before.

Why in the hell had he thought they could handle this? When every instinct he had told him otherwise?

"We can't do this."

"Why not? I cry when I'm happy, Vince. Everything feels so right. You, me."

"God, Colleen, do you know how lucky I feel to be here with you? But—"

"But what?"

Frustration welled inside him. The honest truth was that he wasn't sure what he felt for her, but even he, clod that he was, knew that was the last thing Colleen needed to hear when she was naked in his bed. Just as he knew without a doubt she didn't give her heart easily.

"I…care for you."

"That's okay, Vince. I can live with that. Would you please turn out the light and come back to bed?" She held out her hand to him, her eyes reflecting a deep vulnerability. And though she denied it, he was aware that the wrong person or the wrong motives could cripple her emotionally.

"*I* couldn't live with that. You deserve so much more than I can give you."

"Let me be the judge."

"I can't. You're not objective. You've never believed you deserve the best. You've settled for crumbs when you should have demanded the whole damn cake. All I can give you is crumbs, just like everyone else in your life. If you can't look out for yourself, then it's up to me."

"Do you really believe that?"

"All I know is what I can and can't give. I can't promise the kind of love you're looking for. The kind of love you deserve. I would be a real lowlife to take advantage of you."

"I'm an adult. You're not taking advantage of me. What's this really about, Vince?"

How could he explain what he didn't really understand himself? "I know I'll hurt you, Colleen. Not if, but *when*. I always hurt the people who care about me most."

He thought about what loving him had cost his mother. She'd believed his promises and ended up paying with her life. "I'm not sure I'm capable of the forever kind of love."

"Or do you think you're not *worthy* of the forever kind of love?" Her voice was soft, regretful.

When he didn't answer, Colleen sat up. Her gaze was steady.

Vince looked away. He couldn't handle the truth he saw in her eyes.

He was a fraud. Always had been. Always would be. And she knew it. The rescuer needed rescuing.

CHAPTER TEN

COLLEEN CLOSED her bedroom door with a click, though a part of her would have preferred to slam it.

Tears streamed down her face unchecked. Tears of hurt and loss and disappointment.

Plucking Scooby-Doo off the dresser, she fingered his soft ears. She sat on her bed and hugged the stuffed animal close. It was no substitute for having Vince in her arms, but some comfort just the same.

Vince was wrong. Her feelings for him wouldn't go away simply because he refused to acknowledge them, or God forbid, return her love. He did't seem to realize it was much too late to warn her away.

Colleen swiped the moisture off her cheeks. The overwhelming sense of loss was fading, quickly replaced by anger. How could he presume to know what was best for her? Who did he think he was to dictate what she did and didn't deserve? He'd treated her like a child and it hurt.

What's more, she couldn't call him on his logic. How could she convince him he was a better man than he seemed to think? Or maybe that was what he intended. How noble he must feel, saving helpless little Colleen from the big, bad wolf.

So where did she go from here? She figured there were two choices. One, stay as far away from him as possible until he left. It was the easier solution. Certainly taking the path of least resistance was more comfortable for her.

The second plan was more daring, a choice the old Colleen would have been unable to make. But the new Colleen lifted her chin, squared her shoulders and anticipated the challenge. Contrary to what Vince wanted her to believe, it wasn't her fragility holding them back—it was his. She would just prove to him that they were *both* strong enough for this relationship.

THE NEXT MORNING was hell. Colleen hadn't worked out the specifics of her plan even after her second cup of coffee. She sat at the table, wondering how to convince a man's man like Vince to confide in her. Convince him that he had issues of his own. Denial was macho; touchy-feely implied weakness.

Her strategy session was interrupted by Vince's arrival, his hair still wet from his shower. Her heart ached at the dark circles under his eyes. But she resisted the urge to apologize, to promise not to push him to get involved. It might work in the short run, but she was a long-run kind of woman.

"Coffee's ready," she said.

He mumbled something that approximated thank you and poured himself a cup. "I'm sorry, Colleen.

I haven't been a very good guest or friend. I should have insisted we keep it strictly platonic."

She rose from the table, rinsed out her coffee cup and placed it in the dishwasher. Turning to Vince, she said, "I'm sorry, too. Because you're throwing away something special in the name of protecting me. I think if you're honest with yourself, you'll admit that's a load of bull."

"I've got to do what I think is right."

"Yes, you do. So do I. And that means standing up for what *I* believe is right. You should at least give a relationship with me a shot."

"It wouldn't work. I wish you'd just forget about it."

"Do you? Really?"

Vince hesitated, the coffee cup suspended at chest level. "Yes. It's best for everyone."

"Talk to me, Vince. Help me understand."

"There's nothing to talk about. Just let it go."

Colleen studied him, trying to see beyond the stubborn mask into his heart. His mouth was set in a determined line, but there was the barest hint of a lost little boy in his eyes.

She would figure it out. Determination seemed to be one of the better qualities she'd inherited from her father. "But—"

Vince crossed his arms over his chest.

It would be useless to pursue the matter in his present mood. But that didn't mean she had to give up completely. Colleen started to leave the kitchen, but glanced back at him and said, "Oh, and if you think my sister is a determined woman, wait 'til you see me in action."

She hummed a little tune as she strolled into the living room. It felt good to take destiny into her own hands.

She barely noticed the sound of a key in the front door and was surprised when Violet tiptoed in, carrying her shoes. Wearing a slightly rumpled black maternity cocktail dress, her sister was absolutely radiant.

"I was trying to be quiet. Thought you might still be asleep." She flushed like a guilty teenager.

"No, we're awake. Is Ian coming in? I'm looking forward to meeting him."

"No, he was in a hurry to get to his book-signing. We woke up late."

Woke up late, or never went to sleep?

Either way, her sister looked rejuvenated. Ian had obviously been the best medicine for her.

Colleen wished she glowed like Violet did. And she would have, too, if Vince hadn't put the brakes on their lovemaking.

Violet frowned. "What's wrong? You look tired. And sad."

"Nothing's wrong. I didn't sleep well last night." That was the truth at least.

"Are you sure? Did something happen while I was gone?"

"Vince took me to the baseball game last night. We had a terrific time." Colleen stifled a sigh. Not nearly as great as it could have been, though.

"Is Dad okay? You would have called me if he got worse, wouldn't you?"

"Yes, I would have called."

Nodding, Violet stretched, smiling benevolently. "Just wanted to make sure. I think I'll go take a nap. Ian's coming by this afternoon to take me to visit Dad."

"But—" Colleen protested.

"Maybe that will give you a break. You look like you could use some R&R, little sister."

If she only knew.

VINCE WISHED to hell that Violet hadn't picked now to play the dutiful daughter. It meant Colleen stayed home from the hospital and hung around the house all afternoon.

Not only did her presence have his conscience making a racket, he was tempted to take it all back— tell her he cared about her, wanted a future together and invite her to his bed.

Though she wore a baggy, smiley-face T-shirt and loose jeans, she had the same effect on him as if she'd been wearing lingerie.

He'd caught glimpses of her doing lurid things like washing clothes, vacuuming, typing. No matter how mundane the chore, she was downright sexy. She dusted, and he visualized her naked in his bed. She loaded the dishwasher, he saw her naked in his bed.

She scrubbed toilets and she was again naked in his bed, on her hands and knees no less.

As a result, he was walking around with a perpetual erection and a thoroughly black mood. He didn't know how much more of this he could take.

He'd tried to find something to do outside, but everything was now shipshape. Flopping on the couch, he clicked the remote, looking for CNN. Nothing like international news to dampen his desire. Lord only knew what X-rated activity Colleen had planned next. Polishing furniture maybe?

Vince nearly groaned aloud when she entered the room a couple minutes later. She wore a long, black leotard and might as well have been nude for real this time. The stretchy fabric hugged her in ways that should be outlawed.

Swallowing hard, he couldn't take his eyes off of her as she unrolled some sort of foam mat. "I hope you don't mind. I do yoga to unwind."

"Um. Sure." It sounded harmless until he saw what was involved. Some sort of salute the sun thing, or so Colleen told him. Then other contortions that actually made him blush.

He tried to focus on the news, but his eyes were drawn to the woman in black. Once he got past the sexual possibilities of the positions, he admired her fluid grace. She was downright perfect. Way too good for him.

Leaning his head back, he closed his eyes. Loss squeezed his chest. Colleen had offered herself to him. For as long as he was in L.A., maybe longer. Maybe a lifetime. And he'd refused. When every nerve cell in his body hollered at him to accept. The irony was that if she'd been any other woman, he would have slept with her in a heartbeat. But because she was special, he wouldn't go there. He had to be one twisted bastard.

The phone rang, making him jump. He reached across the end table and answered. "It's for you," he said, carrying the receiver to Colleen.

"Hi, Daddy." She frowned, no longer serene.

From what Vince could hear, Sean wasn't happy. It seemed Violet had bailed again.

Colleen's knuckles were white where she held the receiver. Her mouth was a tight line, the corners trembled.

He ignored his instinctive need to kiss away her troubles.

"I'm sorry, Daddy. I know you're disappointed."

She listened to more of what Vince assumed was complaining. Glancing at her watch, she said, "I can't make it in time for visiting hours today. I'll have to see you in the morning."

The selfish old goat wanted her to drop everything and run right over. Anger burned in Vince's gut. The guy had a lot of nerve.

"Okay, I'll see you tomorrow. Love you, Daddy. Bye."

Vince commented, "You're not going, are you?"

Colleen shook her head. "I guess Violet only stayed about five minutes. Said hello, introduced him to Ian and left."

"At least he saw her."

"He wanted to talk with her. He wants to know she still loves him."

"That's what he said?"

"Not in so many words. It's obvious though. In some ways, I wish Violet would just tell him what he needs to hear. It would be so much easier that way."

"Easier, but not honest."

"No, not honest. And I might be just as hesitant to forgive if I were in Vi's shoes. It's hard for me to reconcile myself to the fact that he used to hit her. I keep thinking back, wondering if I knew and just blocked it out." She hesitated, her eyes dark and troubled. "All I remember is hiding in the bathroom when things got loud and being really, really scared."

Vince reached out to brush the hair from her eyes, but didn't follow through. He couldn't touch and comfort and still draw a distinct line between them. Everything that seemed to be black and white was blurring into shades of gray. Especially his feelings for Colleen.

"You've got to let them work it out their own way."

Colleen sighed. "I suppose you're right. Sometimes, I wonder what life would have been like if Daddy hadn't been a drinker. Kind of like that movie where it shows the ways Gwyneth Paltrow's life would have been different if she'd taken another train. Would Mom and Dad still have divorced? Would Violet have left? Would I have made different choices, graduated college, started a family?"

Vince swallowed hard. He'd often thought about

changing the past. Wondered what his life would have been like if he could go back and make different decisions.

"It's better just to accept what happened and move on." Even to his own ears, he sounded a little desperate, a little defensive. Had he really moved on? Somehow he had the feeling he might never get past the effects of the past.

Colleen tucked her legs under her on the exercise mat. "I guess I'm not very good at that. I wish I could snap my fingers and make it all better for Vi, for Dad…for me."

"That's not so much of a stretch from what I want for you. I'm trying to protect you, Colleen."

She softly replied, "The difference is I'm not dying. I'm capable of taking care of myself."

Vince made a noncommittal noise in his throat.

Colleen shook her head. "But you'll have to figure that out yourself." Rummaging through her purse, she finally withdrew a tiny address book. "I'll call Violet on her cell. See what happened at the hospital."

"I want to talk to her when you're done. I think Ian's last signing was this afternoon. If he flies out in the morning, maybe we'll drive home then."

She ignored him, but he could tell from her frown that she'd heard him. After chatting for a few minutes, she hung up.

"Hey, I wanted to talk to her," he protested.

"Call her if you want." Her expression was bleak. "But I found out what you needed to know. Congratulations, you got your wish. You guys are leaving to-morrow morning when Ian leaves. That ought to make you very happy."

It should have made him happy, but it didn't.

CHAPTER ELEVEN

COLLEEN PACED the length of the living room. This wasn't the way it was supposed to end. Dad was supposed to apologize to Violet, they'd forgive, hug and everything would be fine. They'd be a family again. All the talk of letting them work it out in their own time was useless if Violet wouldn't stay to see it through.

She turned to Vince. "You can't let her leave like this."

"I told you, it's Violet's decision, not mine. Besides, I have a life to get back to."

"Yes, that's right. Your conscience is clear. And you have a life. One that doesn't include me." Her words came from a hollow place in her heart.

"This isn't about us."

"You're right. But maybe it should be."

Colleen saw her hopes disintegrating before her eyes. Violet and Vince would leave tomorrow morning, *poof,* as if they'd never been there. Life would go back to a routine of transcribing and hospital visits. No sister, no lover. Nothing.

Loneliness washed over her, as if they'd already left. She couldn't let it happen. "So you're going to help Violet run away again. Do you realize that if she leaves now, all our efforts were for nothing?"

"She said goodbye to your dad. That's going to have to be enough."

Shaking her head slowly, Colleen said, "You really don't get it, do you? As far as you're concerned, you've done your job. Violet's seen Dad and stayed healthy, so hey, let's hit the road. We haven't even come close to helping Violet. She's not going to resolve this until she confronts Dad. And he *needs* to apologize. Help me convince her to stay one more day?" She stepped closer, grasped Vince's hand. "Please?"

His face softened. "I'm not going to try to sway her decision one way or the other. But if Violet decides to stay, I'll call work and let them know I need another day."

"Thank you. You won't regret this." Colleen hugged him.

He stood stock-still, his arms at his side, until she released him. Then he seemed to draw a deep breath.

COLLEEN WATCHED Violet put the finishing touches on her sandwich—a small, midafternoon snack for a woman who seemed to eat constantly.

"Ian sounds like a great guy," Colleen commented.

"He is." Violet beamed, but her smile quickly faded. "I just wish he could have stayed longer. It really helped having him here…when I saw Dad."

"How'd the visit go?"

"It was kind of a shock. He's lost so much weight I almost didn't recognize him. The voice is the same, though."

"He didn't say anything about being sorry?" Colleen glanced sideways at her sister.

"Not a peep."

"What in the heck did you talk about then? The weather?"

"Yes, actually we did. I introduced him to Ian and Dad asked to see pictures of Rose. That was about it. Then the silence got uncomfortable and we left."

Colleen shook her head. She was trying really hard to stay out of the middle, but it was looking more and more like *somebody* needed to do something. She managed not to voice her opinion. Instead, she asked, "Are you still planning on leaving tomorrow?"

Her sister nodded.

Okay, staying out of it wasn't an option anymore. She wouldn't tell her sister what to do, she'd just gently lead her to the right thing. "Do you feel like you've reached any sort of…understanding with Dad?"

"Oh, I understood him a long time ago. He's a mean, selfish old bastard."

"But he's a mean, selfish, *dying* old bastard. Maybe you could give him a little more time?"

Give me *more time?*

"I gave him plenty of time."

"He said you only stayed five minutes. That's hardly giving him a chance to make amends."

"Look, I'm not going to hang around his hospital room indefinitely while he tries to find it in his black heart to apologize to me." Violet slapped her sandwich on a paper plate and headed toward Colleen's room. "Now, if you'll excuse me, I need to pack."

Colleen followed close behind. "I'm not saying you have to stay indefinitely. Just give it another day or two."

Violet kept walking.

Colleen couldn't allow her to leave. Violet was supposed to make everything right—at least that's what big sisters on TV did.

Desperation flowed through Colleen like a slow-acting poison. "Don't you wonder what he'll say? What he remembers?"

"I don't want to know."

"Maybe he'll tell you something that will help you with *your* kids."

Violet hesitated. She set the paper plate on the dresser and pulled out her suitcase.

"You know, find out where Dad went wrong. Things he'd do differently."

"Not beating me would have been a good start."

"Don't you want to know *why* he beat you?" Colleen asked.

"He didn't need a reason. Like I said, he's a mean, selfish old bastard. Dying doesn't change a thing." She grabbed clothes from the dresser and tossed them in the suitcase.

A thought gnawed at Colleen, one that had bothered her for years. Her voice was soft when she said, "Don't you wonder why he was so mean to you and not me?"

Violet stopped folding a shirt. She wouldn't meet Colleen's eyes.

"Because you're perfect. I was the one who always did the wrong thing."

The defeat in Vi's voice tore at Colleen's heart. Guilt followed. Guilt that maybe she had somehow been to blame.

Colleen pushed the emotions away, intent on her mission. She had to focus if she wanted to reunite her family. "Do you beat Rosie when she makes a mistake? Even if she makes you mad?"

"No."

"How about when the new baby comes? If it makes better choices than its big sister, will you beat Rosie then?"

"That's ridiculous."

"Yes. It is."

"Besides, I'm a better parent than Dad ever was."

Colleen nodded. "You are. But I would think you'd want to be more informed. Want to know exactly what caused his abuse, how it can be avoided and how you can keep from passing it down to your children, no matter how unknowingly."

Violet frowned. "I'd *never* hit my children."

"What if Dad told himself the same thing? I really doubt he set out to use you and Patrick as punching bags."

Sighing, Violet closed her eyes and rubbed her temples. "You're giving me a headache and I can't think."

Colleen pressed on. "Traveling will only make your headache worse. Why don't you lie down for a minute? Then you can decide what's best."

"I think I will lie down."

Crossing her fingers, Colleen left her old room and shut the door behind her. She hoped Violet would take a long nap—until the next morning.

She closed her eyes. *I'm sorry, Vince. I tried to stay out of it, really I did.* But there was just too much at stake.

Glancing at her watch, she headed toward the kitchen.

Vince came in from the backyard, an old dish towel draped across the back of his neck. He used the corner to wipe sweat off his face. "Screen door's fixed."

"Thank you. You've been a big help."

"No problem." He pulled a water bottle from the fridge, opened it and drank almost half.

Colleen watched, fascinated, as a bead of sweat trickled down his jaw, then his neck. She was almost sorry when he finished the water.

Tossing the bottle in the trash, he asked, "Is Violet packed?"

"No, she's napping."

"A short catnap, I hope."

Colleen shrugged. "Who knows with pregnant

women? She mentioned that she didn't feel very good—headache or something."

"Any contractions? Swelling in her legs? I don't think headaches were on the list, but I could be wrong."

"She seemed fine, besides the headache. Just tired."

Vince touched her arm. "Colleen."

"What?"

He hesitated for a moment, then shook his head. "Let me know when she wakes up. Thought I might take a look at your air-conditioning unit. Could probably use a tune-up." He turned and went outside.

Apparently he'd do anything to keep from being alone with her.

Trying to follow Vince's lead and keep busy, Colleen baked a batch of Violet's favorite muffins for breakfast the next morning. With every minute that went by, Violet and Vince were that much closer to staying the night.

It was nearly five o'clock when Vince came in again. "How's Vi?"

"Still sleeping. I don't think you should wake her. The doctor specifically recommended rest, remember?"

Vince swore under his breath. "That means we're stuck here another night."

Colleen nodded. A small victory at last.

"I better call work then."

"I'm hoping Vi changes her mind and intends to

go see Dad again tomorrow morning." She slung her purse over her shoulder. "I sure will be glad to get my car back." Frowning, she considered the logistics. "Maybe I'll ride back with you to Echo Point tomorrow morning to get my car. In the meantime, how about I borrow the van. I'll pick up some steaks for dinner."

"Wait a minute, I'll go with you after I make my phone call."

Colleen studied his face, wondering why he wanted to spend time with her all of the sudden. Judging from his resigned tone, it wasn't for the pleasure of her company.

"That's not necessary."

"Yes. It is. It'll be dark soon and you shouldn't be out alone at night."

She didn't know whether to be touched or irritated by his concern. "Do you do this with your sisters, too? The buddy system after dark thing?"

"No need. It's safe in Echo Point. L.A.'s dangerous."

"Not if you're careful."

"Sometimes being careful isn't enough."

VINCE SIGHED with relief. The dishes were clean, the kitchen was quiet and he was completely alone after a tense evening with Colleen and Violet. He'd insisted on doing the after-dinner cleanup, suggesting Colleen and Violet make it an early night. He'd like to think the offer was a result of the good manners his sisters had drilled into him, but he knew, deep down, it was because he was afraid. Afraid for Colleen, afraid for himself and afraid of the memories circling like vultures.

Vince turned out the kitchen light, thankful he'd put a stronger bulb in the bathroom night-light—he could at least follow the dim glow from the kitchen to the living room without tripping.

Approaching the couch, Vince hesitated. He could hear Colleen's even breathing in the quiet house. She was asleep. It had been a tough day on all of them.

He stepped closer and tucked the lightweight cotton blanket under her chin. Then he stood there, unable to move. She was so beautiful, so real. He reached out and touched her hair, where the blond strands fanned across the pillow. They felt silky and full of life, just like her. He smiled sadly, glad nobody was there to see him say goodbye to what might have been. Loss settled in his chest, dense and heavy.

Shaking his head, he forced himself to move on to his room, where the full bed seemed very large and empty.

As he dozed intermittently, images from the day flashed through his mind. Colleen leaning close to him in the grocery store as they conferred on the best cut of steak. Colleen standing on tiptoe to kiss him. Colleen trying to convince him that love was enough, that *he* was enough to make her happy.

"Vince, would you tell the studio audience exactly why you can't commit to a woman?" Colleen's voice hung in the air.

He started to sweat. The hot lights hurt his eyes. He squinted, trying desperately to see Colleen.

The spotlight moved. There, he could see her, standing with her back to the audience. She looked like she meant business in her dark green pantsuit, her hair pulled tightly back from her forehead.

And beyond, his sisters sat in the front row. All three of them wore that superior, Vince-is-a-complete-commitment-phobe-but-we-tolerate-him-anyway expression.

He sank into a cushy chair. Glancing around for some sort of clue, he noticed the set was arranged to look comfortable and homey, as if they were in someone's living room. He craned his neck to see the huge letters outlined in lights behind him. Dr. Phyllis Live!

Colleen stepped closer, the cameras following her every move. She chose the cushy chair next to him. "So what's it going to be, Vince? Can you say those three important words to me? Or are you a hopeless excuse for a man?"

He tried to speak, tried to explain, but no words came out.

The women in the audience booed. It echoed in his brain as they faded into nothingness.

Vince opened his eyes, disoriented in the dark. Groaning, he sat up in bed and glanced at the clock— 2:00 a.m. Just a dream.

Hopeless excuse for a man.

The women's chant followed him as he headed for the bathroom. A glass of water helped his parched throat, but did little to assuage the remnants of the dream that made him feel like a real lowlife.

Once he was in bed again, he fidgeted. Great, just great. Now he'd be up all night. And it would be a long drive home in the morning....

A ball field came into view. A familiar aroma tickled his nose. It was one he associated with sunshine and happy times—the odor of a leather glove after a close game.

Then he heard the sound of solid contact between bat and ball.

Vince shielded his eyes from the sun and watched the ball arc high in the air.

Time stood still, his teammates were at their positions, frozen in time. Joey Peterson on first, Ricky White pitching. It was good to see his two best friends again.

The fly ball headed toward center field.

"I got it," Vince called. The right fielder backed off to let him make the play.

He raised his glove, made a textbook catch. He threw to second base....

And suddenly the odor of diesel fuel and day-old tacos assaulted him.

The baseball diamond disappeared, as did the grass and sweet sunshine.

The sky grew overcast. Gray.

He glanced around. Espinoza's gas station. How in the heck had he managed to get there?

A maroon Impala screeched into the gas station,

stopping beside a familiar-looking baby-blue Grand Torino. The woman pumping gas looked familiar, too.

"Mom," he shouted.

But she didn't hear him. She placed the nozzle back on the pump and turned toward the Impala.

The driver rolled down the window and said something.

His mom shook her head.

The guy was wearing gang colors. He held a gun. There was a flash. His mother fell, as if in slow motion.

"Mom," he yelled.

This time she heard him and looked up. The fear in her eyes was replaced with love.

Vince ran to her, but it was as if he were slogging through mud. She reached for him, her eyes imploring him to help. But her arm dropped back to the asphalt before he could reach her.

Tears were hot on his cheeks as he stood over her, rhythmically smacking a baseball into the pocket of his cowhide glove, over and over and over. He pulled off the glove and flung it to the ground, his gut roiling at the odor of sweaty leather. Sirens wailed, car horns blared, and he couldn't seem to move. Couldn't seem to call out for help.

CHAPTER TWELVE

COLLEEN HEARD a noise that didn't fit the regular nighttime sounds of the settling house. Violet? Vince?

She shifted, trying to find a more comfortable position. It was impossible. So, she waited. Barely breathing for fear she'd miss the noise if it came again.

And it did come again. Half groan, half plea. Baritone.

Colleen exhaled slowly. Thank God. She was terrified Violet had gone into labor.

All the same, she tiptoed to Violet's door to make sure. Peeking in, she was relieved to find her sister sleeping deeply, her breathing even and slow.

Colleen quietly closed the door and tilted her head to the side. The noise was definitely coming from Patrick's room.

Hurrying down the hallway, she hesitated outside the door. But the sound was so grief-stricken, she rushed in.

Vince was asleep, but thrashing. He was covered in sweat, murmuring something. She caught a word here and there. *Don't. Please. No! Mom.* The last was a long, drawn-out cry that raised the hair on the back of her neck.

She moved to his bedside, avoiding his thrashing legs. She grasped his shoulders. "Vince."

He didn't seem to hear her. Tears coursed down his face. He was in terrible agony.

"Vince," she called, louder this time.

He mumbled something in response.

"Wake up."

His eyes fluttered open briefly, then closed.

She waited to see if he'd fallen into a peaceful sleep. If so, she'd tiptoe back to the couch and he'd never know she had been there.

Moments later, the thrashing and muttering started again.

"You're safe, Vince." She grasped his arm and shook him. "It's just a dream. Wake up."

His eyes opened. He stared up at the ceiling. It was hard to tell if he was conscious of his surroundings.

"It was just a dream. It's okay."

Vince started. "What're you doing here?" he mumbled. "Should be asleep."

"You were having a nightmare."

He knuckled the sleep from his eyes, squinting at the alarm clock. "Three o'clock? Sorry I bothered you. Go back to bed."

Instead of leaving, she sat on the edge of the bed. "Do you want to talk about it?"

"No. Want to go back to sleep."

Colleen sighed. "I'm not going to leave you alone like this."

"It's okay. I'm fine." He sounded more like himself.

But Colleen didn't want to leave. She wanted to stay with him. To be there for him. To hold him.

"Shhh. Move over."

"Huh?"

"I said move over. I'm coming in." What she'd do when she got there, she had absolutely no idea.

"I'm not an invalid."

"I know you're not. I just want to be with you."

"It's not a good idea."

"Probably not, but the couch makes this bed feel like heaven. My back will never be the same."

He hesitated. "So you're here to sleep? That's all?"

"Yes."

He grunted and moved over, turning his back to her.

She slid between the sheets. They were deliciously warm from his body heat. Sighing, she decided this was definitely much better than the couch. And possibly the only chance she might have of spending the night in the same bed with Vince.

She smiled wryly in the dark. All she wanted was to be near him for however long he'd let her, in whatever manner of closeness he would allow.

"Vince?"

"Hmm."

"Tell me about your nightmare."

"There's nothing to tell. I don't remember it."

"You're lying," she said.

He rolled over to face her. "You're not going to let me sleep, are you?"

"No. I'm not. Not until you tell me about the nightmare."

He sighed heavily. His breath was warm on her face, his body tantalizingly close in the small bed. "I'll tell you about my dream if you promise to let me take the couch tonight."

"Okay. I promise." It bothered her that she had to blackmail him into confiding in her. She wanted to share everything with him. His pain was her pain, his joy, her joy.

Vince closed his eyes, shutting her out, his face awash with grief. Slowly he told her about his dream, the gas station, his mother's carjacking, her death.

"I had no idea." She raised up on her elbow and stroked his face as if he were a small boy in need of comfort. "That's horrible. There's more, though, isn't there?"

He grasped her hand, stilling the caress. "Don't. I can't do this if you touch me."

She let her hand relax in his. "Okay, but tell me."

He didn't release her hand and she took that as a good sign. Especially since he seemed unaware of the contact, as if it were natural for them to be in the same bed, talking, with her hand grasped in his, pressed tightly to his bare chest.

"I should have been there, Colleen. I promised I'd go with her and I didn't."

The raw regret in his voice sent chills up her spine. "You weren't responsible. You were only a kid."

"I was ten. Old enough to keep my promises."

"But not old enough to take on armed men."

He squeezed his eyes shut. "Don't you think I know that? Anybody in law enforcement would advise against a citizen confronting someone who has a gun. Particularly a kid, but..."

Vince opened his eyes and she felt as if a barrier had been stripped away. His gaze was shadowed with guilt and a vulnerability that touched her.

"But?"

"But I was a kid who felt responsible long before I was a law enforcement officer." He sighed. "I just can't shake the feeling that I could have done something."

"Have you ever talked to anyone about this?"

"Nobody. You're the first."

Emotion flooded through Colleen at his admission—a love so strong it scared her and the knowledge that she would do anything to help him.

She freed her hand from his and stroked the tense lines near his mouth. His face was just inches from hers. Leaning closer, she kissed him, gently at first, then deepened the kiss.

He groaned, pulling away. "You've got to go."

Colleen had spent her whole life letting others dictate how she would feel, what she would do, what kind of life she would lead. No more. The time had come to take control. She knew in her heart Vince cared for her, or could if he would only allow himself. She wouldn't let him backtrack or put up walls. "I love you," she whispered.

"You've known me less than a week. You can't love me."

"Time doesn't matter. I know what I feel and I'm not leaving."

"I can't handle this right now, Colleen."

"That's too bad. Because I'm not going anywhere. I'm in the same house, the same bed and you can't just wish me away like the rest of the women you've dated."

"You don't get it, do you?" His voice was bitter. "Even after I told you what happened to my mom? I'm not the guy you think I am. I've failed every woman who ever loved me."

Colleen placed her hand over his heart. "How do I convince you you're not the guy you say you are? Some guy who breaks promises and lets people down? The Vince I see here," she tapped his chest, "has more heart than he will probably ever know. And I'd trust him with my life."

"That's the problem. I don't want you to entrust me with your life. It's too big a responsibility."

"Not really. Because then you entrust me with your life. It's an even trade."

Vince smiled sadly. "You're making this very difficult."

"You're wrong. I intend to make it impossible for you to shut me out. I passed difficult a long time ago."

"Look, we live hundreds of miles apart. It wouldn't work even if I were the kind of guy you think I am." He traced the line of her shoulder. His featherlight caress raised goose bumps.

She longed to touch him, love him. But she forced herself to be content with the warmth of his chest beneath her resting hand. "I'm not asking for promises. I'm asking you to quit protecting both of us for just one night."

He was silent for what seemed like hours, his eyes closed tight. His heart beat beneath her palm, wild and erratic.

"Please?" she whispered.

He groaned and pulled her close.

THE FIRST gentle rays of daylight filtered through the blinds.

Colleen opened her eyes and found Vince watching her.

"Morning," he murmured.

"Morning." Colleen thought it would be a glorious day.

He absently trailed his fingers along her rib cage.

Colleen shivered. Every nerve ending in her body came alive.

"I've been watching you sleep. You are so beautiful."

Colleen blushed at his compliment and at the memory of all they'd shared the night before.

Drawing the sheet back, Vince's gaze roved from head to foot. "You're absolutely perfect, every bit of you."

Swallowing hard, Colleen's throat went dry.

Vince's gaze was warm, a hint of amusement lurked in his voice. "Why so shy? Even after last night? Especially after last night."

"I didn't give you a choice, did I?" In the cold light of day, it was hard to believe she'd been so persistent in pursuing him. But she was glad, just the same. "I'm not usually like that."

"You don't see me complaining, do you?"

"You were last night."

"Last night I wasn't sure it was a good idea. Now I know it was a *very* good idea."

She reached up and traced his jawline.

His voice was husky. "You're the best thing to happen to me in a long time. But—"

"But what? You're still wondering if you should have done the noble thing and protected me? Look at me." She spread her arms wide. "You made love to me and my heart's still in one piece. *Your* heart is still in one piece."

He hesitated. "Just know I care. And I wouldn't intentionally do anything to hurt you."

Colleen plucked a square packet off the nightstand. Tearing it open, she murmured, "Then make love with me again."

Vince groaned. "I'm afraid you're going to regret getting involved with me. But I can't tell you no." he took the packet from her outstretched hand and put on the condom. "Come here," he whispered, rolling onto his back. He drew her down on top of him, kissed her slowly, languidly, as if they had all the time in the world—and he intended to use every moment to the fullest.

They moved as if under water, in rhythm with the tides. It could have been days, it could have been hours, but Colleen lost all track of time. Lost track of everything but Vince. He was inside her, she moved with him, claimed him. They were perfect together.

I love you, I love you, I love you.

CHAPTER THIRTEEN

VINCE KISSED Colleen lightly on the head and crept out of the bedroom.

He went in search of coffee. Thankfully, the kitchen was empty. He needed time to think.

Gazing out the window, he lifted his face to the warm sunshine streaming in. An unfamiliar frisson of hope sang in his blood. Maybe, just maybe, he could make things work this time.

The night with Colleen had been surreal. He'd never connected with another human being the way he'd connected with her. It was as if she saw past all the outer stuff right to his core. And still loved him anyway.

Love.

What a scary thought.

He shook his head.

What about him? Sure, he cared for her. Damn near adored her. But love?

Vince sighed, turning away from the window. He'd convinced himself long ago that he was incapable of loving a woman, of sustaining a relationship.

But Colleen made him wonder if he'd underestimated himself. Wonder if maybe he could get past his fear of failing her. Get past the pulse-pounding certainty that something bad would happen to her if they got serious. Somehow for the first time he realized love and commitment and death had become all tangled up to him. And he wasn't quite sure how to untangle them. For Colleen, though, he was willing to try.

She made him feel more alive than he'd ever thought possible. They'd made love with an intensity that had amazed him—world-weary, love-'em-and-leave-'em kind of guy that he was. He'd buried himself in her over and over, striving to become one being. As if he knew the pieces fit together in one cohesive whole that had nothing to do with body parts.

Shaking his head, he admitted he had it bad for her. The poetic bent of his thoughts was proof enough.

"It's about time you woke up." Violet's voice jarred him as she entered the kitchen. She poured a glass of milk and returned the carton to the refrigerator. "I think Colleen left for the hospital without asking if I wanted to go along." Her voice was tinged with hurt.

"Um. She's not at the hospital."

"She's not out back, she's not in the bathroom so she has to be at—"

"My room." He attempted to keep his voice level, afraid an embarrassing level of wonder might shine through.

"Your room?" Violet squeaked.

Vince nodded. He met her accusing glare and didn't flinch.

"What, she's changing the linens or something?"

"No. She's sleeping." He brushed past her to get the milk for himself.

Violet grabbed his arm and swung him to face her. "She's vulnerable right now."

"She's also a big girl." Colleen shuffled into the kitchen. "And can take care of herself."

"She sure can." Vince whistled in appreciation.

Colleen had pulled on a tight white tank top and a pair of very short plaid boxers. Her legs went on for miles.

She gave him the biggest smile he'd ever seen.

Violet clucked like a mother hen. "Colleen, your hair's a mess. Don't you want to clean up?"

"Nope. I want breakfast. *Lots* of breakfast."

Stifling a chuckle, he admired the way she stood up to her older sister. Proclaiming her independence had been a long time coming. "I imagine you *are* hungry." He winked at her and pulled a frying pan from the cabinet. "You probably worked up quite an appetite. Fried eggs okay? Over hard?"

Violet's shocked expression was priceless.

The amusement shining in Colleen's eyes was even better. She looked like one very satisfied woman, her skin, her eyes, her smile all glowing in the morning sunshine. "Perfect."

He met her gaze, hoping he could telegraph with-

out words how much she meant to him, double en-
tendres aside.

Her eyes widened.

Violet sputtered and choked on her coffee.
"Since I'm, um, obviously not needed here, I'll go
get ready for the hospital." She sidled out of the
room.

Vince barely noticed her leave.

"Did she say what I thought she said?" Colleen
asked.

"Huh? I wasn't paying much attention."

"She's going to see Daddy again."

"That's…good." He was distracted by how very
little her tank top left to the imagination. The outline
of her areolas teased him, tempted him to give them
the attention they deserved. With his lips, his tongue.

"It's *very* good news."

Vince forced his gaze upward. The wicked gleam
in Colleen's eyes told him she knew exactly what he
was thinking.

"Sleep well?" he murmured.

"Never better." Her cheeks grew pink.

Reaching across the counter, he touched her breast,
rubbing his thumb across the nipple, never taking his
eyes off her face. "You're beautiful." His voice grew
husky. "Especially when you blush. All over."

She tipped her head to the side in question.

He brushed his fingers along her jawline. "I always wondered if you blushed all over. After last
night, I know you do."

"I've always hated it. That I blush at the drop of a hat."

"Oh, don't hate it. That would be a shame. 'Cause now every time I see you get embarrassed, I'll visualize how pretty you look naked and blushing all over."

She rolled her eyes. "Oh, great, now I'll have that to add to my social phobias. Not only will I be embarrassed that I'm blushing, I'll be doubly embarrassed that I know exactly what you're thinking."

"Kinda sexy, don't you think? Our own private code." He leaned farther across the counter and kissed her. "Makes it really difficult for me to concentrate, though. On anything but taking you back to bed."

She returned his kiss. Shy, blushing Colleen tangled her hands in the hair at the nape of his neck and pulled him partway over the breakfast bar.

His breathing grew shallow. His head swam. Balancing on the breakfast bar while making love could be a challenge, but one he definitely wanted to try.

He swept mail and papers off the counter with hands that seemed made of wood. But his mouth was hot and pliable, inviting Colleen's investigation.

"Do I need to get out the garden hose?"

Vince grunted, confused. What he wanted to do with Colleen didn't involve lawn implements.

Something stabbed him between the shoulder blades. He yelped. Swinging around, he raised his fist, ready to do battle with an unseen assailant.

His breathing slowed, he lowered his arm.

"What the hell are you doing?" he demanded,

eyeing Violet cautiously. The fork she wielded looked deceptively benign, but he knew it was sharp. He'd bet he had the imprints in his back to prove it.

"Getting your attention." She smiled sweetly. "You're burning the eggs, among other things." Waving the fork in the general direction of the stove, she placed it on the counter. "And we're going to miss morning visiting hours at the rate you two are going."

Shaking her head, she turned and left.

Vince glanced at Colleen.

She shrugged.

"Um. Sorry about the eggs."

"I'm sure they're delicious." She ran her tongue over her bottom lip.

Vince barely refrained from vaulting over the counter to take up where they left off. "You're an evil woman."

And he was toast. Absolute toast.

"I have my moments."

Vince scraped up what was left of the eggs. "We'll call them a blackened Cajun scramble."

Colleen's laughter rang out, a beautiful sound that warmed his heart. "Let me grab some plates."

While she set the table, Vince poured juice. "So Violet's going to the hospital?"

She nodded. "This is the best day ever."

"I gotta hand it to you, I didn't think you'd get her back there. Especially without Ian." His gaze followed Colleen as she set the table. Her movements were sure and graceful. He stepped up behind her and wrapped his arms around her waist.

Colleen sighed, leaning her head against his shoulder. "I wondered for a while myself. But she's a fighter. She likes to tackle things head-on."

"That'd be the Vi I know. Though since we started this trip I'm not sure I know her at all."

"I wonder if I *ever* knew her."

"It's kinda cute, the way you looked up to her." He lifted the hair off of her neck and kissed her nape.

Colleen shivered. "It's a little-sister thing."

"I can see why it was hard for you when she left."

She turned to face him, resting her palms lightly on his chest. "Especially since I kept waiting for her to come home. First, my dad told me she'd visit on Christmas break. Then he said after she graduated. Finally he quit talking about her at all."

"And your mom?"

"She left shortly after that. Moved to San Diego. Remarried. Forgot about me."

"Surely she visited you. Saw you on school breaks?"

"Nope. Gave Dad full custody." The sadness in Colleen's eyes was deep and dark.

"Aw, sweetheart, that must've been tough," he murmured.

"Sometimes it makes me sad. Until Vi came home, I thought I'd lost everyone except Dad."

"I think I understand a little better. Wish I could be more help than I am."

"You've done so much already, just by being here. I've been thinking maybe I'm trying too hard with Violet. Maybe it's not helping that there's always someone with her when she visits Dad."

"That's the only way you can get her there. Either you or Ian."

Nodding, Colleen said, "I figured I'd take her into the room today. Stay a few minutes and find an excuse to go out to the car. Or down to the commissary or something."

"You think she'd let you out of her sight?"

"This time should be easier. I'm hoping she won't need me at all. I'm just kind of a familiar, nonthreatening crutch."

"Sweetheart, you are way more than that, at least in my book. I guess your plan is worth a try. There's probably stuff your dad doesn't want to say in front of other people."

"I don't know what else to do. Will you ride over with us?"

"I've got some projects I'd like to tackle here." He nuzzled her neck. "But I'll take you out to dinner tonight—a real date."

COLLEEN PULLED into the driveway and parked behind an unfamiliar Lexus. She and Violet had been at the hospital most of the morning.

"Expecting company?" Violet asked.

"No. Maybe somebody visiting Vince? Long-lost cousin or something?" Colleen sighed. "I'd hoped to whisk him away for a romantic picnic lunch."

Violet eyed Colleen. "I worry about you. Worry that maybe you and Vince are taking things too fast."

She gave Violet a quick hug. "Thanks for being concerned about me. But I'm not going to live in fear of what might or might not happen. Vince makes me happy."

"I know. You make him happy, too. I just can't help being a bit protective."

"It means a lot. That you care enough to worry about me."

"I've always loved you, little sister. Resented the hell out of you, granted, but always loved you." She smoothed Colleen's hair away from her face. "And much as I tried to put you out of my mind all those years, there was an empty spot in my heart. I couldn't allow myself to believe I missed my bratty sister or worry about how you were doing. It was easier to think Dad would always treat you like a princess."

Colleen couldn't speak. The lump in her throat was too huge. She nodded, hoping Violet understood how much it meant to hear her say that.

Violet's eyes were bright with emotion. She cleared her throat. "Um, I'm glad things seem to be working out for you and Vince—he's a terrific guy. He's got some issues, but then again who doesn't?" She shrugged, smiling wryly. "If he's what you want, then go for it with everything you've got. A wise woman once told me that the tens in life don't come along very often. And when they do arrive, you have to grab them quick. It looks like Vince might just be your ten."

"Thanks, Violet. I really…care for him." She felt like a preteen admitting a crush. But she couldn't bring herself to tell Violet she'd fallen in love with him. Real live, adult, trial-by-fire love.

"I know, pumpkin, it shows."

Colleen's eyes misted. "You used to call me that when I was a kid. Pumpkin."

"When I braided your hair."

"In a French braid. I felt so grown-up and elegant."

"And now you *are* grown-up." Violet cleared her throat. "Let's go inside."

"You go on ahead. I need a couple minutes out here by myself. Maybe if I'm lucky, Vince's mystery visitor will have left and I can have him to myself. There's a place I'd like to take him in East L.A."

Violet shook her head. "Not an area of town where I'd take someone for a romantic meal."

"It's not the food. I want to take him by a baseball field where he used to play when he lived there. Thought it might help him sort some stuff out."

Violet raised an eyebrow. "I hope you know what you're doing."

"I'm not sure about anything. I just know that I care about Vince and want him to be happy."

"Then that's good enough for me." Violet patted Colleen's arm. "You've got a good heart. Which reminds me, I want to thank you for all the trouble you went to bringing me back here. I know you meant well."

"I want you to be happy, too."

Violet nodded. "That hasn't changed. When you were a little girl, you'd get upset when we fought. You wanted everyone to get along. Then when things got really ugly, you'd disappear. I used to hide, too, but once Patrick was gone, it just wasn't possible."

Colleen sighed. "I wish there was some way we could heal and be a normal family."

"Face it, we'll never be a normal family. The best we can do is deal with it and move on. I intend to make sure none of this stuff ever touches my kids."

"Things didn't go any better with Dad today?"

Violet shook her head. "Mostly we watched Jeopardy! together. But I've tried. That will give me some peace when he…you know…"

"Dies."

"Yes. But I owe it to myself and my family to give it my best shot. I called Vince from the hospital and he agreed to stay 'til Monday. If you don't mind having us that long? Or I can get a hotel."

Excitement bubbled up inside Colleen. "Monday? Are you kidding? I'd *love* to have you here. *Both* of you."

Violet opened the car door. "Thanks, Col, you're a gem. I'll tell Vince you'll be in soon. I don't blame you for wanting a few minutes all to yourself out here. We've pretty much turned your life upside down."

VINCE PACED in front of the window. Why the hell was Colleen taking so long? Violet had said she'd come inside in a couple of minutes. Needed some time alone. He wondered if something had happened at the hospital to upset her.

He wanted to go check on her, but was afraid World War III might break out here if he did. Vince watched the two women sitting at opposite ends of the living room, completely still. Violet studiously ignored their guest, while the other woman pretended she wasn't aware of it.

"Um, it looks like Colleen might be a while. Can I get either of you ladies something to drink?" He would have given his right arm for a shot of tequila for himself.

"No, thanks, Vince."

"No, thank you," the other woman murmured. She wasn't what he'd expected. Her tailored pantsuit looked expensive, her perfume smelled expensive and her voice, softly modulated, *sounded* expensive, as if she belonged at a country club in the 'burbs.

Vince resumed pacing.

"It's good to see you, Violet. You're looking well," the woman said.

Violet shrugged.

"When are you due?"

"In about six weeks."

"Is your husband in town? I don't think I've ever met him."

"No."

Vince raised an eyebrow at Violet's terse response. He had to give the other woman credit for being tenacious, though. She didn't seem inclined to quit.

"And you have a daughter. How is she doing?"

"Fine."

"I'd love to see some pictures."

Vince cringed. Judging from Vi's pinched expression, she was getting ready to tell the woman exactly where she could shove those pictures.

The sound of the door opening was music to his ears. The cavalry had come to save the day.

But Colleen stopped in the doorway, staring at the woman on the couch.

"Mom. What're you doing here?"

CHAPTER FOURTEEN

COLLEEN COULDN'T believe her eyes. Her mother was the last person she'd expected to see in her living room.

"I received the messages. About your father. I—I thought it would be a good idea to come."

Colleen waited for a smart-aleck comment from Violet. When it didn't come, she glanced at her sister.

Vi sat ramrod straight, her face averted, her lips trembling.

"I don't know what to say." That was the truth. Because a few of the things running through her mind weren't pretty.

You sure took your damn time.

Why bother now?

Nothing better to do? Things slow at the country club?

Her mother cleared her throat. "I realize this is awkward. But you said… Well, it sounded like your father was dying."

"He *is* dying." Colleen couldn't believe the acidic tone coming out of her own mouth. It was as if she were Violet's ventriloquist dummy. Except the emotions were all hers.

"Your latest message made it sound imminent."

Vince went to Colleen and touched her on the shoulder. "I let her know the endoscopic rubberband thing worked, and he's out of the woods."

"So you can go back home now, Mom."

"Colleen Marie Davis, I'm still your mother and I deserve to be treated with respect."

Shaking her head, Colleen brushed away angry tears. "No, you don't. Respect is earned. You ran out on Dad. You ran out on me."

Her throat got tight with the effort of staying in control of her emotions. "I can't do this. I've got to go." She dashed out the door, grateful for the keys clutched in her hand.

She had the van started when Vince threw himself in the passenger seat. Tires screeched as she hit the gas and reversed out of the driveway.

Vince braced his arm against the dash.

Colleen shifted into Drive and punched the accelerator. Vince flew back in his seat like a crash-test dummy.

The specter of an accident was what made her take a few slow, calming breaths.

"You want me to drive?"

"No. I just want to go somewhere else, anywhere else but here. I've waited so long for my mom to come find me, and now that she has, I can't deal with her. Ironic, huh?"

"How about we go get some lunch? You might feel better once you've had something to eat."

"I wanted to take you on a sort of picnic. That was before she showed up."

"Hey, I'm still game. Where do you want to go?"

"We'll pick up lunch first, then I'll show you."

"Yes, ma'am." Vince saluted smartly.

"Thank you," she whispered.

"For what?"

"For being here."

"There isn't anywhere I'd rather be."

And she believed him.

Drawing in a shaky breath, she said, "I—I guess I understand a little better why it's taken Violet so long to come to terms with Dad. And understand her instinct to get as far away as possible. That's the only thing I could focus on." She glanced sideways at him. "I probably seem like a nutcase to you."

He frowned, his tone thoughtful. "No. It makes a lot of sense. Sounds like your fight or flight instincts kicked in big-time."

"Exactly. Not mending bridges, facing the past or dealing with it and moving on. I just felt if I didn't get away fast something horrible was going to happen. So how do I know if I can get past it?"

"You don't. But you have to try."

Colleen didn't like the sound of his solution. It made her feel helpless, as if she was at the mercy of something she didn't quite understand. "One thing's for sure—I owe Violet a big apology. I'm going through hell and I don't have a difficult pregnancy on top of everything else. She probably thinks I'm a hypocrite. And I was never hit, either."

"Um, I'm no expert, but some of my training involved abuse—psychological abuse can be just as damaging."

"My mom didn't abuse me. She left."

"She abandoned you. Same thing."

Colleen's head ached with confusion. She drove by rote, pulling into the parking lot she'd located earlier on a city map.

Easing the gear into Park, she switched off the engine.

"She left us because my dad was a drunk."

Vince nodded. "That's valid. But she was your mother, for God's sake. She never tried to reestablish a relationship with you. Was never there for you. Never checked to make sure you were properly cared for. In my book, that's abandonment."

Colleen froze. Intellectually, she'd known her mother had abandoned her, but having Vince spell it out explained a lot. She wasn't crazy. Her mother had neglected and abandoned her when protecting her daughter should have been her first priority. A wide chasm of grief opened up, threatening to overwhelm her. "My mom could have come back. But she never did."

Colleen's anguish radiated through Vince. He gathered her in his arms, maneuvering around the steering wheel and console between them.

He expected tears and was prepared to hold her through the storm.

But she didn't utter a sound.

He tipped her face up and was surprised to see that her eyes were dry, her expression stark.

"If you need a shoulder to cry on, I'm here."

"I don't need to cry. I need to forget for a while."

She drew his head down and kissed him.

He returned the kiss for a moment then he pulled away. "That's not the answer, Colleen."

She sighed, brushing her fingers along his mouth. "I know. It seemed like a good way to forget, though."

"Believe me, I'll make love with you any time, just about any place, but it's gotta be for the right reasons. Escape isn't one of them." He rested his forehead against hers. "Okay?"

"Okay." Colleen's voice was husky, but stronger.

"Now, didn't you say something about a picnic?"

She straightened and looked out the window. "Yes, we'll eat lunch over there." She pointed toward some bleachers by a baseball diamond.

Vince started to sweat, realizing for the first time exactly where they were. He'd been too distracted by Colleen to notice. This place wasn't safe. It made him want to roll up the windows, lock the doors.

But Colleen seemed determined to eat lunch there. She opened the car door, grabbed the fast-food bags, her pop and got out.

He couldn't let her go out there alone.

Stiffly, he picked up his pop and followed her.

She headed toward the pathetic excuse for bleachers. The metal frame was rusted, the wood slats old and decrepit and the view dismal.

Colleen climbed to the top and gingerly sat down.

"Watch out for splinters," he warned.

She patted the seat next to her.

Vince sat in the spot she'd indicated. "How'd you manage to find this place? I didn't tell you where it was."

"Process of elimination and the Internet. Wonderful tool."

"I'm not used to the view from here." He surveyed the field through the rusted chain-link backstop.

"What position did you play?"

"Center field."

"I would like to have seen that. I bet you were cute."

"Please. Some respect here. I was very serious about the game. I was anything but cute."

"How serious?"

"I was going to be a major league player."

"You and about every other kid in America."

"But I meant it. Baseball was all I could talk about, all I could think about."

"Interesting that it's involved in your nightmare. Must've had a profound influence on you."

"It doesn't take a shrink to figure that one out." He wished she'd leave his nightmares out of it.

"So enlighten me. How are the two connected?"

Vince shifted in his seat. He had the sinking sensation he might never be the open kind of guy Colleen wanted. It was okay when it was *her* problems they talked about, but not his. He was supposed to be the problem-solver, the rescuer, dammit.

"How long has it been since you've seen your mother?" he asked, hoping to divert her.

She raised her chin. "Don't change the subject. And don't answer a question with a question. What gives?"

"I told you already, I was supposed to go with my mom the day she died."

"So what's that got to do with playing baseball?"

Sighing, he surrendered to the inevitable. "I knew my mom hated going shopping by herself. She said it always made her feel better to have a man along— you know moms, they build up your self-esteem. Anyway, some of the guys wanted me to play ball, so I begged off at the last minute."

"That's a natural thing for a kid to do. Why won't you accept that there was nothing you could have done even if you were there? You might have been killed, too."

Guilt lodged in his chest, a dull ache after so many years. Add shame for being a selfish little brat and he had one hell of a pity party going. "I broke my promise to her, thought only of myself. And she got killed."

She rested her head against his shoulder. Softly she said, "Wow, that's a heavy load to carry. Especially for a kid."

Vince nodded. "I haven't played baseball since. Day before yesterday was the first time I've put on a ball glove in twenty years."

"You gave up something you loved so much? As penance?"

He shrugged. "I dunno. Every time I'd put on my mitt, I'd get a sick feeling in my stomach. Really bad."

"Kind of like how I felt when I saw my mom just now. Is that why you shut down on me at the Angels game? Baseball brought it all back?"

"Maybe." Vince unwrapped his burger even though he had very little appetite. "It's not something I think about too much. As a matter of fact, if I can keep from thinking about it, I don't get that sick feeling in my stomach. No impending doom."

"It's called denial, Vince. It's so easy to see it in someone else…the not thinking about it part. Denial may work for a while, but it will eventually come back to bite you on the butt. Look at what happened to me today."

"My mom died, Colleen. There's no way I can talk to her and make it right. No way she and I can move on from this. It's permanent. And I'll have to live with that guilt for the rest of my life."

COLLEEN BREATHED a sigh of relief as they pulled into the driveway after their picnic. Then she smothered a pang of loss.

The Lexus was gone. Her mother was gone. Again.

She opened the passenger door a crack and leaned over to give Vince a goodbye kiss. "I'm sorry I tried to tell you what to do. I seem to be really good at that."

"You're forgiven. I just need to run to the hardware store real quick."

"I'm beginning to think the hardware store is a means of escape for you."

"Hey, I'm seriously outnumbered at your house. Sometimes I need to go to a male domain and absorb all that testosterone. I'll be back in about an hour so you guys can take the van to the hospital."

She turned to wave goodbye, but her heart was dropping to her toes. He was leaving her here to deal with the fallout alone.

She squared her shoulders and marched up the driveway.

The front door was locked.

She rang the doorbell.

Nobody answered. Colleen fished around in her purse and came up with her keys.

"Violet," she called, as she opened the door.

No answer.

She went through the kitchen and out the back door. "Violet?"

No one there, either.

When she returned to the kitchen, she found a sticky note on the counter. Violet and Mom had gone to the hospital together.

She barely noticed the note flutter to the floor. Her fingers, her mind and her heart were all numb.

They'd done exactly what they'd done before. They'd left her.

Sinking to the floor, Colleen let the tears flow down her face until they dripped off her chin. The awful, horrible feeling of being tossed aside like a piece of garbage expanded inside her chest. But it wasn't today's thoughtless act that immobilized her. It was the betrayal years ago. First Violet, then her mother.

They'd stayed away because Colleen hadn't been worth coming back for. They knew it, she knew it. The only person who didn't know it yet was Vince. And he'd figure it out all too soon.

"COME ON, PRECIOUS GIRL, wake up," a familiar female voice said.

Colleen was gathered into warm, loving arms. She didn't want to wake up. She was having the most wonderful dream—one where her mother still lived with them and called her pet names.

"What's she doing on the floor?" Violet's voice was tinged with concern.

Colleen felt her lips curve in a smile. Violet was here, too. Now her world seemed complete.

A male voice asked, "What's wrong? What happened? Is she hurt?"

It was a pleasant voice. But out of place somehow.

"Hey, sweetheart, wake up."

Colleen managed to lift her eyelids a fraction.

Vince's face wavered in front of her.

She was safely ensconced in someone's lap. Someone who smelled like—

"Mom." Her eyes flew open the rest of the way.

As she looked up into her mother's face, it was if the years faded away. She had the same gentle smile, the same sadness in her eyes.

Colleen struggled to sit up.

"Are you okay?" Vince asked, helping her stand.

"Yes. I guess I was exhausted. I sat down on the floor for a minute and I must've fallen asleep."

Vince cupped his hand around her face. His fingers lightly traced her cheek. "You've been crying."

"Um. I'm just tired."

"Vince, would you please take her in the living room to sit down? I'll bring her some tea or hot cocoa."

"Sure thing, Mrs. Davis."

"Peralta. I remarried. But why don't you call me by my first name. Maria."

Remarried. Colleen came back to the present with a jolt. It had been a wonderful dream while it lasted.

Vince led her to the couch. "Sit down."

She complied.

He sat next to her, putting his arm around her shoulder. "You want to tell me what happened?"

"It's nothing. Really."

"How come you were crying?"

She couldn't meet his gaze. Couldn't admit to what a wuss she'd been just because she wasn't included in the trip to the hospital.

"I'm just overtired. Somebody kept me up late last night." She tried to chuckle but it came out more like a croak.

"In that case, I'll let it slide. Looks like you'll get plenty of sleep tonight. I think you'll have a full house."

"Why?"

"Your mother. Won't she want to stay here? Or will that be awkward?"

"God, I hope she doesn't want to stay here. I'm not sleeping on that couch again. I have every intention of joining you again tonight—I don't care who knows it."

"Shhh." He pressed his finger to her lips. "No need to announce it. You are welcome in my bed, anytime, day or night. I want you to know I'll give this thing with us my best shot. Long distance, if need be, after I go home."

Colleen snuggled against him, savoring his warmth. "That's all I've ever wanted. For you to give our relationship a chance."

Vince bent down to kiss her, gently nibbling on her lower lip. "Can't wait for tonight." His voice was husky, his eyes intense.

"Here you go, Colleen." Her mom held out a steaming cup of tea.

Colleen tried not to show her disappointment at being interrupted. "Um, Mom, I'm sorry about running out on you earlier. You kind of caught me by surprise."

"I know. I kind of surprised myself by coming here."

There was a long pause.

Colleen didn't know what to say. She had day-dreamed so often of the moment when her mother would come looking for her and it was nothing like this. She'd imagined them falling into each other's arms, crying tears of joy. Then they'd catch up on each other's lives, her mother would apologize profusely for missing most of the important milestones of Colleen's life and they would become best friends and confidantes.

Instead, she stared at the woman and couldn't think of a single socially acceptable thing to say.

Her mother looked equally ill at ease.

The seconds ticked by.

Colleen glanced at Vince, hoping he'd rescue her.

He shrugged and smiled encouragingly.

"Um, how's Dad doing?"

"Violet says he's much better. He looked pretty weak to me. It was hard seeing him like that."

Colleen nodded in agreement.

Why was this so damn hard? She thought of the countless times she'd hoped and prayed her mother would come back. When she'd had her first period, first date, first just about anything, she'd longed for a warm, reassuring mother to confide in.

Now the woman was a stranger and Colleen didn't much want to make polite chitchat with her.

Colleen shifted uncomfortably.

Her mother brushed imaginary lint from her navy blue slacks.

Colleen cleared her throat. "Um, did Violet get a chance to talk to him? Alone?"

"I went in by myself at first. Violet said something about finding the cafeteria and joined me later."

"What'd Dad say?"

"He was surprised to see me, to say the least. But it was a good visit. We both needed to make amends." Her smile was sad. "We left some things unresolved when we divorced."

"What things?"

"Colleen Marie Davis, that is none of your business."

"Yes, Mom," she meekly replied. "Where's Violet?"

"She went to lie down."

"I thought we'd all go to the hospital together." Glancing at her watch, Colleen stood abruptly. "Oh my gosh, visiting hours are almost over. I'll let Violet sleep. You're coming, aren't you?"

She turned to her mother.

"No, Colleen. I'm not going back to the hospital. Your father and I have said all we needed to say."

"But…you just got here."

"I had intended to return home today. But I've decided to stay on until Sunday. I want to spend time with you girls."

"You mean you want to spend time with Violet, don't you?"

"That's not fair, Colleen."

"It's the truth though." She stood there, staring at her mother, the years peeling back. Once Violet left for college, there was no reason for Maria Davis to stay. Certainly not for the third-grader who stood at the window and watched her mom load suitcases in the car.

And not for the girl who watched her dad storm out of the house, his face purple, yelling and screaming, throwing a half-empty beer can at the receding taillights. The same child who watched him sit down and drink himself into a sobbing mess. And then mopped the kitchen floor where her dad peed all over himself.

"It's always been the truth, Mom. I was the throwaway child. Violet was the one you cared about. Oh, and Patrick. You loved them with your whole heart. There just wasn't anything left over for me, was there? Not even after Patrick died."

She didn't wait for her mother to reply. Gathering her purse and car keys, she turned to Vince. "I'll be back in time for that dinner you promised."

"Stay. Maybe you can talk it out."

"There's nothing to talk about." Colleen rested her hand on the doorknob.

Vince's voice was urgent. "You can't keep running away. Even you said it will come back to haunt you."

She turned. "I'll have to take that chance. Would

you help my mother find a decent hotel? I don't want her sleeping in this house. She gave up that right a long time ago."

COLLEEN CREPT into her dad's hospital room. He was asleep.

Pulling a chair close, she studied him. Even in sleep, he looked sad, bitter. The corners of his mouth turned down in a perpetual frown, the skin around his neck sagged. He'd always been a big man, but now he weighed barely one-twenty-five. And on his now-scrawny frame, he carried a grotesque belly, bloated by the fluids and toxins his body was no longer able to process on its own.

His eyes opened.

She grasped his hand. "Hi, Daddy, I'm here."

He weakly patted her hand.

"You saw Violet? And…Mom?"

Nodding, he struggled to sit up.

"Here, let me." Colleen used the remote control to maneuver the bed in to a more comfortable sitting position. Then she fluffed his pillow and tucked it behind his back.

"You're a good daughter, Colleen."

Her hands stilled.

How long had those words controlled her? Her whole life? All those straight-A's, meals she'd cooked when she wasn't yet tall enough to reach the top cupboards, friends and parties and dates she'd forgone. Just to hear a bit of praise from a man who didn't believe in positive strokes. Except now, when the life was draining out of him.

She wanted to scream at the unfairness of it all, demand back the years she'd given up while caring for him.

But she didn't. She was a good daughter. Besides, she owed it to him for staying with her after everyone else had left.

"Thank you, Daddy."

CHAPTER FIFTEEN

VINCE SMOOTHED Colleen's hair from her face. Her breath was warm and gentle on his bare chest, where she rested her cheek. An overwhelming wave of protectiveness washed over him.

"Better?" he asked.

"Mmm." She nodded. Her eyelids fluttered closed. "*Much* better."

"This was a terrific idea. Though I would have enjoyed taking you out some place nice for dinner, fast food certainly has its advantages." He glanced at the fast-food wrapper dangling off the edge of the bed. "I much prefer making love to eating in a fancy restaurant."

"Sure. Fast food." Her voice sounded drowsy, content.

He stared at the ceiling, amazed at the turn his life had taken in less than a week. Commitment to one woman didn't terrify him now as long as that woman was Colleen.

Vince only wished he could take on her pain for her, relieve her of the burden. But he couldn't. All he could do was be there for her.

"I love you," he whispered into her hair.

She raised her face to him, her smile wobbly. "Did you say what I thought you said?"

Vince nodded. "I love you." The words felt natural.

"I love you, too." She drew his head down for a long, searching kiss.

A brilliant idea popped into his head. "D'you ever think about moving to a small town. A place like, say, Echo Point?"

"It's a lovely place, but there isn't an ocean. I doubt they need many marine biologists or have the facilities to train them. How about you, any desire to give San Diego a try?"

"San Diego's kinda big…."

COLLEEN KNEW something was wrong before she opened her eyes.

Vince's muscles twitched, he threw a leg over her hip. She dodged an elbow a few seconds later as he rolled over.

He muttered something.

She rubbed his back, hoping to lull him into a deep, dreamless sleep.

It didn't work.

Vince thrashed and moaned.

"Vince, wake up."

"No…please…Mom."

It was just like before.

Grasping him by the shoulders, she shook him hard. He stopped thrashing for a moment. Then resumed.

"No…please…not Colleen."

Colleen froze. The hairs at the nape of her neck prickled. He was dreaming about her.

How in the world could she wake him without getting nailed by a flailing arm or leg?

She went to the bathroom and poured a glass of cold water. Returning to his side, she dipped her fingers in the water and flicked it on his face. That did the trick.

His eyes opened, he reached toward her side of the bed.

"I'm here, Vince."

He turned his head, wiping sleep from his eyes. "What're you doing up?"

"You were having another nightmare. I couldn't wake you. So I got some cold water to sprinkle on your face." Colleen blotted his face with the sheet.

"Another nightmare?" He fell back against the pillows. "Now I remember. The same dream I had the other night, only this time…"

"This time?"

"You were there."

"What happened?"

"Mom was on the ground, dying, pleading with me to help her. Then she changed into you. You reached out to me while you bled out. And I couldn't do a thing."

Colleen shuddered. She wasn't superstitious, but didn't like the tale anyway. "It's over now."

She placed the glass on the nightstand and went around to her side of the bed.

The sheets were cool on her skin. She shivered again. Colleen wasn't sure if she was cold, in shock or entertaining the Irish second sight. Whatever the reason, her teeth chattered.

"Cold?" Vince wrapped an arm around her and drew her close.

"You need to deal with this, Vince."

"Like you're dealing with your mother?"

"I'm not doing a terrific job of it. But I'm trying, while the opportunity presents itself. Maybe you could lay the groundwork while you're in L.A. At least it's a start to healing."

"I healed a long time ago."

"No, you didn't. It's scabbed over, but the wound is still there. And every time it breaks open and bleeds, your life—and the lives of everyone around you—is going to be turned upside down. I learned the hard way. Your issues with your mom's death will taint the good things in your life. Like us. It's all interrelated."

"All that interrelated stuff may mean something to you, but it doesn't to me. I'll be fine once I get back to Echo Point."

"Have you thought about seeing a counselor?"

"I've *seen* a counselor." He turned away from her. "And it didn't work."

Colleen wished she could see his face. "You can't shut me out when things go bad. That's not how a healthy relationship works."

Vince rolled over to face her. His mouth was compressed into an angry line. "You knew up-front that

I wasn't good at relationships. What do you want from me?"

"I want all of you. Not fifty percent, or seventy-five, or even ninety. You can't give this relationship your all if there's a part of you living in the past."

"Sweetheart, you *already* have me one hundred percent. Digging up all that old stuff won't change it."

"I wish I could be sure," she murmured.

"I haven't seen you jumping right in to resolve things with your mom."

She sighed. "I'm not really sure where to begin, or if I even want to."

"Isn't that kinda how Violet feels?"

She peeked up at him. "So if Violet is trying, the least I can do is try?"

"Something like that." He leaned over and kissed her. "And I can't ask you to do something I'm not willing to do. How about I try to work on some of my stuff, if you'll try to figure out a way to face your mom?"

"You make it sound so easy."

"I *know* it's not easy. Like I know you are brave and kind and sincere. You'll find the right way."

Her heart warmed at his words. It amazed her that he viewed her that way.

"I wish I could be as sure as you are. Did you really mean it? You'll work on your problem, too?"

He nodded. "Uh-huh."

"Promise?"

"Promise."

"I INVITED MY MOM over for a barbecue this evening."
Colleen swallowed hard. "I thought maybe she and
I might get a few minutes alone to talk. About, you
know, past history."

Vince raised an eyebrow. He carefully folded the
newspaper and placed it on the coffee table. His expression was bland. It was his poker face. "Okay.
You're sure you want to do this?"

Colleen nodded. "Positive."

She only wished she was half as positive as she
sounded. Her tummy did flip-flops, she couldn't
seem to get enough air. Hyperventilation was a distinct possibility.

"Come here and sit." He patted the couch cushion
next to him.

When she was seated, he gently grasped the back
of her neck. "Put your head between your knees."

It helped a little, but not a lot.

"Colleen, nobody's pushing you to do this. As a
matter of fact, I'd prefer you didn't. I hate to see you
hurting."

She believed him. Pain was evident in his voice.

"I'm not doing this for you. I'm doing this for
me." Her words were muffled by her legs.

"What can I do to help?"

"Rewrite family history?"

"Sorry. I'm a mere mortal. No supernatural powers."

"What in the world are you doing, Colleen? Is
she hurt?"

Colleen raised her head to look up into Violet's

perplexed face. "No, I'm fine. I—I was a little light-headed so Vince told me to put my head between my knees."

"You didn't hear me coming in the door and I must've made enough noise to wake the dead." She balanced a paper grocery sack on her hip, two more lay at her feet. "I stopped by the store and picked up a few things. Mom said you'd invited her for a bar-becue tonight."

"What'd you get?" Vince deserted Colleen to peek in the bags. "Mmm. Steaks, hamburger, potato salad and, drumroll please, brownie mix."

"We've been eating up all Colleen's food this week, so I thought I'd do a little shopping."

"Works for me." He reached for his wallet. "Here, let me give you a few bucks. I eat more than my share."

"No way, buddy. Ian will pay for your half. He'll pay in ways that would make you blush." She wag-gled her eyebrows and handed a bag to Vince. "But make yourself useful. Take this to the kitchen."

"Yes, ma'am. You Davis women are a forceful lot these days."

"And don't you forget it," Violet said.

Once he was out of earshot, she grabbed Colleen's arm. "I wanted to talk to you alone," she whispered. "Mom and I have done a lot of talking, and I under-stand some stuff I was too young to understand when I lived here."

"And your point is?"

"Everything's not as black and white as I thought.

I—I'm trying to give her a chance. Maybe you can, too?"

Colleen stiffened. "Of course I'll give her a chance."

COLLEEN COULDN'T remember being more nervous. Not even when she'd asked Brad Johnson, star quarterback, to the Sadie Hawkins dance. She hoped her mother wouldn't reject her nearly as cruelly as Brad. His laughter still haunted her during difficult social situations.

Making love with Vince always calmed her nerves, but that was out of the question right now. He was busy getting the grill lit. Besides, Violet was hovering like a mother hen.

"For goodness sake, Violet, would you please sit down. You're making me nervous."

"I'm just so excited. Wouldn't it be nice if the three of us could eventually be friends. You know, long lunches, shopping trips, maybe visit the spa together."

A pang of longing swept over Colleen. Those were the same things she'd dreamed about and thought she could never have. It was all within her reach. If she didn't blow this visit with her mother. If she could keep a lid on her resentment.

But Colleen knew that burying her feelings would be a mistake. If they had any chance at all of building a close relationship, she had to be honest with her mother. And that included owning up to the bitter resentment she'd never outwardly acknowledged.

The doorbell pealed.

Violet jumped up to answer.

Colleen couldn't move. She sat there on the couch like a hunk of petrified wood.

She was petrified all right. Clapping her hand over her mouth, she stifled a giggle at her pun. *I'm a poet and don't even know it.*

Hearing her name, she glanced up to see her mother standing in front of her.

Pull yourself together.

"Thank you for inviting me, Colleen," her mother said. "I'm so very glad you're giving me a second chance."

All sorts of rude responses jostled to be first out of the gate. It created a logjam between what Colleen knew she should say and all the things she shouldn't. "Um. Yeah."

"I brought dessert. Your favorite. German Chocolate cake."

"It's Violet's favorite. I hate German Chocolate cake."

That wasn't quite true. At least not until today.

Colleen stood and glanced around, looking for a means of escape. This wasn't going to work.

Her mother frowned. "I could have sworn it was your favorite."

"Maybe when I was eight. But a person's taste buds change every seven years. And you weren't around *then*."

Her mother's eyes were filmed with sadness. "You're right, I wasn't. I can't change the past. I—I can only say I'm sorry."

"That's all you can say? Why, Mom? I want to know why you left. Why you never visited. Was I that horrible? I tried so hard to be a good girl. Dad noticed. But never you. I thought for a while if I was smart enough, pretty enough, *perfect* enough, you'd come back. But you never did." She ran out of breath, only partially horrified at the stuff that had come out of her mouth.

"I couldn't, Colleen. I had to save myself."

"You could have taken me with you." The cry came from deep inside, wrenched from a dark, pitiful place.

Her mother reached out to touch her cheek, but Colleen jerked her head away.

"I could barely take care of myself. By the time you came along, I didn't have anything else to give."

"I would have taken care of you," Colleen whispered. After all, she'd taken care of her dad.

"Oh, precious girl, you couldn't have. It wasn't a matter of not being perfect enough. It was that I was so sick. I—I tried to commit suicide."

Colleen blinked.

"I knew then I needed to leave. Make a clean start. See if I could rebuild my life. Violet was gone, Patrick was gone." Her voice grew rough with unshed tears. "And you seemed…okay. You adored your dad. I knew he'd treat you decently, unlike the older kids. So I did something selfish. I survived. And I could do that by forgetting this life ever existed. I moved to San Diego and worked really hard to put all of you out of my mind. But it never really happened. Every birthday, every milestone, I was there in spirit."

"What about when you remarried? You could have come for me then. Or was that too much bother?"

"I didn't want to disrupt your life."

"Bull. You didn't want to disrupt *your* life."

Tears gathered in her mother's eyes.

"You were always too perceptive, Colleen. You're right. I'm not being honest with myself. Or with you. I didn't want to do anything that might endanger what little peace I'd found." She shrugged. "Not very pretty."

"No, it's not." Violet walked back into the room. "You didn't tell me that part. I can't imagine giving up Rose for any reason." She put her arm around Colleen's waist. They made a united front for the first time Colleen could remember.

Their mother lifted her chin. "How very fortunate you are. That you grew up strong. Made good decisions."

"I didn't have a choice. I do know one thing, though—you abandoned us both in different ways. With me, it was a little less obvious. You may not have left physically while I was growing up, but you left emotionally. When Dad beat us, you looked the other way. Pretended it didn't happen. You could have stopped it, you know."

"I wasn't strong enough. And I was a mess. I wish with all my heart I could go back and change that. But I can't. I intended to apologize and I've done that. You two will have to decide whether you will allow me back in your lives. I have no control over that."

"Yeah, just like you had no control over Dad abusing us."

Sadly shaking her head, their mother replied, "I've learned to accept that I have regrets I'll live with for the rest of my life. But I did the best I could at the time."

She placed the cake on the coffee table. "Now, I'd like to thank you for inviting me to dinner and hearing me out. I don't think it would be a good idea for me to stay. You know where I can be reached. I love you both, for whatever it's worth."

She turned and quietly let herself out the door.

Colleen went to the window and watched her get into her car. Her dad wasn't there this time to throw things at the retreating taillights. But Colleen's overwhelming sense of loss was the same.

White-hot anger roiled inside her. "How dare she come into our lives after all these years and toss around a few apologies, expecting us to welcome her with open arms."

When Violet didn't answer, Colleen turned away from the window. Her sister had left the room.

They'd come full circle. Her mom and her sister had once again abandoned her.

Colleen's gaze fell on the coffee table. She picked up the cake and heaved it against the wall. It was satisfying to watch the gooey frosting creep down the wall like some sort of toxic slug.

She'd lost control, made a huge scene and been anything *but* the good daughter. It had been a long time coming.

Colleen nodded, hoping she'd taken a step toward releasing the sad, lonely eight-year-old deserted by almost everyone she loved.

CHAPTER SIXTEEN

VINCE FOUND Colleen standing in the middle of the living room.

"What the hell?" There was cake all over the place. Chunks of chocolate pastry littered the floor, coconut frosting smeared the wall.

Colleen turned to him. "I did it." Her eyes were open, but it was as if she looked right through him.

Somehow he couldn't reconcile the evidence with his beautiful, patient Colleen. "An accident?"

She raised her chin. "No. I did it on purpose."

"What happened? All Vi said was that you needed me and I better come quick."

"I don't like German Chocolate cake."

"I figured that much. Looks kinda like overkill, though."

Colleen nodded. "Exactly. I wanted to kill someone. I was so mad, so hurt…"

Vince exhaled slowly. He stepped close and tugged her into his arms. "It's gonna be okay. Tell me what happened."

Her voice expressionless, Colleen recounted the meeting with her mother.

Letting out a low whistle, he said, "I'm glad you didn't hold it all in, but maybe a little moderation?"

She shook her head. "Oh, *all* of it needed to come out. At least now I have some answers. I'm just not sure if I can handle them." She leaned into him, resting her forehead against his chest.

"Hey, I'm here for you. So's Violet."

"I know," she murmured. "I thought I'd feel better, but now I just feel lousy."

"See? Sometimes this confronting the past stuff just causes trouble."

"I was so sure."

"I bet the books made it sound all cozy and reaffirming. But I'll tell you, there are some things that were too crummy for me the first time they happened. There's no way I want to relive them."

"But you do. In your dreams."

Vince swore under his breath. "Okay, I give. I'm not the best person in the world for dispensing advice. But I worry about you. Because I love you."

Colleen raised her face. Her eyes were moist, her lips trembled. "I'll never get tired of hearing you say 'I love you.' Never."

He bent his head to kiss her. He meant it to be a tender kiss, a promise to love her forever, but she responded with a passion that blew his mind. Groaning, he pulled away. His breathing was ragged, his self-control shot. "Can't. Not now. Violet's awake."

"Violet's going for a drive." The soft response came from behind him.

Glancing over his shoulder, he saw her, keys in hand, eyes warm with understanding.

"And I intend to be gone for at least an hour."

VINCE WATCHED over Colleen as she slept. The tear-stains on her cheeks made his chest tighten. He gingerly brushed the hair from her brow, trying not to wake her, but needing to reassure himself that she was really there and essentially in one piece.

He loved this woman more than he ever thought it possible to care for another human being. But loving her so intensely invited all sorts of terrifying scenarios to creep through his imagination. He realized he would gladly die to protect her. And he hoped to hell he never let her down.

The really hokey part was wanting to make everything right for her. Chase away all her troubles. Logically, he knew he shouldn't do that even if it were possible. She was an intelligent, vital woman, who deserved to determine her own destiny. He only hoped he was strong enough not to interfere.

COLLEEN DRESSED quietly and left the bedroom. Placing a note on the kitchen table, she grabbed the keys from the hook. She avoided looking at the mess in the living room, a very real reminder of her loss of control. There would be plenty of time to clean it up when she got home.

It only took a few minutes to reach her mother's hotel. She tapped lightly on the door.

Her mother appeared almost immediately, as if she'd been waiting.

"Hi, Mom. We need to talk."

"Yes. We probably do. Come in." She opened the door wide.

Colleen followed her into the tasteful, understated room. She spotted the suitcase open on the bed.

"Running away again?"

Her mother lifted her chin. "No. I'm going home. Where I belong."

This wasn't the mom she remembered. The mother from her childhood had been fragile and frazzled. This woman's quiet dignity made Colleen feel ashamed.

"Look, I'm not here to judge you."

"Yes, you are. I can see it in your eyes."

Sighing, Colleen wished she could just slink back to Vince's bed. But she needed to finish what she'd started.

"Did I do something? To make you leave when I was a little girl?" Her voice was small, uncertain and she hated it.

"No, it had absolutely nothing to do with you. My marriage wasn't good to start with." She paused. "It deteriorated until I could barely look at your father for fear he would see the disgust written all over my face. I figured that if I loved him enough, he wouldn't drink. Over the years, I think I realized he would have been an alcoholic no matter what I did. It hurts, though, to see him like he is."

Colleen nodded. "It shocks me every time I visit him. Even though the changes came on gradually for the most part. Sometimes it makes me downright mad."

"That's okay, Colleen. It's okay to be angry with him, angry with me. I just hope someday we can find a way to be in each other's lives again."

"That's all I've ever wanted. And now, I can't seem to forgive you." Her words rose from a dark, hollow place inside her.

Her mother sighed. "Sometimes forgiveness takes a long, long time. Sometimes you have to forgive yourself first."

"I—I don't understand."

"You will. When the time is right." She placed her palm on Colleen's cheek. Her eyes were bright with unshed tears. "But always know, precious girl, that I want you to be happy. I'll be thinking about you every single day. And praying, too."

"Thank you. I just hope it isn't too little, too late. Have a safe trip back, Mom." Colleen ran all the way back to the van.

VINCE SAT on the couch, staring unseeingly at the newspaper open on his lap. He glanced at his watch. Two minutes later than the last time he'd looked.

Where was she?

Colleen's mom had called to make sure she got home okay. Said she was upset when she left the hotel. That had been over an hour ago.

He'd turned on every light in the kitchen and living room, but it still seemed dark and ominous. All sorts of scary scenarios flashed across his mind and Colleen was in terrible danger in each and every one.

Where could she be?

Should he call the hospitals?

The mere thought brought on a cold sweat and visions of a waiting room, a surgeon in scrubs talking to his dad in low, earnest tones.

Shaking his head to rid himself of the images, he tried to convince himself he was overreacting. But he couldn't help remembering how dangerous this city was. Especially for a woman alone.

That gnawing in his gut was back. He didn't think he could handle it if something happened to Colleen. She had become the light of his world in only a few short days. And yet it was hard to remember when she wasn't in his life. She was so much a part of him that he felt they'd always been together.

The sound of the door handle turning a few minutes later was the most joyous sound he'd ever heard.

Jumping up, he was at the door by the time Colleen stepped over the threshold. He surveyed her from head to toe. She didn't look injured. She just looked defeated.

"Hey, where have you been?" He wrapped his arms around her.

"Driving."

"Just driving? Your mom called over an hour ago to make sure you got home. We were worried. Violet was worn out so I promised I'd wake her when you got home."

"I'm fine. Really." She pulled out of his arms and went to the window, where she stared out into the night.

"I thought something happened to you." He kept his voice even, devoid of the panic he felt.

"I needed time alone. I guess I should have called." Her voice was listless.

"What happened?"

"I don't feel like talking about it."

"It might help."

"I'm not trying to shut you out. I just can't talk about it now."

"This is tearing you apart, Colleen." He couldn't quite keep the uneasiness out of his voice.

"Yes. It *is* tearing me apart."

"Why won't you let me help?"

"Because some things I have to do by myself." She went to the coat closet and pulled out her pillow and blankets. "I'm going to sleep in my room tonight, on the floor."

"But—"

"I can't, Vince. Not tonight."

"We'll just sleep. Let me hold you."

"No. I need my space." Her eyes empty of all emotion, she looked past him as if he weren't there.

He didn't kiss her, didn't hug her. The stiff set of her shoulders told him she didn't want his touch.

"Okay. If that's what you need."

Watching her walk down the hall and close her

bedroom door behind her was one of the hardest things he'd ever done. His instinct was to follow her and pound on the door until she let him in.

But he knew he'd lose her if he did something stupid like that. She was in a place where he couldn't reach her. A place from which only Colleen could rescue herself.

Frustration boiled inside him.

He was a rescuer. That's what he did best. First, as a cop, then a sheriff and later a son. How did he rescue someone who didn't want to be saved?

Slowly, he headed to the guest bedroom. Alone.

He undressed and brushed his teeth as if on autopilot. The bed was cold and lonely when he slid between the sheets. He shivered. Not so much because of the room temperature, but more because of the emptiness waiting to swallow him whole.

He'd been there for Colleen. He'd been there for Violet. Tried to protect them. And now it seemed neither of them needed him.

Self-sufficiency was a good thing, right? Then how come he couldn't get over this dread?

Vince tossed and turned. He reached for Colleen but found only space. Finally, he dozed.

It seemed like only moments later when he shot to a sitting position, breathing heavily. Sweat beaded his face, trickled down his back, turned the sheets into a damp, soggy mess.

He glanced at the clock and realized he'd been asleep for over an hour. He had relived the nightmare again. Only this time it had been different. Worse. Instead of reliving the past, he'd been in the present. Colleen drove the van, Violet her passenger. They'd stopped at the gas station in his old neighborhood. Colleen had started to pump gas. An Impala parked beside them and she hadn't seemed to notice it. Neither had Violet.

He'd opened his mouth to yell a warning, but nothing came out. He'd been completely helpless, rooted to the spot and unable to warn the woman he loved.

Vince had awakened before the inevitable happened—two people who meant the world to him destroyed while he'd been helpless to prevent it.

"VINCE, HONEY, wake up." The voice was soft, loving.

"Sleep. Jus' a few more minutes, Mom." He pulled the covers over his head.

"It's important. You've got to wake up."

He was rudely jostled awake.

Vince sat and flipped the covers away in one motion. "Colleen. What time is it?" He squinted at the clock.

"It's early. I've got to go to the hospital. Violet's coming with me."

"Too early." He noticed she was fully dressed, her hair in a tidy French braid. "How come so early?"

"There's a problem. Dad's got a fever. They think he might have an infection."

He was having a hard time processing the information. Her worried frown told him it might be severe.

"What kind of infection?"

"The doctors aren't sure. They're running some tests. It might be peritonitis. That's why we need to get to the hospital right away."

"You need me to drive?"

"No. But Vince, I need you at the hospital with me. I—I'm at the end of my rope. I was up all night thinking about the situation with my mom. Couldn't sleep, couldn't figure out what I should do. My emotions are still raw this morning."

Her plea shook him. She finally needed him to rescue her and there was absolutely no way he could do it, no matter how badly he wanted to help. "I *am* here for you. And I'll be right out in the parking lot for you, too."

"That's not what I meant. I need you there, with me, the whole way. *Inside* the hospital."

"You're overreacting. This infection might turn out to be nothing."

"I have a bad feeling about it, Vince."

He reached over and cupped the back of her neck. "Hey, you're overtired. You said your emotions are raw. You're probably jumping to conclusions. I'll drive you two over there and wait in the van."

"Then if things aren't looking good with my dad, you'll come inside with me?"

Vince couldn't refuse the plea he saw in her eyes. He hesitated, then nodded. "If things go south, send someone for me. I'll be there in a heartbeat. Okay?"

"Okay," she murmured. She pressed a kiss to his lips. "Thank you."

He wanted to believe he could be there for her. That if he wanted it badly enough, he could make it happen. He felt a renewed sense of purpose. "Is Violet ready?"

Colleen nodded.

"I'll throw on some clothes and we'll hit the road."

It was barely a half hour later when they arrived at the hospital. Vince was surprised to see that the parking lot was full at such an early hour. Finding a parking space was only marginally easier than during regular visiting hours.

"It'll be okay," he said to Colleen. He set the parking brake and went around to the passenger side. Opening Colleen's door, he kissed her pale cheek. Her eyes were deep, dark pools of worry.

"I'm here for you."

She nodded, grasping his hand in hers. She gripped his hand tightly, almost as if drawing strength from him. Then she let go and the connection was broken.

He opened the sliding door and helped Violet out. "You get too tired, take a break and stretch out on the back seat. Sometimes those waiting rooms get kind of claustrophobic."

Violet stood on tiptoe to kiss him on the cheek. "Thanks, Vince. You're a good guy."

Vince was back in rescue mode and all was right with the world.

CHAPTER SEVENTEEN

VINCE DECIDED he would never conquer his aversion to hospitals by hiding in the van. He had the will so there certainly had to be a way.

Exiting the vehicle, he activated the car alarm, pocketed the keys and headed toward the hospital. It felt good to be taking positive action.

However, his steps slowed as he approached the entrance. The sliding glass doors looked like a beast with a cavernous mouth, waiting to devour him.

People go in, but they don't come out. Wasn't that the catchphrase for one of those old horror movies they showed on late-night TV?

He resolutely pushed the thought away. Lots of people came out of hospitals to lead full lives. It just hadn't been what he'd personally observed. And from everything Colleen and Vi said, Sean Davis wasn't coming out again, short of a miracle.

Forcing his feet forward, the blast of air-conditioning sent chills along his arms. He kept moving. One foot after another, until he reached the information desk.

The white-haired volunteer smiled warmly and asked how she could help him.

How *could* she help him? Magically snap her fingers and heal Colleen's father? Then he wouldn't need to be here at all.

But she was only a mere mortal, a volunteer at that.

"I'm visiting and I forgot the room number. Sean Davis."

She punched in the name on the computer and frowned.

"And your relationship to Mr. Davis?"

If they were screening visitors, then it was bad. Really bad. And Colleen would need him now more than ever. "I'm his," Vince paused, "son-in-law. I'm meeting my, um, wife here."

"Mr. Davis has been moved to ICU. The elevator down the hall and to the right will take you directly up to the ICU waiting area."

Vince gulped. He forced himself to head in the direction she indicated. He even managed to push the elevator button. But when the doors opened, he couldn't go in.

His mother had been in ICU for three days before she died. He'd spent hour after hour there with his dad and sisters, along with assorted aunts, uncles and cousins. Though they'd been careful not to let him hear their whispers, he'd overheard enough to piece together the truth. It wasn't safe for a woman out alone in the city. His mother had been easy prey. Everyone probably knew of his broken promise.

Knew that it was his fault she was dead. If she hadn't been alone, it wouldn't have happened.

He'd buried the guilt. Become a police officer so he could stop bad guys from hurting someone else's mom. And then he'd been involved in a robbery in progress call at a convenience market. The suspects had come out firing and an innocent woman was caught in the cross fire. He held her hand and comforted her as she lay on the hot asphalt of the parking lot, bleeding profusely, waiting for the ambulance to arrive. He'd managed six hours in the ICU waiting room, but that didn't stop the inevitable. The woman died and he'd never been the same since.

No, he couldn't do another stint in an ICU waiting room. Simply couldn't do it. Turning on his heel, Vince went back the way he came.

The white-haired lady looked at him inquiringly when he passed her desk.

"Left the flowers in the car," he mumbled as he hurried by.

He knew as well as she did that they wouldn't allow flowers in ICU. Any excuse would do, though.

Vince rubbed grit from his eyes as he emerged into the sunlight. He was *not* going to let this thing cripple him. He'd sit outside the entrance on one of the nice, comfy stone benches. If Colleen needed him, he'd be close.

COLLEEN COULDN'T stay inside the hospital another minute. She needed Vince. Stepping outside, she shaded her eyes. How could it possibly be sunny when her world was falling apart?

Then she saw Vince's dear, sweet solemn face.

"Thank God, you're here."

He was by her side in seconds.

"What's wrong?"

The concern in his voice set loose the tears she'd been holding back. "They started IV antibiotics, but they think Dad's gone into septic shock."

Vince wrapped his arms around her and drew her close. "I'm sorry, sweetheart."

"It gets worse."

"Tell me," he murmured.

She soaked up his strength and his love. *This* was what she'd needed so desperately.

"I—I tried to calm Violet down, but she got all upset and crying. I did everything I knew. But she was just out of control."

"Where is she now? Tell her to come down here and we'll take a nice, relaxing walk."

"They admitted her. She's gone into labor. I'm so scared. I don't want her to lose this baby. And I don't want to lose her." Panic lumbered through her like a great, clumsy elephant.

Vince swore under his breath. "Did you call Ian?"

"Not yet."

"I'll call him. That's at least *something* I can do."

His face was bleak as he spoke to Ian. Then emotion after emotion flashed: guilt, frustration, fear.

And dammit, it made her mad. Where was Vince

when she needed him? Up to his eyeballs in unresolved issues. She needed his strength, she needed him by her side. And it looked like he could fulfill neither.

"He's catching the next plane." Vince clipped his phone back on his belt.

"Good. Vi needs him. Just like I need you."

"Aw, sweetheart, I'm here for you." He pulled her into his arms.

"I'd like you to be there with me when I talk to the doctors. They're going to want me to make decisions on treatment for Dad—Violet, too, until Ian gets here. Your support is important right now."

"I tried, Colleen. I really tried. I can't do hospital waiting rooms."

"How about the maternity ward?"

He shook his head. "Anything past the reception area and I freeze."

"You said you love me. What if we eventually get married? Will you be waiting in the parking lot while I give birth?"

"That's not fair."

"Yes. It *is* fair. I love you. But I want someone I can share the good times and the bad. Both of those sometimes include hospitals."

"I can be there for you—what?—ninety-nine percent of the time? Are you saying I don't love you enough if I can't give one hundred percent *all* the time? Nobody can do that. It's a fairy tale."

Shaking her head, Colleen fought a wave of sadness. "I don't expect a fairy tale. I expect you to try to do something about a situation that's obviously causing you pain. And I expect you to love me enough to *want* to be there one hundred percent."

"I *can't.*"

"Then you're not nearly the man I thought you were." Colleen's heart was heavy as she turned on her heel and went back into the hospital, not even trying to brush away the tears coursing down her face.

She stopped by the maternity ward on her way to ICU and let the nurses know Ian was on his way.

According to the nurse, Violet was receiving an IV to stop the contractions. The nurse promised to locate Colleen if her condition changed.

In the elevator, Colleen covered her face with her hands. It wasn't supposed to end this way. Dad and Violet hadn't forgiven each other and the three of them weren't a nice, little solid family unit. They were still groping blindly for some way to reconnect.

The minutes seemed like hours as she waited for some news of her father.

Colleen felt a hand tentatively touch her shoulder. *Vince!*

She turned. "Oh, it's you. What're you doing here?"

"Vince didn't think you should be alone," her mother said.

"He called you?"

"Yes. He cares about you very much."

"I know he does." Colleen sighed. "That doesn't help much, though, when I need him in here with me."

Her mother shrugged. "I guess I'm all you've got. He's right, you shouldn't be here alone. You can tell me to go to hell if you want, but I'm staying put. If you need anything, let me know."

Colleen shook her head, watching her mother make herself comfortable at one end of the waiting room, pulling a crochet hook and yarn from her bag.

Shaking her head, Colleen wondered when she'd taken up crocheting.

Then her father's doctor came out the swinging door. His expression was serious. "Your father is in grave condition. We've not seen a substantial change since we started the antibiotics."

"What're we looking at if they don't work?"

"We'll try to find another drug. Unfortunately, our choices are limited by your father's liver disease. We have to be careful of toxicity."

Colleen bit her lip, but the words came out before she could stop them. "He's terminal, for God's sake. What does it matter if the drugs are toxic to his liver? Did he worry for the last forty years about alcohol being toxic to his system? Hell, no."

"You're overwrought. Why don't you get a cup of coffee? We'll see how he does over the next several hours."

"I'm not overwrought. I'm pissed off. There's a difference."

The physician cleared his throat. "Um. Yes, I guess there is. Might I suggest decaf?"

Colleen opened her mouth to really lay into him when she noticed the twinkle in his eyes.

"Yes, doctor, I think that might be a wise idea," Colleen replied.

Turning to her mother, she was annoyed to see her raise an eyebrow. "Don't say it. I know Sister Agnes would not approve of my language."

"That's not what I was thinking. I was admiring your spirit. And your ability to stand up for yourself. You expressed yourself quite well, as a matter of fact."

"Hmm. Well. Good. You want to go with me to get coffee? We can check on Violet, first. And I promise I'll get decaf."

"Oh, don't do that, dear. I find you highly entertaining in your present mood."

"I'll take that as a compliment."

"It was meant as one. You said what you were thinking. There's absolutely nothing wrong with that. If I'd done that years ago, my life might not have been such a mess."

VINCE WAYLAID Colleen's mom as she exited the hospital. "How's Colleen doing? Violet? Mr. Davis?"

"Young man, you should go ask Colleen yourself."

"But—"

"You have issues. I know. We all do. Now what are you going to do about them?" She brushed by him without another look. When she returned a half hour later with Violet's overnight bag, he pretended he didn't see her.

Instead, he stepped behind a hefty nurse taking a smoking break. Pulling out his wireless phone, he punched his speed dial number for the ICU nurses' station. Next call would be the maternity ward. It was a sorry way to keep up to date on both patients' conditions.

COLLEEN PACED the waiting room, trying to elude the awful sense of loneliness threatening to overwhelm her.

She tried to tell herself that she wasn't alone. Her mother shuttled between the ICU waiting room and the maternity ward. And Ian's arrival had eased her worries about her sister's treatment. Her brother-in-law was a tall, nice-looking man who refused to leave Violet's bedside. Colleen had liked him instantly.

So she shouldn't feel so alone.

Her heart ached to be by her father's side, but the staff wouldn't allow her to see him yet. And her heart ached to be with Vince. Only his touch, his reassurance would fill that scary, empty place inside her.

"Why don't you sit for a while? You're going to wear a path in the carpet," her mother suggested. She held Colleen's gaze while her hand moved at a rapid, steady pace, looping yarn around the crochet hook.

Colleen went and sat next to her. "How long have you been doing that?"

"Crocheting? Years and years now. It calms my nerves."

"What're you making?"

"An afghan. Next I'll work on a blanket for Violet's baby and another especially for Rose."

Colleen blinked at the wistful note in her mother's voice. She didn't know whether to be pleased or irked that her mother wanted to be a grandmother when she'd opted out of mothering.

Clearing her throat, she said, "Rose is a real character. I think I fell in love with her the minute I set eyes on her. Imagine that. I'm an aunt."

"And I'm a grandmother."

"Mom?"

"Hmm?"

"Do you love this guy you married?"

"With all my heart." Her eyes shone. "I miss him."

"He's not like Daddy?"

Her mother shook her head.

"No. He's always been there for me. Never let me down."

They sat in silence for a few minutes, broken only by an occasional page over the speaker system.

"Mom?"

"Hmm?"

"I'm glad you came today."

Her mother's hands stopped, she placed the half-finished afghan and yarn in her lap. Reaching out, she grasped Colleen's hand. "So am I, dear. So am I."

VINCE HAD HAD enough inaction. He was a protector, dammit, and he'd failed miserably with Violet and Colleen. He was stuck out here in the parking lot and there wasn't a damn thing he could do about it.

He wanted to march right through those doors

and make sure Colleen was okay. But dread clawed at his stomach. Something horrible would happen if he so much as set foot in a waiting area.

Maybe if he could hold Colleen in his arms, they could lean on each other. She'd seemed so defenseless. His urge to protect her was almost undeniable. Unfortunately, his survival instinct was stronger. Los Angeles meant danger, waiting rooms meant certain death and his fight-or-flight instincts were in full force.

A gentle touch on his arm brought him out of his own personal hell.

"Vince?" Colleen's mother looked tired.

"Yes, ma'am?"

"The doctors were unable to stop Violet's labor. Her water broke. They've decided to perform an emergency C-section."

Vince's world tilted. "The baby?"

"It's touch-and-go."

He swore softly. "Sorry, ma'am, about the language."

"That's all right. I feel the same way." Her voice was husky. "I'm going to the chapel. You know what they say, where two or more are gathered in His name…"

He nodded, watching her turn and go back inside.

Squeezing his eyes shut, Vince wanted to scream at the heavens. Why did this happen to Violet and Ian? They were wonderful, devoted parents. They didn't deserve this.

And Colleen would be heartbroken, too. She would feel responsible even though Violet herself had made the choice to come to L.A.

He ached to have Colleen in his arms so he could reassure her, reassure himself.

Flipping open his phone, he started to dial her cell number, but then he remembered all cell phones were turned off in the hospital.

He *had* to reach her. Had to make sure she didn't claim any guilt over this disaster. After all, he was as responsible as anyone. It had been *his* job to keep Violet calm and healthy.

Vince paced, his mind working frantically.

CHAPTER EIGHTEEN

COLLEEN KNEW the doctor had bad news the minute she saw him approach, his face devoid of expression. She started to tremble before he was close enough to speak.

Glancing wildly around for something, some*one* to hold onto, she remembered her mom had gone to the chapel. Colleen would have to face the news, whatever it was, alone.

"Doctor?"

He grasped her cold hands. "I'm sorry."

"Sorry?"

"Your father didn't make it, Colleen. The peritonitis was too advanced."

"Try one of the other drugs. One of the more toxic ones."

His gaze was gentle, understanding. "He's gone, Colleen. There's nothing more we can do."

The bottom dropped out of her world.

The doctor led her to a chair. "Is there someone I can call for you?"

Shaking her head numbly, she replied, "No. Nobody."

"Your mother?"

With tremendous effort, Colleen was finally able to string together her fractured thoughts. Her mother had been there, but she'd gone somewhere. Where? She concentrated hard. "In the chapel."

"I'll send someone for her. I'm sorry, dear." He touched her shoulder then strode away.

He had to be wrong. There was no way her father could be dead. They had so much left to do, to say.

Clamping a hand over her mouth, she was able to mute the keening noise she was making to a moan. Her dad had been alone when he died. The man who had been father, mother, sibling, all rolled into one had died without anyone who loved him alongside.

Alone.

The word echoed through her brain. Her shoulders slumped, it was an effort to remain upright in the generic waiting room chair.

She was now truly alone.

Except Vince.

She needed to be with him. An overwhelming instinct prodded her into action. She rose, her feet moved, taking her to the elevator. The Lobby button was cool beneath her fingertip. Her feet took over again when the elevator doors opened. Across the lobby and out the doors.

She shivered. It was cold, so cold. Looking at the sky, she saw low, angry clouds hiding the sun.

"Colleen."

Vince moved to her side. "I'm so glad to see you.

I've been out of my mind with worry, wondering what was happening. The nurse wouldn't give me any information on your dad or Violet. Are they okay?"

"He's…gone, Vince." Saying the words aloud brought a rush of pain. "And I didn't get to say goodbye."

Vince took her in his arms, but his body was stiff, unyielding, anything but comforting.

"Did you hear me? Dead."

"I'm so sorry," he whispered against her hair.

"He was all alone. I *should* have been there with him."

"Shhh. He knew how much you cared."

"You don't understand. There was so much left undone."

Vince's voice was husky. "I understand way more than you think."

She wrapped her arms around his waist, trying to absorb his strength, his warmth. Still, she shivered.

"Will they let you see him?" he asked.

"I—I don't know."

He leaned back, held her gaze. His voice was urgent. "Remember you told me you thought my mom could see me from heaven and would be proud. I think the same thing is true of your dad. You can talk to him now. Tell him how you feel. Tell him all the things you wanted to but didn't get the chance."

She nodded slowly. "But I'm afraid." Glancing up in his face, she asked, "Will you come with me?"

"I…can't."

"No, I guess not." It felt as if her heart shriveled and died. She was genuinely alone. "Goodbye, Vince."

Vince watched Colleen turn and walk back into the hospital, and it just about tore him apart. He started to call out to her, but stopped himself. What could he offer her now? Certainly not what she needed—someone by her side, supporting her, loving her, through some of the worst hours of her life.

Her pain echoed inside him, bringing back memories he'd half forgotten. The raw grief he saw in his dad's eyes whenever he mentioned his mother. How they'd visited the scene of the shooting and his dad had thrown himself to the asphalt, red roses falling to the ground. How he'd grasped his father's arm and helped him to his feet, leading him to the car without a backward glance.

They'd never discussed it afterward, his father's lapse in self-control. After that, Vince hadn't been able to share his grief for fear it would be too much for his father to bear. And he'd never said goodbye to his mother. One minute she was in the hospital bed, the next it was empty, remade for the next occupant.

Pacing, he ran his hand through his hair. Would it have made a difference? The opportunity to say goodbye? To talk about his grief, his guilt?

He'd told Colleen it would help her. He had to believe his own words, had to take a chance just as he'd asked Colleen to take a chance.

Nodding, he shoved his hands in his pockets and headed for the van.

VINCE RIPPED the No Trespassing sign off the chain-link fence. Espinoza's Garage was dilapidated and deserted.

He'd driven there as fast as was safely possible, filled with an urgency he didn't understand. He also didn't understand why he was compelled to grab the baseball glove out of the back seat when he got out of the van. But he obeyed.

Glancing around, he noticed a large sign nearby that proclaimed this to be the future site of a brand spanking new convenience store/gas station, one of thousands owned by a national chain.

Huge chunks of asphalt littered the parking lot, apparently torn up by the yellow backhoe nearby. Demolition was the intent, not restoration.

Vince hooked his fingers through the chain-link and leaned against the fence. A chilly wind bit at his back. This wasn't what he'd expected. He'd half hoped the station was long gone, already replaced by a strip mall or fast-food restaurant.

But this sleeping beast, trapped between the old and the new, baffled him.

He waited for the sick feeling to start. He was at the scene of his mother's murder, the place that most represented danger and loss to him. So where was the horrible dread he'd felt since he arrived in Los Angeles?

He needed to get closer. He needed to get inside.

Looking upward, Vince eyed the top of the fence. Barbed wire running the perimeter would be a deterrent to most. But not a cop trained to work the streets of South Phoenix. He tucked Sean Davis's glove inside his windbreaker and was over the top and on the other side in seconds, nursing a scratch on his hand where he'd skimmed the wire.

He was grateful they hadn't torn out the pumps yet. Number three was where his mother had been. He forced his feet to take him there, one step after another.

Standing on the spot where she'd died, he felt nothing. Absolutely nothing. The only memories sparked were those of his dad falling to his knees, red roses spilling from his outstretched hands.

But today wasn't about his dad. Today was about Vince.

He sucked in a deep breath and forced himself to focus.

Studying the pavement, he realized his mother's blood, so easily recognizable the day after her death, had been obliterated by new stains. Coffee, oil, maybe even someone else's blood.

Vince closed his eyes, trying to visualize the place as it had been twenty years ago. It was too quiet today. No clanking of tools in the repair bay, no vehicles coming and going, no honking horns.

The mitt was solid and reassuring against his chest, where he had it snuggled like a baby koala clinging to its mother.

Vince pulled out the glove. His talisman of failure. He had to face this stuff from the past before he could give Colleen his all. She needed him and he needed to be with her.

He refused to admit defeat. He had to believe what he'd told Colleen was true. That his mother could hear him, see him. That he could tell her goodbye.

The baseball glove was warm from his body heat, making it more malleable than it had been when he first found it in the shed. He forced his fingers into the grooves left by another's hand. His hand started to sweat. As each minute went by, the glove began to conform to his hand.

Vince moved a few paces away from the pump to where he stood in his nightmares.

The breeze ruffled his hair. He smelled rain. It had been overcast the day when he'd accompanied his father to see where his mother had died. He supposed it was something his dad had needed in order to process his grief. But this was the place where the ten-year-old Vince had stopped feeling his grief, bottling it up and tucking it away.

Vince frowned. He'd had his ball glove with him that day, too. His most prized possession, he'd kept it with him those interminable days in the hospital.

Weird how it had become all convoluted in his mind. Baseball, death, guilt and sorrow.

COLLEEN TIPTOED into the ICU room, surprised at how little her father had changed in death. But the silent machines confirmed that he was really gone, not just sleeping.

Maybe she should have allowed her mother to accompany her. But instead, she'd suggested Maria Peralta wait in the maternity ward so they wouldn't miss any news of Violet's condition.

Colleen moved to the bedside. She looked down at her father and grasped his still-warm hand in hers. "I'm here, Daddy. It's Colleen."

His eyes remained closed.

"I believe you can hear me…wherever you are. They won't let me stay long. I wanted you to know how much I love you."

Colleen's throat felt raw, but she continued. "We had some good times, didn't we? You know what, I went to an Angels game the other day. They won. You would have loved it. I remember when you used to take me to the games. I was a just a little bitty kid. I miss that."

There were other things she missed as well, but none of them were destined to be. All she'd ever really wanted was to have a father like the other girls. A father who was big and strong and would console her when she was sad, protect her when she was threatened and encourage her to be the very best she could be.

And year after year she'd wished her dad would quit drinking and become that kind of man.

Pulling up a chair, she wondered when she'd given up hope of receiving more from him. Maybe she never had. Maybe that's why she'd stayed to care for him instead of starting her own life. And now it was too late. His death meant that no matter how hard she worked, no matter how devoted a daughter, she couldn't earn a daddy who loved her.

Colleen pulled her knees up to her chest and hugged them tight to her body. She was such a hypocrite. She'd told Vince he needed to handle his issues if he wanted to have a future. But what had she really done to face hers? She'd brought Violet back home, so Violet could fix everything. That's what she'd really wanted. She'd figured her big sister could make anything right.

Instead, Violet was in the maternity ward, fighting for her life, fighting for her baby's life.

And it was time for Colleen to handle her own battles. She'd needed to resolve this just as badly as her sister. And now it was too late.

An overwhelming sense of emptiness washed over her. She wiped the tears from her face and stood. Leaning over the bed, she tucked the sheet up under his chin and said, "I'm sorry I wasn't here. I hate that you were alone."

Studying his face, she had to admit he looked peaceful, or as peaceful as he was capable. He didn't look like someone who had died alone and scared.

"You know, Daddy, I'll always be grateful that you stayed to raise me." Her voice was soft, intimate in such a sterile environment. "I know it must've been difficult at times. But…I feel like you should have encouraged me to spread my wings and build a life for myself as an adult, instead of urging me to stay."

Colleen suppressed a sharp pang of betrayal. Anger soon followed, surprising in its intensity.

"And hitting Violet, I'm glad it's not my place to forgive you for that. B-because I'm not sure I could. You hurt her. Tore our family apart. Alcohol was *the* most important thing to you. Not me, not my mother, not Patrick or Violet. Not even your own health. And I *hate* that."

She was confused by the jumble of conflicting emotions she had for her father.

"But you were there for me in your own way." Colleen smoothed a wisp of gray hair off his forehead, smiling sadly.

"There will be a huge hole in my life now that you're gone. Goodbye, Daddy. I love you."

COLLEEN WENT to the maternity ward waiting room. She quietly approached her mother. The older woman's fingers moved with blinding speed, manipulating yarn and a hook to create something beautiful.

Stopping short, Colleen studied her mother. She was still an attractive woman. There was a contentment about her that had been missing all those years ago.

"Hi, Mom." The words sounded so natural.

"Hi. Are you okay?"

"I guess."

"Is there anything I can do?"

"No. I've just got a bunch of stuff to work out in my mind."

"That's understandable. I'm here if you need me."

"Mom?"

"Yes?"

"Are you sad? About Dad?"

Her mother looked at her over the top of her reading glasses. "Yes, I am. He was a big part of my life for many, many years. And I mourn what might have been, too."

Colleen nodded. "Sometimes I get mad. Weren't we important enough for him to quit drinking?"

"To you and me, the choice seems simple. Unfortunately, for him it wasn't. But know, precious girl, your father loved you as much as he was able to love anyone." She paused, her eyes held a faraway look. "You should have seen him the day you were born. I think he was the proudest dad I've ever seen."

"Really? How was he when Violet was born?"

"He was...disappointed."

"Did he want another boy? I guess he was used to girls by the time I came along."

Her mother made a noncommittal noise. "I'm sorry you've had to go through this. Your dad died way too young."

"Yes, he did." Colleen's eyes blurred, but she wiped away the moisture. She felt adrift, as if she were a boat cast out to sea without a rudder or anchor. She needed the man she loved. "I'm going outside for a couple minutes. To talk to Vince. Let me know if anything changes."

"Certainly. I want you to remember, though, that

your father chose his own path. You should choose yours."

Colleen thought about it all the way down to the lobby. Her mother was right—she would have to choose.

She was so lost in thought, it took her a minute to realize she'd stopped near the lobby information desk. People walked around her, apparently unaware that her world had changed irrevocably. What to say to Vince when she got outside?

She veered into the gift shop and wandered through, her thoughts racing. Her path had converged and tangled with Vince's—and she wanted them to stay permanently intertwined. If his path had run parallel to hers, they would have never met. Could she expect that they would learn and grow at exactly the same pace, in the same way? Hell, no. But she'd told him he needed to deal with his past if they were to have a future. She'd as much as told him he was abnormal if he didn't heal on her schedule. That if he didn't give her one hundred percent all the time, he didn't love her enough.

Pretty much what she'd told herself about her dad. She'd signed over so many years of her life, giving a hundred percent and then some, and it hadn't changed him one bit. All her ministrations had simply made his ride a little smoother—the end result was the same. And she'd given up so many opportunities.

If giving her heart to Vince was dependent on his following her arbitrary schedule, then maybe she didn't love him as much as she thought.

Colleen shook her head. She loved him completely. He was there when she needed him. He protected her, loved her and encouraged her to do her very best. All the things she'd wanted so desperately from a father who simply wasn't capable of loving that way.

It was there in front of her face. How could she have missed it?

She needed to be with Vince, needed to apologize to him for being so foolish. Raising her chin, she left the gift shop.

Her heart felt lighter with each step that took her closer to Vince.

The big glass doors whooshed open.

Colleen stepped outside, surprised to see storm clouds rolling in. How many hours had it been since she'd been out here? She couldn't even remember.

Glancing around, she looked for Vince, but couldn't find him. Had he gone for a walk?

Maybe he was in the van?

Colleen went to the van, or where the van had been this morning. There was now a small, red import in the same spot.

He was gone. Really gone.

He'd been there all day and she'd simply taken for granted that he would stay as long as she needed him. That's how much faith she had in his love for her. Too bad she hadn't been able to demonstrate her love for him, unconditionally accepting him for the terrific guy he was, baggage or no baggage.

In shock, she returned to the hospital and made her way to the maternity ward.

"He wasn't there," she told her mom.

"An orderly brought this for you just after you left." Her mother handed her a note.

Colleen's hands were shaking as she unfolded the piece of notebook paper. She frowned as she read it.

"That's odd. He went to the gas station."

"What's so odd about that?"

"We had a full tank this morning."

VINCE REMOVED the baseball glove. It hadn't worked. Not even a twinge in his gut. Sure, the gas station made him sad, but nothing like the panic he felt in his dreams.

The aroma of sweaty leather teased him. An odor that had been such a big part of his life until he was ten. He associated it with the end of a game, when he'd felt on top of the world.

Vince's stomach started to grumble.

These days, sweaty leather had a darker association. Failing his mother.

He glanced down at the pavement and saw a crimson blotch spread across the concrete. It looked like new blood.

"Help me." His mother's voice was whisper-soft.

Turning, he tried to locate her. But she wasn't there.

What if he'd been wrong? What if this place wouldn't heal him? Maybe it was simply a piece of real estate.

Vince turned the thought over in his mind. The corner lot *was* just a piece of real estate where a tragedy had occurred. Like a hospital was, on a larger scale, a piece of real estate where tragedies and miracles both occurred. Years from now, both places might be demolished, turned into something else. The tragedies and miracles would live on only in the people who remembered them.

The answer was inside him. *He* had the ability to heal himself.

He walked a few paces to where he'd imagined the bloodstain. He thought of his mom and her love for him. He'd been a fortunate kid to have her for ten years. He'd been fortunate to have other loving relatives to step in and fill the void left by her death. Seeing Colleen's family struggle to reconnect made him thankful he had three meddling sisters who cared enough to tell him when he screwed up.

Vince glanced at the sky, enjoying the breeze that ruffled his hair. The sun peeked out from behind the clouds and kissed his face. He heard the sounds of horns honking, sirens blaring. Smelled the aroma of day-old tacos and diesel fuel. And smiled at the beauty of the day.

Squatting, Vince addressed the concrete in front of pump number three. "Goodbye, Mom." He kissed his fingertips and pressed them to the stained ground.

CHAPTER NINETEEN

COLLEEN PACED from the door to her mother's chair and back again.

"You're going to wear a hole in the carpet, dear," her mother commented.

"I need to do *something.* I'm so worried. They won't tell Violet, will they? About Dad?"

"They assured me that's our responsibility. Her doctors agree that now isn't the time for bad news."

"No, it isn't. I'm scared, Mom. What if she loses the baby? What if Violet isn't strong enough—"

"Your sister has the best possible medical care. We need to keep positive thoughts."

Colleen nodded. "I'm trying to stay positive, but with everything that's going on, it's hard. I'm worried about Vince, too. He left without a word and I'm not sure he's coming back."

Her mother continued to crochet, but she looked up to say, "He'll be back. Love's like that. Sometimes you have to sit back and watch someone you care about struggle. You can't do it for him. He'll have to work it out on his own."

"So what do I do in the meantime?"

"Wait. Be here for him when he comes back."

"What if he doesn't come back? Just hops the next plane to Phoenix? Or what if something happens to him? That gas station's in a rough neighborhood."

"He can take care of himself. Have a little faith."

"I'm trying, Mom. But it's so hard."

"I know it is, precious girl."

There was a commotion from the direction of the operating room, as several doctors and nurses wheeled an incubator into the hall. Ian, dressed in scrubs, was right behind them. His gaze never wavered from the incubator.

Colleen craned her neck, but couldn't see a bit of her new niece or nephew.

The obstetrician came through the doors seemingly hours later. He removed his mask. "Violet is doing well. Her blood pressure has stabilized, she's alert and responding. They'll be taking her to a room shortly.

"And the baby?" Colleen asked.

"He's small, but he's a fighter. The fact that he's breathing on his own is a good sign. The pediatrician will give him a thorough examination and we'll have more information."

"He? I have a nephew?"

"You sure do."

VINCE'S RESOLVE stayed strong until he pulled into the hospital parking lot. Then, it wavered only a bit.

As he walked up to the entrance, sweat trickled down his back, saturated his collar, beaded his upper lip. He'd spent so much time out here, it seemed comfortingly familiar. The inside was a different story.

Keep moving, keep moving.

And he did. Past the information desk, where a bald gentleman greeted visitors.

The controlled chaos of the hospital assaulted his every sense. The intercom was a nonstop command post for information. Nurses bustled, an orderly pushed a patient in a wheelchair, a second orderly pushed a gurney—all he saw was an adult covered from chin to toe in a white sheet and a cascade of black hair. Vince told himself the hospital was just a piece of real estate. Yes, the woman on the gurney reminded him of his mother, but he'd said goodbye. He'd released himself from the past. And he knew, absolutely *knew* his mother would have approved.

The thought sustained him as he boarded the elevator and watched the doors shut. He wasn't trapped. The elevator car was taking him to Colleen.

His breathing slowed, his pulse stopped pounding. This was really going to be okay.

ICU or the maternity ward?

He'd never been the kind of kid to enter the water an inch at a time. He'd been the first kid to jump in the city pool on the opening day of the swimming season, reveling in the shock of cold water against his skin. No guts, no glory.

He punched the button for ICU.

The car picked up speed. Or so it seemed to Vince. He arrived at the appropriate floor all too quickly.

Stepping out of the elevator, he glanced around. A sign pointed him toward the waiting area.

Images flashed before him of another ICU waiting room. Hushed voices, loved ones waiting for fate to give the thumbs-up or thumbs-down.

Vince shook his head, trying to remember that miracles could happen here, too. He scanned the room. No Colleen, or anyone else he recognized for that matter. He debated checking in at the nurses' station, but decided against it. They might just throw him out on his ear if they found out he wasn't really Colleen's husband.

Instead, he took the elevator to the next floor. Maternity. The waiting room here was a whole other story. Happy families celebrating a joyous occasion. Here and there he detected a hint of worry. Those were the ones still waiting.

He heard Colleen's voice before he saw her. She and her mother were on the far side of the room. He headed in her direction.

When he was a few feet away, she glanced up, her gaze locked with his. He saw everything he needed in her eyes.

Love, understanding, wisdom and the need to be alone with him, to love him privately.

That Grinch, heart-growing-two-sizes emotion gripped his chest. He'd never let a piece of real estate separate them again.

She flew into his outstretched arms and hugged him fiercely.

"You did it. You're here."

"I did it. I'm here with you, whatever happens."

She stepped back and surveyed him, frowning. "Are you okay?"

"I am now. This is for you." He handed her the single red rose.

Colleen smiled with bemusement. "Thank you." She tucked her hand in his. "I was wrong, Vince. I had no right to force you into something you weren't ready for."

"Force is a little too strong. We'll say you gave me a nudge in the right direction."

She nodded. Stepping closer, she slid her arms around his waist.

"You achieved mortality today." Her eyes sparkled with excitement.

"I did some scary stuff, but I wouldn't call it achieving mortality."

"I would. You have a new godson. He's small, but he's got ten fingers, ten toes and a set of lungs to rival Pavarotti. The neonatal specialist says he's darn near perfect."

Vince picked her up and swung her around. His whoop of joy bounced back at them from the sedate, sea-green walls. He ignored the few raised eyebrows. "That's the best news ever."

"There's more."

"More?"

"His name is Edward Vincent Smith. Edward was Ian's father's name. And Vincent is for the baby's godfather."

"They named him after me?" he murmured.

Nodding, Colleen said, "Because they want him to grow up to be brave and loving just like you."

Vince didn't know what to say. His throat got all scratchy. He felt honored beyond words. "I haven't been very brave lately."

"Oh, yes, you have. More than you give yourself credit for."

"Come on, let's go see my namesake." He craned his neck to see around Colleen.

"Coming with us, Maria? We're gonna go see the baby."

She nodded and smiled. "You two go on ahead. I'll be there in a minute."

He pulled Colleen by the hand, following the arrow directing them to the nursery.

They waited for what seemed like an eternity to see the new baby, and then only caught a glimpse of him through the viewing window. He was one of several infants in incubators lined against the wall of the nursery.

"He's beautiful," Colleen breathed.

"He sure is." Vince nodded, his throat scratchy again.

IT WAS AFTER ten when Vince and Colleen arrived home. Vince thought his brain might explode with all the stuff he'd experienced in one day.

But glancing at Colleen, he knew she had to be even more disoriented and exhausted than he was. She was pale, her eyes shadowed.

Vince grasped her elbow and guided her toward his room. "You need some sleep."

Colleen sat on the bed and stifled a yawn. Tugging on the hem of her shirt, she struggled to pull the shirt over her head. "I hope my mind can quit racing long enough," came her muffled response.

"Here, let me help." He tenderly removed her clothes and replaced them with one of his soft, clean T-shirts.

Colleen accepted Vince's ministrations with gratitude. She clambered into his bed and was immediately immersed in his scent. The sheets, the pillowcases, the shirt she wore, they all smelled of Vince.

He tucked the covers up under her chin. "Sleep tight."

She didn't have the energy to ask if he intended to join her. Rolling onto her side, she dozed almost immediately.

But somewhere through the haze of half sleep, she felt the mattress dip under Vince's weight. His warm naked body eased against hers, he wrapped his arm around her waist.

She slept, a deep dreamless sleep, safely cocooned in his arms.

WHEN COLLEEN AWOKE, weak rays of sunlight peeked through the blinds. She bolted upright. "Oh no. I didn't mean to sleep this long. I've gotta get—"

"Back to bed and relax. I called the hospital." Vince raised up on his elbow, his hair boyishly mussed. Glancing at the bedside clock, he said, "About an hour ago. Ian said Violet had a restless night and will probably sleep for an hour or two this morning in between feedings."

"Is everything okay? The baby?"

"Everyone's fine. Ian said the baby's having a hard time feeding. They just need some peace and quiet to settle in."

She eased back on the pillows, grateful for a reprieve from telling Violet about their dad.

Vince reached over and brushed the hair from her eyes. "And I called your mom. She offered to call your dad's distant relatives with the news."

Colleen nodded. "That would be great. Dad made all the other arrangements himself years ago— wanted to make sure the services were exactly the way he wanted. I can't imagine having to do all that in the middle of everything else."

Vince nodded.

She suppressed a bubble of excitement. "Maybe I'll get to hold the baby today. Is it wrong to want to celebrate the baby's arrival when my dad just died?"

"You enjoy that little guy as much as you want. Don't let anyone tell you different. It doesn't take anything away from your feelings about your dad."

Grasping Vince's hand, she kissed his palm then lifted it to her cheek. "You always know how to make me feel better. Thank you."

"No problem, sweetheart." He traced the line of her jaw. "Now, why don't you go back to sleep? I'll wake you in time to shower and reach the hospital after lunch."

"I need you more than I need sleep. Join me?" She opened her arms to him.

"I thought you'd never ask."

Colleen reveled in the sheer perfection of making love with Vince. They tasted and teased, made promises and laughed. And afterward, Colleen rested her cheek against Vince's chest, listening to the strong, steady beat of his heart. "No dozing off. We need to get dressed in a couple minutes."

"I'm just resting my eyes."

"Sure you are." She hesitated for a moment. "Vince, what happened yesterday? At the gas station?"

He draped his arm over her hips. "I quit running from the memories, from the guilt. I guess something you said made me realize I never got to say goodbye to my mom. At the hospital, they whisked her away immediately. At the funeral home, I was too freaked out. And when I visited the murder scene with my dad, he pretty much fell apart and I stuffed away all my feelings after that."

"I'm glad you've come to terms with it." She trailed her hand over his biceps. "You love me no matter what, right?"

He nodded. "Yep. No matter what."

"Even if I'm a huge fraud?"

"Hmm. That's a tough one. How huge? Like tent dresses, that kind of thing?"

Colleen poked him in the ribs. "Be serious. I'm trying to let you know some of my biggest faults so you can make an informed decision about us."

Vince threw back his head and laughed. "An informed decision has nothing to do with love, sweetheart. You're stuck with me, so quit trying to wiggle out of it. Tell me about this fault of yours."

"First I tell Violet she's got to let Dad make amends if she wants to move on with her life. Then Mom shows up and I can't seem to practice what I preach. I as much as tell her to get out of town."

"I can see where you might consider that a little inconsistent. I still love you, though."

"And then there's you."

"Me?"

"I tell you to confront your past, deal with your issues."

He nodded. "Very good advice."

"I tried to force you to handle it before you were ready, but I couldn't seem to follow through where my dad was concerned. And now I'll never have the chance to talk to him in a human, one-on-one kind of way. I'm really good at telling other people what to do. So how come I can't follow my own advice?"

"Simple, Watson. You're too close and have too much at stake. Besides, there are times when a little harmless pretending can be a good thing. Maybe it wouldn't have done any good to tell a dying man he was a crummy father. You'll face that stuff when the time is right."

"I hope you're right. Because I want a happy, healthy future that includes you. I don't want to screw it up with my issues."

"I should be so lucky to have you screw up my life with your issues for the next fifty or sixty years."

"You mean that?"

"Every bit." He gazed into her eyes. "I know the timing really sucks, but will you marry me?"

Colleen took a deep breath. She couldn't think of a better time for a proposal. A new beginning to negate the finality of death. "Of course I'll marry you."

CHAPTER TWENTY

COLLEEN STEPPED inside the hospital room and gazed at the two occupants.

Violet held a very small bundle to her breast. The bundle had a shock of black hair and made loud sucking noises.

Colleen smiled, and tears blurred her eyes. It was a new, wonderful memory that went a long way toward replacing some of the old, unpleasant ones.

"Hi," she softly said.

Violet glanced up. Her eyes radiated joy and wonder.

"Hi. Want to come see your nephew?"

Nodding, Colleen moved to the bed, looking down on the most miraculous thing she'd ever seen. "He's beautiful," she breathed.

She watched the little fingers flex on her sister's breast. The baby's eyelids fluttered, as if he were dreaming. His sucking slowed, then finally stopped.

Violet gingerly lifted him to her shoulder while rearranging her nightgown. She rubbed his tiny back.

Then he did the most amazing thing: her nephew burped.

Colleen couldn't help but smile in awe. There was a real person housed in that small body. A person who would call her Aunt Colleen and let her spoil him rotten.

"Do you want to hold him? We should have a few seconds before the nurse comes back. They don't want him out of the incubator for long."

Colleen's arms reached out, while her mind said no. "He's so tiny. What if I hurt him?"

"He's tougher than he looks. You'll do fine."

She moved closer to accept the precious being Violet placed in the crook of her arm.

He wriggled, then he made soft snuffling sounds.

Her insides melted on the spot as she started swaying from side to side in some instinctive kind of maternal dance. Colleen knew without a doubt that she and baby Eddie would get along fine.

Her gaze locked with Violet's in a magical moment of bonding. A bonding that made Colleen all the more reluctant to break the spell by imparting bad news.

She cleared her throat. "Um, I have something to tell you. Ian offered and that was really sweet, but I'm the one who dragged you here, so I need to be the one to tell you."

Violet raised an eyebrow. "Go ahead."

"Dad, um, passed away while you were in labor and everything was so touch-and-go. We all agreed you didn't need the news then. And after that I—I fig-

ured you deserved some happy time with Eddie."
Colleen glanced out the window. "I guess I was being
a little bit of a coward, too."

The silence prodded Colleen to look at her sister.
Expecting hysterics, she was surprised to see a sad
acceptance in her eyes. "I know about Dad. I forced
the news out of Ian before he left to get Rosie. I
knew something was wrong and wouldn't rest 'til I
knew. And when I asked about Dad, he and Mom
changed the subject."

"Are you…okay about it?"

Violet sighed. "I'm not sure what I feel. I'm disappointed everything wasn't resolved all neat and
tidy. But I tried, I really did. And I'm going to have
to be satisfied with that."

Colleen nodded. "I'm sorry I pushed you so hard.
After Mom came back, I understood a lot better what
you were up against. It was pretty arrogant of me to
think I knew what you needed."

"Arrogant's a little strong. And you meant well,
pumpkin." Violet's eyes narrowed. "You've changed
you know. In just a week. You've grown up, little sister. Is it Vince?"

"Vince is the frosting on the cake…um…so to
speak."

"Not German Chocolate, though." Violet grinned.

"You're not going to let me forget that, are you?"

"Nope. That's what siblings are for. To keep you
humble."

"Thanks. I'll remember that."

Baby Eddie made smacking sounds in his sleep. She jiggled him just a bit and he settled in.

"Vince was my anchor in all this craziness. I *hope* I've grown. I want our relationship, our future, to be so much more than what our parents had. I'm scared as hell that I'll repeat their mistakes, but with Vince I feel so incredibly lucky. I think we'll make it."

"I *know* you will."

A nurse bustled in and scooped Eddie from Colleen's arms.

"Time for this guy to go back to the nursery."

The cold, empty space where he'd nestled left Colleen feeling somehow incomplete. She gave the baby one last longing glance as the nurse placed him in the clear plastic bassinet and wheeled him out the door.

VINCE FELT disconnected as he watched Sean Davis's casket being lowered into the ground. He'd never met the man who had affected his life so profoundly.

Sean Davis had raised Colleen and for that Vince would always be grateful. But forgiving him for the horrible things he'd done might be a long time coming.

Vince glanced at the woman standing next to him, gripping his arm. Even in grief, Colleen was beautiful. Her eyes brimmed with tears, but she stood tall. She could face her troubles head-on, bend, but not break.

He was an incredibly lucky man.

Glancing at Violet, he wasn't surprised to see that

Ian had wrapped an arm around her waist to support her. She was barely out of the hospital. Baby Eddie—or little Vince as he liked to think of him—would be released in the next couple days.

His future mother-in-law stood between the two women, holding each daughter's hand, making a chain of three.

Maria cleared her throat, wiping away a tear. "Girls, your father had something he wanted me to give you, but I'll wait 'til we get back to the house. There are some things he asked me to explain, too."

Vince suppressed a wave of uneasiness. Whatever the news was, he and Colleen would handle it together.

COLLEEN POURED hot tea for all of them. She was more an iced tea type, but for some reason a cold drink seemed too frivolous for the occasion.

Her mother sipped her tea, sitting in the same place at the kitchen table where she'd presided for so many years. Violet and Ian sat on one side of her, with Colleen and Vince on the other.

"This is a hard discussion to have with you girls, but it was your father's dearest wish, so I promised I would do this." She pulled two thin envelopes from her purse, handing one to Violet and one to Colleen. "These are what he called 'love letters' to his daughters." She smiled sadly. "His mortality apparently encouraged him to be more sentimental."

Violet snorted.

Colleen watched Ian take his wife's hand in his.

"Your father and I didn't see eye to eye on a lot of things. But I can tell you unequivocally, he loved both you girls. It just wasn't in him to express it."

Colleen turned the envelope over in her hand, noting her father's handwriting. "I'll read mine later. I don't think I can do it now."

"Me, either," Violet said.

Her mother nodded. "That's fine. There was also something he wanted me to tell you that he knew he wouldn't be able to bring himself to write down. You both have commented on the disparity in the way he treated you. I carry my own guilt about that, but this isn't the time for it. He wanted you to know his reasons, wrong though they were."

Colleen held her breath.

"When your dad and I met, I was dating another boy. I loved him dearly and your father knew that. My parents didn't consider the other boy good enough for me. His family had recently arrived from Mexico and was very poor…." She twisted a napkin in her fingers and stared at her tea cup. "Your father was a little older, had a good job, so he seemed like a better choice to them. I allowed my parents to persuade me to accept your dad's proposal."

"Oh, Mom, how horrible," Colleen said. She squeezed Vince's hand. She couldn't imagine being coerced to give up Vince. It would be like taking out her heart and stomping on it.

"Your father was a good man. He made me laugh, I enjoyed his company. I thought it would be enough…so we married. But it became apparent very quickly that it wasn't enough. By that time, I was pregnant with Patrick and longing for my lost love. Your dad could sense how unhappy I was and the reason for it. He became very jealous, accusing me of all sorts of horrible things. When Patrick was born, his coloring was more like the Ruiz side of the family, a bit like Eddie. Sean took one look at the full head of black hair and decided Patrick wasn't his child. Two years later, his reaction to Violet was the same. But when Colleen came along, she looked so much like Sean that he *couldn't* deny she was his daughter."

"How did you live like that for so many years?" Violet asked.

Maria's smile was sad. "Not well, as I'm sure you remember. The guilt was horrible. I was never unfaithful to your father in a physical way. But here—" she placed her palm over her heart "—I never quit loving Miguel. And the more your dad drank, the worse it got. Until finally, I just shut down inside."

Colleen reached over and grasped her mother's hand.

"After Patrick died, I wasn't sure I wanted to live anymore. I left, I got help." Maria's voice was soft.

"And Miguel? Did you ever see him again?"

Her smile was sweet. "Yes. I contacted him once I was better. He's my husband now."

"The restaurant owner?"

"Yes. He worked hard, got an education and succeeded. But I would have loved him even if he hadn't."

"Wow." Colleen couldn't quite assimilate everything in one chunk. "It's quite a story."

"Yes, it is. There was no excuse for your father to treat you badly. Both of you. But he was a sick man long before his liver failed. I hope you will find it in your hearts to forgive him. And forgive me, for my part."

"Why didn't Dad just leave after Patrick was born?" Violet asked.

"He said he loved me too much to leave."

Colleen's memories shifted now that she knew so much more. Everything made sense. The truth wasn't necessarily more palatable, just more understandable. And her father, for all his faults, had been a sad, tragic casualty of unrequited love and his disease.

"Are you going to read your letter now?" Colleen asked Violet.

"I'm not sure if I'll ever be ready to read it."

"Me, neither."

"Give it some time," her mother said. "You may feel differently after you've had a chance to heal."

EPILOGUE

Echo Point, Arizona
Six months later

COLLEEN FOUND a quiet corner in the courtyard and took a few seconds to compose herself amid all the revelry. The mariachi music faded, along with the laughter and boisterous chatter.

She searched the sky above the flat adobe roof of Violet's home, but saw only a gorgeous pink and gold sunset. She'd once told Vince that she thought deceased relatives could see loved ones from heaven. Could her dad see her, today, on her wedding day?

Colleen knew Vince had moved behind her before he said a word. There was some sort of sixth sense that connected them—she guessed love gave them a heightened awareness of each other.

"Whatcha looking for?" he asked, kissing the top of her head.

"I don't know. Maybe a sign? You know, that Dad was watching up there somewhere?"

Wrapping his arms around her, he said, "Those

were beautiful things he said about you in his letter. Every bit of it the truth. I wondered about your opening it the day before the wedding, but it turned out be a good thing. His words were a wonderful wedding gift."

She smiled. "Yes, a gift. Violet still hasn't opened hers. Maybe once I tell her how terrific an experience it was—"

"You're doing it again," he whispered.

"Okay, okay. She'll decide on her own. Happy?"

"Delirious. You're one special woman, Colleen Moreno."

"Mmm. I don't think I'll ever get tired of hearing that." She continued to search the sky. "I still can't help thinking there should be some kind of sign from above."

"I know what you mean. I hope my mom can see us. She'd adore you, you know."

"Maybe they're up there together." Colleen chuckled at the thought.

Vince raised his champagne glass high. "To our parents," he whispered in her ear.

"To our parents."

Their reprieve didn't last long. Violet called to them. It was time to cut the cake.

"I think our peaceful moment is over," Colleen commented.

"Yeah, but we've got thousands of peaceful moments ahead of us."

"Only thousands?" She raised an eyebrow.

"Well, yeah. Once we have children, I hear peace and quiet cease to exist."

"No doubt." She nodded toward Rosie, chasing several of Vince's nieces and nephews, weaving in and out between the round dinner tables. They banged into one table, squealed excitedly as the table skidded a few inches, and continued their mission of effervescent destruction.

Glancing up at Vince's face, she wished she could take a picture of his grin. He loved those kids as his own. "You're going to miss them, aren't you?"

He nodded. "Yeah, I kinda like the little ankle biters. But we'll come back and visit. And I bet we can persuade our respective sisters to bring them to see the ocean, say, in August."

Colleen laughed. "No doubt. I imagine San Diego starts looking pretty good when it's a hundred degrees outside. I hate taking you away from the town you love so much, though."

"I'll learn to love San Diego, too. Come on, sweetheart. We have a cake to cut."

"Yeah, just what those kids need is more sugar."

They started across the courtyard when Colleen stumbled. "Darn, I think I tripped over my train."

The cream-colored, off-the-shoulder Vera Wang knockoff made her feel like a fairy princess. Unfortunately, she kept tripping over the skirt. She lifted the hem to inspect the damage.

"It looks okay." She frowned. "But what's this." Leaning over, Colleen took a closer look at the lump at her feet. Dusk had fallen quickly and it was difficult to see in the fading light. She picked it up and turned it over in her hands. A white orb dropped out and rolled a few feet away, to rest at the base of a lovely mesquite tree.

"Look, Vince. It's a baseball glove. You don't think—"

"It's a sign from above? Hardly. One of those kids probably dropped it."

"I guess you're right. Would you grab the ball so nobody trips over it?"

"Sure thing, sweetheart." He picked it up and looked at it under the light of a paper lantern. "You're not going to believe this."

"What?"

"It's an Angels baseball."

"Angels. Ha-ha. Very funny." She pointed upward. "After we were discussing signs from heaven."

"I'm not kidding. It's got the logo. Look." He handed her the ball.

She sucked in a breath. "Wow. Coincidence?"

"Probably. Give me the mitt and we'll see if we can find the owner."

He frowned when she handed him the glove.

"What's wrong?"

"It feels…familiar." Attempting to tuck his hand inside, he shook his head. "Too small."

"Come on, you two, the natives are getting restless. There will be an all-out revolt if you don't cut the cake soon." Violet stood before them, hands on hips. She looked gorgeous in her rose-colored matron of honor dress. Their mother was close behind her, every bit as beautiful.

And holding her mother's hand was the distinguished Miguel. A kind, gentle man, it was obvious he loved her mother heart and soul. For that reason, if nothing else, Colleen loved him, too.

"We wouldn't want a revolt. Come on, Vince, the cake awaits." Colleen grasped his hand and led him to the rectangular table where their wedding cake was displayed.

"Hey, first, has anyone lost a baseball glove?" He held it aloft. Glancing around, he said, "Nobody?"

"There's some printing on it. It looks like a name," Colleen pointed out.

His eyes narrowed as he read the script. "Here." He shoved the glove at her. "You read it. You'll never believe it otherwise."

"It belongs to…." The printing looked like that of a fourth-grade child. "Vince Moreno." She gulped, glancing around, but the onlookers didn't seem to be paying attention. "It's the sign we were looking for," she murmured.

Vince held her gaze. Then smiled slowly. "I believe it is."

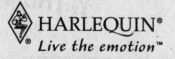

Receive a FREE hardcover book from

HARLEQUIN ROMANCE®

in September!

Harlequin Romance celebrates the launch of
the line's new cover design by offering you
this exclusive offer valid only in September,
only in Harlequin Romance.

To receive your
FREE HARDCOVER BOOK
written by bestselling author
Emilie Richards, send us four
proofs of purchase from any
September 2004 Harlequin
Romance books. Further details
and proofs of purchase can be
found in all September 2004
Harlequin Romance books.

*Must be postmarked
no later than October 31.*

Don't forget to be one of the first
to pick up a copy of the new-look
Harlequin Romance novels in September!

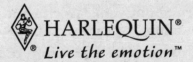

HARLEQUIN®

Live the emotion™

Visit us at www.eHarlequin.com

HRPOP0904

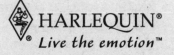

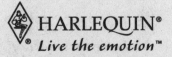